Shadows on the Ivy

**Center Point
Large Print**

**This Large Print Book carries the
Seal of Approval of N.A.V.H.**

Shadows on the Ivy

Lea Wait

Center Point Publishing
Thorndike, Maine

To my daughters, Caroline Childs, Ali Gutschenritter,
Becky Wynne, and Liz Wait, whose lives prove
every day that adoption was the right choice;

To Bob Thomas, who shows me that time can increase
wisdom, worth, and wonder, as well as love;

And to Susanne Kirk, who is patient, enthusiastic,
and encouraging, and Sarah Knight, who is always there with
answers when I have questions. Scribner—and I—
are lucky to have them both.

This Center Point Large Print edition
is published in the year 2005 by arrangement with
Scribner, a division of Simon & Schuster, Inc.

The text of this Large Print edition is unabridged. In other
aspects, this book may vary from the original edition. Printed
in Thailand. Set in 16-point Times New Roman type.

ISBN 1-58547-531-9

Library of Congress Cataloging-in-Publication Data

Wait, Lea.
    Shadows on the ivy / Lea Wait.--Center Point large print ed.
    p. cm.
    ISBN 1-58547-531-9 (lib. bdg. : alk. paper)
    1. Summer, Maggie (Fictitious character)--Fiction. 2. Prints--Collectors and collecting--Fiction.
3. Single parents--Crimes against--Fiction. 4. Women college teachers--Fiction. 5. Antique dealers--Fiction.
6. Poisonings--Fiction. 7. Large type books. I. Title.

PS3623.A42S537 2004B
813'.6--dc22

                                                                2004014285

Chapter 1

The Banquet Where the Really Grand Company Were Assembled in the Elfin Hall. *Lithograph by Arthur Rackham (1867–1939) from* Hans Christian Andersen's Fairy Tales, *1912. Rackham was a major Edwardian illustrator who specialized in magical, mystical, and legendary themes. His work influenced the surrealists. This print is of a large room crowded with elves, animal-people, trolls, fairy princesses, and other imaginary creatures who are dining on frogs and snails and sipping from cups overflowing with frothing beverages. 9.75 x 7.75 inches. Price: $70.*

Dorothy and Oliver Whitcomb's home was elegant, their food delicious, and their bar open, but Maggie Summer wanted to be at home sorting prints for next weekend's Morristown Antique Show. Her roles as an antique-print dealer and a college professor sometimes complemented each other, and sometimes conflicted. Today they conflicted.

She shifted her weight from one foot to another, cursing her decision to wear the sexy crimson silk heels that had tempted her at the Short Hills Mall last evening. Women alone on Saturday night should not be allowed to go shopping! Last night the shoes had made her feel young and alluring. Today they just hurt. An hour ago a small blister had appeared on her left little toe.

Her eyes wandered from four of John Gould's prints of hummingbirds that were hanging near the windows to the six hand-colored steel engravings of Burritt's 1835 view of the sky at different seasons that hung over the large black marble fireplace. The Whitcombs were devoted customers of Maggie's antique-print business, Shadows. They were also Somerset College trustees and major donors. When they issued an invitation, she accepted.

The Whitcombs had spent almost as much on framing as they had on the prints, but the result was worth it. The Burritts fit especially well in this room. The delicate figures drawn between the constellations blended perfectly into a library furnished with comfortable leather chairs and couches. Knowledge of the past combined with desire to know the future. Maggie walked closer, admiring the familiar star-defined astrological patterns. As always when she looked at the stars, she looked for her sign, Gemini. Two figures; two destinies.

Did the stars represent her two professions? Or her two emotional selves . . . the self-contained, intelligent, respected woman most people saw . . . or the frustrated, conflicted self she hid beneath the surface? Were either of them the sexy lady in red heels?

Gemini was green in this edition of Burritts. Green for jealousy? Jealousy of those for whom the patterns of life seemed to fall into place so easily. Career . . . marriage . . . children . . . The white wine was taking her mind down paths she didn't want to follow. At least not right now.

Maggie turned her thoughts to business. She had

6

another edition of these Burritt engravings in her inventory at home. Should she pay to have them matted and framed? They'd be much more striking if they were framed, but she'd have to charge considerably more for them. How much more would people pay so they could take artwork home from an antique show and immediately hang it on their living room wall? She might experiment with the Burritts. She could use some good sales. If customers wanted frames, frames she would give them. She made a mental note to consult Brad and Steve, her local framers.

Her next beverage would be Diet Pepsi—with caffeine. And maybe she could scavenge a Tylenol from someone. She sighed, looking around the room again. If only she'd resisted wearing the red heels.

Across the room Dorothy Whitcomb was talking to freshman Sarah Anderson, backing her up against a bookcase filled with what appeared to be nineteenth-century first editions. They were probably just decorator leather bindings purchased by the yard, but in this setting they worked almost as well as the real thing. Neither Dorothy nor Oliver were, to Maggie's knowledge, book lovers. Certainly they weren't antiquarian-book collectors. But major donors to Somerset College should have an elegant library. It was part of the unwritten job description. And no doubt why the Whitcombs chose to host this reception in their library rather than in their equally posh living room.

Sarah's shoulder-length red hair was bouncing as she nodded at Dorothy politely. Twenty-three-year-old Sarah was pretty, but not too patient. She wouldn't listen forever. She had clearly dressed up for this reception. For Sarah, gray slacks and an almost-matching turtleneck was about as elegant as her wardrobe got. Dorothy never seemed to consider that the scholarship students she invited to her "informal get-togethers" (read "cocktail parties") might find dressing for these occasions a financial challenge. Maggie sighed. She should rescue Sarah. Would her feet hold up?

Paul Turk provided a welcome interruption to Maggie's gloomy thoughts. "Help! I know the Whitcombs, and some of the students, but I'm getting weary of smiling."

Maggie lightly touched Paul's arm in friendly understanding. His cologne was an attractive spicy scent, with traces of musk. Not the usual aftershave he wore on campus. Very nice. She moved out of range of the scent. Her life was complicated enough just now.

Paul was the newest member of the American Studies faculty. A corporate dropout, and former Wall Street associate of Oliver Whitcomb's, he'd had the inside track for a teaching opening this fall when he'd decided to capitalize on his master's in American history and exchange his windowed office at an investment firm for a small cubicle at Somerset College. Slender, and taller than Maggie at perhaps five feet ten inches, Paul had started to let his brown hair go a bit shaggy, and the look was good for him, even if it was obvious that he was consciously transforming himself into his vision of what a history professor *should* look like. She suspected the female students she'd seen loitering outside his office were suitably impressed.

Paul's office was next to hers, and she often helped him with "new kid on the block" issues. "It isn't the smiling during these parties that's so challenging," she said, "it's knowing that you have to smile."

He raised his eyebrows and nodded in agreement. "As always, the voice of experience. On your way to the bar?"

"Turning in my white wine for a diet soda."

"And here I was going to pour you one of my perfect Grey Goose martinis."

"Not tonight, thank you," said Maggie as they reached the table of drinks. "But you can do the Diet Pepsi honors. Or maybe I'll just have a Virgin Mary."

"Your choice. Everything's here. I helped Oliver set all this up earlier."

"I'll stick with the Diet Pepsi," Maggie decided. "With caffeine."

Paul reached past empty bottles of vodka and Scotch for the last bottle of Diet Pepsi on the do-it-yourself bar. "Looks as though our fellow guests have been joining us in taking full advantage of the libations." He moved several empties to an overflowing carton beneath the table and replaced them with full bottles.

They moved aside to make room for their host, a big, white-haired man of perhaps sixty whose navy suit had been made to order for his large build. The tailor had succeeded. Oliver looked every bit the wealthy sub-urban gentleman.

"Enjoying yourself, Paul?" said Oliver. "I'm afraid the company here is a bit tamer than what you're used to in New York," he added, giving Paul a knowing cuff

9

on the arm. He opened the bottles Paul had pulled out and refilled pitchers labeled "orange juice" and "Bloody Mary mix."

Paul added to the ice bucket from the chest on the floor next to the table.

"I wish we'd hired someone else to set the drinks up, but Dorothy thought the students would find a bartender ostentatious." Oliver shrugged. "The caterer could have supplied us with someone."

Paul grinned at him. "How could anyone possibly think you and Dorothy were ostentatious?"

"Hard to imagine, isn't it?" answered Oliver with a bit of a twinkle, looking around the mahogany bookcase–lined room that was almost as big as the basketball court in the new gymnasium he had bankrolled at the college. "Dorothy does like to act the grande dame. I'd be just as happy on a smaller stage. But, hell—'if you've got it'—and all that. In any case, have fun. You, too, Maggie." He nodded at her. "I've got to get back to playing host."

Oliver headed across the room toward the college president, Max Hagfield, but was intercepted by a group of students Maggie didn't recognize.

"Those students work out at the gym," Paul answered her unspoken question as they watched. "Oliver will no doubt now expound on the merits of the weight machines he's ordered for the gymnasium." Paul raised his martini to Maggie's cola.

"The *Whitcomb* Gymnasium," she corrected as they clinked glasses and moved away from the bar. Campus gossip reported that Oliver had donated the gym on the condition that he, as a member of the Board of Trustees, could use it at any time, and he'd made sure it contained the equipment he'd preferred at New York's Downtown Athletic Club. The gym had been completed just in time for his retirement. Max Hagfield had eagerly accepted the gymnasium, the weight machines, and any conditions attached to them. "Did Oliver work out that much in New York?" Maggie asked. His large figure didn't appear to have been honed during long workout hours.

"Pretty regularly," Paul said. "But talk to me about the scholarship students who are here tonight. Are they all part of Dorothy's pet project to save the world?"

Oliver Whitcomb had donated the gym; his wife's inspiration was to create a special dormitory for single mothers and their children. No doubt seeing a possibility for great publicity and improved community relations, Max had agreed. Dorothy had spent the past year purchasing a large Victorian house across the street from the main entrance to the college, having it brought up to dormitory code, and, of course, redecorating it. Whitcomb House was now home to six single parents, each with enough living space for the student and one child each. Max Hagfield had required only that the new dormitory be safe, handicapped accessible, and that the single parents it housed include at least one single father. Somerset College must not discriminate against any subset of students. Max's concern for students was exceeded only by his concern for the college's reputation. And his own.

Maggie nodded at Max, who had left his chair, refilled his cognac snifter at the bar, and was now heading

11

toward a group of students by the fireplace.

Max had long since given up the possibility of a berth at a more prestigious university. Instead, he'd tried to elevate the stature of presidency of the community college, so he now saw little difference between himself and his counterpart at Princeton University, a few miles south. For Max Hagfield, Somerset County was his county. Somerset College was his college. The money Dorothy and Oliver Whitcomb donated enhanced the institution; it therefore enhanced Max Hagfield. It was all one and the same.

The students he was now talking with towered over Max. He was shorter than Maggie, and clearly a man who spent more time with his cognac and his tanks of tropical fish than he did in Oliver's new gym.

Max's home was lined with fish tanks, and the small pond in his backyard contained koi and goldfish. His problems with flukes, organic debris, and neighborhood cats were all too familiar to Maggie. There was a small pond in her own yard, and before her husband, Michael, had died last year, he and Max would often temporarily escape parties such as this one to smoke and discuss the challenges of fish maintenance in home ponds. Michael's fish had become trophy catches for seven-year-old neighborhood anglers shortly before his death. Maggie hadn't bothered to replace them.

"All the Whitcomb House students are here," she said to Paul. "They're ambitious young people, and they're taking real advantage of this opportunity to attend college. I doubt any of them would be in school without Dorothy's help." One of Dorothy's requests was for one faculty member to be assigned to all six of the young families. To her delight, Maggie was given that job, so she knew them all well.

On the opposite side of the room Kendall Park, Whitcomb House's token father, was draining a glass of beer and chatting earnestly with another student. If Somerset College had fielded a football team, Kendall, heavily muscled and well over six feet tall, could have played fullback. But Kendall filled most of his hours studying and caring for thirteen-month-old Josette. When Josette's mother had left a note last spring saying California beckoned, she had also left their baby. Twenty-year-old Kendall had become a surprised, but devoted, single dad. Defying all stereotypes about male and female parenting skills, Kendall was among the most concerned and nurturing of the Whitcomb House parents.

Maria Ramirez and Heather Farelli were standing by the antipasto table; Tiffany Douglass, her streaked blonde hair cascading over one shoulder, was wearing a long, patterned skirt and a red blouse cut a smidge—or perhaps two smidges—too low, was talking with a biology professor. Kayla Martin had on a short, orange knit dress that showed off her legs and was filling her glass with red wine. Sarah Anderson was still talking with Dorothy Whitcomb. Or at least Dorothy Whitcomb was still talking to Sarah.

"Dorothy sees herself as their savior," Paul said.

"And she may be. But she gets too proprietary with them. Like inviting them to all of these receptions, and even hiring a baby-sitter for Whitcomb House so they don't have an excuse not to come." Dorothy was supporting the students; they may have owed her, but she didn't own them. Sometimes Maggie wondered if Dorothy understood the difference.

"Dorothy wouldn't tolerate excuses, would she?" Paul said.

"Do you know her well?"

"Not as well as I know Oliver. But she's been very hospitable since I moved to New Jersey. I didn't know his first wife at all."

"First wife? When he moved here and started donating to Somerset College, Dorothy was his wife."

"Oliver and Dorothy were newlyweds when I first went to work for Oliver's firm. They've only been married six or seven years."

"I remember hearing that he has adult children."

"A boy and a girl, from his first marriage. They're in their late twenties and live on the West Coast. They grew up over in Bernardsville, where Oliver used to live. He sold their old house and bought this one for Dorothy. 'A new house for a new marriage' is how he put it."

Maggie and Paul both looked at Dorothy, whose gold turtleneck and form-fitting black silk slacks matched the drama of her short blonde-tinted red (or was it red-tinted blonde?) hair. She was still holding Sarah Anderson in conversation.

"How much younger is Dorothy than Oliver?" Maggie was curious, and Paul didn't seem to mind sharing what he knew about them.

"He retired at sixty; I think she's in her midforties."

"Really? I thought she might be older," said Maggie. "She doesn't look it, but she has a sort of attitude that says . . ."

"She's pretentious as hell, you mean," Paul said, grinning. "Absolutely. If she knew that attitude would make people assume she was older, she'd drop it as fast as she'd drop a manicurist who smudged her nails. But I suspect no one's ever had the guts to tell her."

"And I'm certainly not going to be the one," said Maggie. "But I do think I'm going to rescue poor Sarah. Dorothy's been talking at her for long enough."

"If you're going to play Good Samaritan, I'll return to the herd. I know a couple of students over by the window. I'll go and act professorial."

"Sounds like a plan." Maggie glanced toward Geoff Boyle and Linc James, two other professors, and headed for Sarah and Dorothy. She concentrated on not limping. The blister must be getting worse. And she really shouldn't stay much longer; she had to organize prints before her morning lecture, and she should pack her van. Not to mention the joy of replacing these blasted shoes with a pair of cozy fleece slippers.

"Have you ever taken Aura to a children's theater performance?" Dorothy's hair was blocking Maggie's view of Sarah's reaction. "Perhaps we could arrange for tickets for all of you some weekend."

"That's a lovely idea, Dorothy," Maggie interrupted. "As long as it isn't near exam time! Maybe after the holidays. Sarah, have you tried the roast beef? It's delicious. Dorothy, your caterer has done wonders with the horseradish sauce."

Sarah slipped away with an appreciative nod at Maggie.

"We do have a wonderful caterer, don't we?" agreed Dorothy. "And nothing too fancy. We wanted the young people to feel right at home. I'm so glad everyone from Whitcomb House could come, and some of the students Oliver has met at the gym, too." She gestured at a group near the French doors that opened onto the patio in warmer weather. "And, of course, some of the faculty. Students mixing with faculty *is* part of the college experience, don't you think?"

"I enjoy getting to know my students," Maggie said. "It helps me plan classes so the material I cover best meets their needs."

"That too, of course." Dorothy held a glass of sparkling water, and her pale pink nails—not a smudge in sight—were reflected in the crystal. "Young minds meeting"—she glanced at Maggie—"more mature ones. Culture being passed from one generation to another. That's what this is all about, isn't it?"

Most students at the community college were living at home and working part-time. Many supported families. A cocktail party at Somerset County Community College was not a humanities seminar at Yale. Maggie glanced around the room. Few students were conversing with professors; most were taking full advantage of the free food and open bar, and talking with each other.

"I think perhaps a beautician . . . ," Dorothy was saying.

Maggie focused in on the red hair and the pink nails

16

again. "Oh?" she said noncommittally. What had Dorothy said?

"A beautician, and then perhaps an interior decorator, would make marvelous guests for those Monday-night seminars you organize for the house, don't you think?"

Maggie spent every Monday evening at Whitcomb House, bringing with her an expert in an area she hoped the students would find helpful—childhood nutrition; legal issues related to single parents; financial planning; time management. The sessions were usually full and lively, since they always included at least some of the six children whose existence qualified their parents for residence at the house.

But a beautician and an interior decorator? Just what six struggling young parents who were exhausted from child care and studying would need. "Maybe later in the year," Maggie compromised. "The women might enjoy having makeovers. Especially if we found someone who could donate makeup for them."

Tiffany Douglass was the only one with any expertise in that area, Maggie realized. Tiff always looked ready for a photo session. Maria, Heather, Kayla, and Sarah had more . . . natural . . . styles. Unless you counted Maria's seven earrings and nose ring or the vine tattoo on Heather's right leg that climbed past all parts of her visible to the general public.

"Oh, I'm sure it could be arranged that the girls get some free makeup," Dorothy said.

Thank goodness she'd found something of value in Dorothy's suggestion, Maggie thought. She'd discouraged Dorothy's last two brainstorms—a catered Halloween party and sterling silver flatware—and Dorothy had been hurt.

"And don't you think Santa should visit for Christmas?"

Maggie sighed inwardly. The Whitcomb House students felt indebted enough to Dorothy for room and board and tuition; they didn't need reminding that they had little money for Christmas gifts. Especially when Dorothy visited at least once a week, leaving presents each time she came. It was nice for the kids, but hurtful for the parents who couldn't provide toys themselves. "I'll talk to everyone and see what their Christmas plans are. Some may want to stay at the house; others have family they'll visit."

"Poor Sarah. She has no one. Oliver and I were thinking of inviting her and Aura to spend the holidays with us." Dorothy and Maggie watched as Sarah poured herself a glass from a pitcher labeled "Bloody Mary mix." She didn't add vodka.

"I'll talk to her," said Maggie. "But don't make any plans until I do."

"Of course not." Dorothy squeezed Maggie's arm. "I'm sure you'll find a good way to introduce the idea to her. So she won't feel we're being patronizing."

A trace of insight? Maggie wondered as Dorothy headed for the bar to refill her sparkling water.

So far as Maggie knew, Dorothy didn't have any children, and clearly the young Whitcomb House students and their families were filling that role for her. They are for me, too, Maggie admitted to herself. She enjoyed the kids at Whitcomb House, from the youngest, Kendall's

Josette and Maria's eighteen-month-old Tony, to the oldest, Mikey Farelli, who at six would be too old next year for his mother to qualify for residence at the house.

Sarah's daughter, Aura, and Kayla's daughter, Katie, were favorites. Both four years old, they quickly became a team: masters of intrigue and disguise; experts at making costumes out of anything they found, from couch pillows to napkins. Last Monday Aura and Katie were princesses, dressed in their mothers' half-slips and balancing Beanie Babies they'd liberated from Mikey Farelli's collection on their heads as if they were crowns. Aura's pale red-gold curls and Katie's black ones bounced as the girls giggled and pranced in front of Whitcomb House's most recent guest, a Montessori teacher there to give the young parents advice about early childhood education.

Wonderful kids. And their parents were learning parenting skills from each other as well as from the college. Only Tiffany's Tyler, who was two, seemed less cared for than the rest. There was always someone to clean him up and head him in the right direction, but that person wasn't always Tiffany. Tiffany had missed more of the Monday seminars than anyone else, too. Where did she spend her evenings? Based on her American Studies grades, not at the library. Maggie sighed. Tiffany had skipped Maggie's "Myths in American Culture" class again last Friday. Maybe Tiff was doing better in her other classes; she should find out and then have a serious talk with her. Soon. Scholarship students had to keep up their grades.

As Maggie watched, Sarah joined Tiffany at one of

the bookcases. Sarah looked unsteady. Maybe her earlier drinks had been stronger than Bloody Mary mix. Tiffany guided Sarah to a chair.

It wouldn't be good for the Whitcombs to see one of "their" girls drunk. Maggie crossed the room quickly.

"Sarah, are you all right?" Maggie bent down next to her.

"No. It's not June. Don't let Simon know." Sarah looked at her strangely. "But I smell roses." Her body listed toward the side of the chair. "I think I'm going to puke."

"Tiffany, take her arm." Together they helped Sarah stand.

"My head hurts, too. Bad."

Maggie quickly smelled Sarah's breath. No alcohol. But she did smell as though she'd been smoking. Funny; she'd never seen Sarah smoke. "Let's get her out of here." Maggie headed Sarah and Tiffany toward the door.

"Shouldn't we say good-bye to the Whitcombs?" Tiffany said. "I'll go tell them." She dropped Sarah's arm and headed for Oliver.

Maggie just managed to keep Sarah upright. She was becoming weaker, and a puddle of drool was dripping onto the front of her soft gray turtleneck. Please, don't let her throw up on the Aubusson carpet, Maggie thought, just before Sarah's legs gave way and she collapsed onto the floor. Within seconds her limp body was surrounded by curious and well-meaning guests. "Give her some space!" Maggie commanded firmly. She knelt and took Sarah's wrist. The pulse was too rapid to count. Dangerously rapid.

"What's the matter with Sarah? Is she drunk? What can we do?" Dorothy looked aghast. "She seemed fine—"

"Call 911," interrupted Maggie. "Now."

Chapter 2

(Untitled.) Soft 1906 lithograph of beautiful woman in profile, auburn hair pinned up, wearing an elegant green evening dress and gloves, her poised figure outlined by a pale yellow cameo printed frame. Classic "Christy Girl" by Howard Chandler Christy (1867–1956). His drawings defined what was considered the ideal American woman in the early twentieth century. 6.75 x 9 inches. Price: $60.

The Whitcombs' cocktail party broke up as soon as the ambulance carrying Sarah Anderson to Somerset Hospital departed, its siren wailing through the quiet suburban streets of a Sunday night in early November.

"Professor Summer, should some of us go to the hospital to check on Sarah?" Kayla Martin was the most dependable of the Whitcomb House residents. At twenty-two, she was also the only one who had been married, proudly signing her name *Mrs.* Kayla Martin. Her former husband even sent occasional child support payments. Kayla brushed her short black curls back from her face. "We have the children to think of, too. What should we tell Aura?"

"Don't worry, Kayla," Maggie said. "You all go back to the house. Just tell Aura her mother was sick and had to see a doctor. I'll go to the hospital. As soon as I hear anything, I'll let you know."

Kayla nodded. "I'll let Aura sleep with Katie tonight. They'll like that. And Sarah will be home tomorrow, won't she?"

"I hope so, Kayla." Maggie turned and almost ran into Dorothy Whitcomb, who had been accepting thank-yous and good-byes from other guests.

"Are you going to the hospital, Maggie?"

"Yes. Someone should." Aura was Sarah's only family. She'd been a child of the foster care system in New Jersey for many years but didn't keep in touch with any of her seven foster families.

"I'll go with you," said Dorothy.

"You don't need to do that."

"Nonsense. I'll take my own car and meet you there."

There was no use arguing and no time to waste. What had happened to Sarah? She'd seemed fine only moments before. Food poisoning? But would it have come on so suddenly? Alcohol? But, at least when she'd seen Sarah, she'd only been drinking spiced tomato juice. Maggie looked over at the bar. It was already closed. Two women from the catering staff were covering and removing the food. They had already disposed of the pitchers containing tomato and orange juices, sealed the liquor and soft drink bottles, and were gathering dirty glasses.

Sarah couldn't have gotten sick from the food. They'd all been sampling the buffet dishes, and everyone else seemed fine.

If all parties could be cleaned up so quickly, Maggie

thought, she might be tempted to entertain more often herself.

The hospital was a ten-minute drive away. Maggie passed fields where show horses grazed during the day. Then the fields and barns gradually changed to small lots filled with split-level homes and modern colonials where grinning jack-o'-lanterns still glowed on porches beneath trees festooned with toilet paper. Two nights ago these suburban streets would have been filled with children dressed as ghosts and witches and Superman and Harry Potter. How did parents come up with those costumes? Maggie had never even mastered the hem-stitch in eighth-grade home economics.

She concentrated on her driving and tried not to think about the work waiting for her at home. Holding down two jobs was often exhausting, much as she enjoyed them both. Teaching American Studies took up her time during weekdays and even some weekends, such as when she had to go to a "must be there" reception. Like today. And when she wasn't at school or preparing for classes, she had to mat engravings or sort inventory items. She called her business Shadows because prints were a reflection of life the way it used to be, a view into the past. The income from Shadows, Maggie hoped, would help frame her future.

Her life had changed in so many ways during the past year. Now a widow for ten months, she'd decided to continue both her academic and antique-print careers, and, if possible, to increase the antiques side of her life to try to compensate for the loss of Michael's income.

The truth was, she missed his monetary contribution to their marriage more than she missed him. His presence in their marriage had been questionable before the car accident that ended it completely.

She was handling everything well—perhaps too well, her friend Gussie sometimes said. Michael's death and the estate issues; the knowledge of his betrayal; getting back into teaching and antiques; even finding a new potential romantic interest.

Maggie smiled softly to herself as she thought of Will Brewer's strength and patience and kindness. The feel of his arms around her.

Will's own antique business kept him on the road most of the time, and his home base was Buffalo, New York, not Somerset County, New Jersey. They'd met at an antique show last Memorial Day weekend. That had been just five months ago, but they'd been closely in touch, or together, since then. His caring filled an empty space in her life. His daily e-mails kept her checking her computer on days when she needed to lean on an emotional shoulder. "I wouldn't have time for a man in my life, full-time," she told herself. There was too much she needed to do first. Will's long-distance caring worked for now and allowed her to maintain her crowded schedule. Unromantic? Maybe. But true.

Or was she finding excuses not to have a man in her life on a regular basis? Michael had frequently traveled on business; there were often weeks when he'd arrived home on Friday after she'd left town to do a weekend antique show. Was she repeating a pattern? Was it simpler to live her life without a man in it?

Maggie shook her head. Her world was the way she needed it to be. Except for those long nights when e-mail messages couldn't take the place of a man to share her bed and to remind her she had a body as well as a mind. Except for those days when she wondered whether Will was really the right person for her after all.

At thirty-eight, Maggie knew her options in some areas of life were limited, and she had almost decided she wanted to be a mother. No. She knew she wanted to be a mother. She just didn't know whether she was brave enough to become a single mother like the women at Whitcomb House. Will had made it clear he wasn't father material. And she wasn't so old that she didn't fantasize about having a husband before she had a child.

Maggie groaned inwardly and shelved her personal issues as she approached the hospital. Tonight she must think about Sarah, not about her own issues.

"Sarah Anderson." The young blonde woman at the front desk looked bored and annoyed as Maggie asked again. "I'm here to find out about Sarah Anderson. She was just brought in by ambulance."

Five or six people sat in the pale green waiting room filled with orange plastic furniture. Maggie could hear voices and machines beeping behind the wall in back of the reception area.

"Are you a relative?"

"We're all Sarah has," said Dorothy, who had just joined Maggie at the desk. "We need to see her. Or her doctor."

"Mrs. Whitcomb, you're always welcome here." The blonde smiled, showing teeth perfected by orthodontia.

"The doctors are with Ms. Anderson now. I'll let them know you're here."

"Thank you. We wouldn't want to interfere in any way, of course," added Dorothy.

Maggie and Dorothy sat next to each other on the hard chairs that lined the waiting room under a mural of ivy climbing a wall.

"You know the woman at the desk?" Maggie asked.

"I'm on the hospital board," explained Dorothy, straightening the pale mink coat she held across her lap. "I try to meet the staff whenever I can."

"Of course," said Maggie. So Whitcomb House was not Dorothy's only pet project.

They sat silently, watching muted CNN on the television hung above the waiting area. A car had been bombed in the Middle East. A software company announced it was going into Chapter 11. The local forecast was for temperatures in the forties, with snow flurries later in the week. Words appeared along the bottom of the screen.

Maggie looked at her watch. Almost eight.

It was another forty minutes before a doctor appeared.

"Mrs. Whitcomb? I'm Dr. Stevens." A tall, middle-aged man with a receding hairline looked down at them. Dorothy and Maggie both stood.

Dorothy shook his hand. "And this is Maggie Summer. Professor Summer. She's Sarah Anderson's campus adviser."

Dr. Stevens acknowledged Maggie's presence with a slight nod. "I'm afraid Ms. Anderson is very ill. She's in a coma."

"Oh, my heavens! What happened to her? What can be done?" Dorothy's voice rose to an almost hysterical note. "She's a single parent, Doctor. She has a little girl. Please don't spare any expense."

"I assure you we're doing everything that we can, Mrs. Whitcomb. She appears to have swallowed something she's had a strong reaction to. We've pumped her stomach, and we've given her atropine. We're admitting her to our intensive care unit and will monitor her condition constantly. Without knowing what she might have ingested, it's hard to predict the future. Right now she's a seriously ill young woman. She has no family?"

Maggie shook her head. "Just a four-year-old daughter. Do you have any idea of what she might have eaten that would make her that sick?"

"We can rule out some things, like alcohol, but it's too early to tell. We've sent the contents of her stomach to our lab for analysis. Could either of you tell me where Ms. Anderson has been or what she has eaten? Does she have any food allergies? Does she take any medications or drugs of any kind?"

"No!" Dorothy's voice was strong, but her natural high color had disappeared from her face. "She doesn't take drugs! She doesn't drink, she doesn't smoke. She's a fine young woman."

The doctor looked at Maggie.

"I don't know if she has any allergies. But as far as I know, Dorothy is right. I've never seen Sarah taking any medications or drugs. And I think she's been in good health. We were all at a party at Dorothy's house when Sarah collapsed. Everyone else was fine when we left. But I'll talk to the students she lives with. They might know more."

"Anything you could find out would be helpful. You can reach me here at the hospital. Have me paged."

"Can we see her?" Dorothy asked.

"Not right now. We're in the middle of transferring her upstairs to the ICU."

Dorothy looked ready to say something else.

"Mrs. Whitcomb, she wouldn't know you were there. It's best to let her be quiet for now, until we have a better sense of her condition. We're doing the best we can."

"You'll call me if her condition changes?"

"I think it would be better if the doctor called me," said Maggie, digging in the side pocket of her purse for a business card. "If anything happens to Sarah, I'm the one who'll have to tell her little girl her mother's not coming home." She paused, suddenly overwhelmed by what she was about to say. She took a deep breath. "I'll be Aura's guardian."

Chapter 3

Wee Willie Winkie. *Lithograph of small boy in nightshirt carrying a lantern through city streets, knocking on windows. Dark blue border of stars with words printed below: "Wee Willie Winkie runs through the town, Upstairs and downstairs, in his nightgown, Rapping at the window, crying through the lock, 'Are the children in their beds, for now it's eight o'clock?'" Delicate pastel version of the old nursery rhyme. London, circa 1890, from* Rhymes

"You! Why will you be Aura's guardian?" Dorothy's concern had suddenly changed to anger. "How did that happen? You've only known Sarah two months!"

Dr. Stevens backed away. "Then I'll call you, Professor Summer. And you will keep Mrs. Whitcomb informed."

"Of course."

As the doctor disappeared through the emergency room's swinging doors, Dorothy turned on Maggie. "Why would she make you Aura's guardian? What have you got to do with Sarah?"

Everyone in the waiting room was looking at them. Maggie put her hand on Dorothy's arm and headed her toward the door to the parking lot. She wouldn't want the college trustee to think she had wielded undue influence over Sarah. But why should Dorothy be reacting so dramatically? Maggie spoke softly as they walked. "Most of the Whitcomb House residents made out wills after we had that legal seminar in September. Sarah has no family, and no close friends outside of Somerset College. She was worried that if anything happened to her, Aura would go into foster care." Foster care could be wonderful or awful. Unfortunately for Sarah, her experiences in the system had been horrendous. She'd never told Maggie the details, but she'd been very clear that she never wanted Aura to be a foster child.

"I'm sure she wouldn't have wanted Aura to have foster parents," Dorothy agreed. "But she could have asked Oliver and me. Then Aura would have had two parents. You aren't even married!"

Maggie swallowed hard, fighting down the urge to be defensive. "Sarah asked me to be Aura's guardian because at the time she couldn't think of anyone else. It was an interim decision. She was young and in good health; she hoped she'd marry in the next few years and her husband would adopt Aura. There was no reason to think her decision would mean anything immediate for Aura. It was just a way to protect her."

Until tonight, Maggie thought. She felt a strong urge to go to Whitcomb House, to hug the little girl with the red hair. To keep her safe. She wanted so much to be a mother, and now there was a child who needed her. She felt the muscles in her shoulders tighten with stress. Aura was still Sarah's child. Sarah would recover. Maggie must control her emotions.

"I'll stop at Whitcomb House and talk to the other students. Maybe they'll know more about Sarah. Something that will help the doctors figure out what's wrong with her."

Dorothy nodded. "Yes. Do that. But"—she reached out and took Maggie's hand—"let me know if you hear anything."

They separated in the parking lot, Dorothy walking toward her navy BMW sedan, and Maggie toward her faded blue van.

She lowered her head to the cold plastic steering wheel for a moment. If only Will were here. She wanted to feel safe and sheltered in his arms; to have his protection; to have him assure her that everything would be all right. A hug couldn't protect you from the world, of course. But it could allow you to pretend for a few precious moments. Had Will written her an e-mail note in the past few hours? Maybe she'd call him when she got home. He was headed for Ohio to do an antique show. He'd probably stop at a motel for the night; it was too cold to sleep in his RV.

She blinked back her tears. She needed a friend. But she and Will had decided to limit expenses by using e-mail instead of cell phones unless there was an emergency. This might be an emergency for Sarah Anderson and her daughter, but there was nothing Will could do about it. She had to handle this herself.

And she had questions to answer. What was wrong with Sarah? Why was Dorothy so agitated? How was Aura coping with her mother's absence? What if Sarah didn't come out of her coma? What if . . . ?

Chapter 4

A Cabinet Meeting—Where Our Betters Rule. *Black-and-white 1896 lithograph from Charles Dana Gibson's (1867–1944)* Americans *portfolio of line illustrations he termed "cartoons." Gibson created "The Gibson Girl," a rival of "The Christy Girl," at the end of the nineteenth century. His work often shows an ironic view of social mores of the period. This illustration depicts eight elegantly dressed and coiffed women sitting around a table, clearly involved in earnest discussion. 11 x 16.75 inches. Price: $70.*

Whitcomb House was a large yellow Victorian trimmed

in maroon that in earlier years had housed the chairman of the Somerset Savings and Loan and his large family. Its wide porch had been restored and its interior redesigned to fit the requirements of both building inspectors and single parents. The elegantly turreted building had a spacious lawn, now covered with drifted leaves. It was hard to miss in a neighborhood filled predominantly with ranch houses and small modern colonials.

The lights were still on when Maggie arrived. The combination of babies, toddlers, and homework assignments almost guaranteed that someone at Whitcomb House would be awake at most hours of the day or night. She knocked on the maroon door covered with cutouts of orange pumpkins and white ghosts.

Kendall opened it. Josette was sleeping in his arms, her black curly hair just visible under a fuzzy pink blanket. Her dad had changed from his dress-up attire of shirt and slacks into a red Somerset sweatshirt and gray sweatpants. He gestured for Maggie to come in, then headed for his room to put Josette in her crib.

Kendall, the only man living in the house, had been assigned the one first-floor bedroom, so none of the women would be in danger of being surprised in their underwear by his need to brush his teeth or dispose of a dirty diaper. Kendall was also therefore the one who usually answered the door and kept unofficial track of who was at home and who wasn't. When Dorothy had designed the layout of the house, she'd assumed that in the evenings most of the parents would be studying at the desks she provided in their rooms. In reality they often left the doors to their rooms open and asked other parents to listen for any trouble, sharing baby-sitting duties while balancing a social life with parental and student responsibilities.

Maggie settled herself into one of the green-and-blue-flowered chairs that matched the living room's couch. The large TV was muted. An episode of *Law and Order* played silently. The other residents must be upstairs.

Across from her, on the long wall above the television set, hung the six Anne Pratt hand-colored engravings she'd helped Dorothy Whitcomb choose for this room, matted in green to go with the decor, and framed in gold. Dorothy had loved the idea that Pratt, who published eleven volumes of botanical prints between 1828 and 1866, was one of the first women to be a successful botanical artist.

"But," Maggie had told Dorothy, "Anne Pratt did stop drawing when she got married for the first time—when she was sixty."

Dorothy had laughed out loud. "Married for the first time at sixty? After spending all those years painting she was probably exhausted. . . . I wonder what she and her husband did for fun?"

"She or her new husband might have needed a tonic. Because when she stopped doing botanical drawing, she started a new career—as an expert in the medicinal uses of plants."

She and Dorothy had agreed that Anne Pratt botanicals had to be a part of a single-parent dorm. It seemed such a long time ago that she and Dorothy had hung the prints. Last summer. When the idea of a dormitory for single parents had been a new, exciting concept. Not a place to look for clues to a mysterious illness.

Kendall was back in a moment. "How's Sarah?"

"She's in a coma."

"I'll call the others? Everyone will want to know."

"In a moment. Kendall, Sarah may have had something to eat or drink either at the party or earlier that made her sick. Does she have any allergies? Does she take drugs of any sort that you know of?"

"No!" Kendall sat down heavily on a tufted ottoman. "She's never mentioned allergies. And no drugs. She's pretty straight. Only drinks occasionally." He hesitated. "She does take vitamins. I heard her talking about vitamin E with Tiffany the other day. And as for food . . . today we shared a pot of minestrone for lunch. Heather's mother brought it over yesterday. No one else is sick."

"And so far as I know, she's the only one who was at the Whitcombs' party who's ill. Does Sarah have any friends outside the house? Does she go out often?"

He shook his head. "She's here most of the time. Friendly, but quiet. Keeps to herself."

"No boyfriends?"

"Not that I've seen or heard of. But like I said—she doesn't talk a lot. At least not to me."

"Who might she have talked with?"

"She and Tiffany are roommates. Tiff might know something. And Aura and Katie play together all the time, so I know Sarah and Kayla are in and out of each other's rooms a lot."

"You'd better call everyone down."

"We're sort of family for each other here. Everyone's been worried."

Kendall called softly up the stairs to where Maria lived with Tony, on the second floor of the attached carriage house. Then he went up the stairs to the rooms on the second floor of the main house to alert the others. Within minutes all of the residents had joined Maggie in the living room.

Maria was wearing bright red-and-purple-striped pajamas; Heather was pulling on a white terry-cloth bathrobe that barely covered her short polyester nightgown. The tattooed vine on her leg climbed even higher than Maggie had anticipated. Kayla and Tiffany were still dressed as they'd been at the Whitcombs'.

"Sarah's been admitted to the hospital. She's in intensive care," Maggie explained. "The doctors pumped out her stomach. They think she took something, or ate or drank something, that made her sick."

"Is she going to be all right?" Kayla asked softly. "She's not going to die, is she?"

"I hope not," said Maggie. She wished she could promise that Sarah would be fine. Soon. "She's in a coma. Do any of you know if she had any allergies?"

Silence.

"What did she take?" said Tiffany.

"The doctors don't know. They're going to test the contents of her stomach; the sooner they know what caused her problem, the sooner they can do something about it. Was Sarah taking any drugs—for medical reasons, or otherwise?"

"She took birth control pills," said Tiffany. "I've seen them on her dresser. And sometimes she took aspirin, when she had a headache."

"And vitamin C. She took vitamin C when she thought she might be getting a cold. And vitamin E sometimes," added Kayla. "But she didn't do drugs. Real drugs."

"She didn't even smoke," Kendall added. "I mean, she didn't smoke anything. Ever."

Maggie wondered if that was true. Sarah's breath had smelled like cigarettes. She also realized that drinking and drugs and smoking—anything—were probably topics these young people were more conversant with than she was. At least these days. After all, she'd been a student once herself.

"Was she depressed? Was there anything unusual about her behavior recently?"

"You mean—'did she try to kill herself?'" Heather's voice rose.

"She wouldn't do anything that took her away from Aura," Kayla said. "Aura is her world. No doubt about that. Sarah had a tough childhood. She didn't want that for Aura."

"Absolutely," added Tiffany. "Sometimes she'd talk. She had plans. She wanted to teach kindergarten. She had some down days, like we all do. It's not easy being a single parent. But she wasn't going to take any pills to mess herself up. No way."

Maggie looked around the room again. Their faces were serious. These young parents had already been through a lot. They knew what was at stake. Tiffany was right; it couldn't be easy being a single parent. Maggie stood up.

"I'm keeping in touch with the doctors. I'll let you all know if there are any changes."

"Can we visit her?"

"Not tonight. She has to rest. And she wouldn't know you were there. I'll let you know when she can have visitors." Maggie hesitated. "How is Aura doing?" She could take Aura to her home; she could give her cream of tomato soup and read her a story; she could . . . "Could I see her?"

"Aura's fine. Sleeping with Katie," said Kayla. "I don't think we should run the risk of waking them. We'll watch out for her." There were nods around the room. "We'll make sure she has a good breakfast and get her to day care tomorrow morning."

They were right, of course. Aura needed to stay here, at least for now. "Taking care of Aura is the best thing you can do for Sarah. She'd want Aura to stay with people she knows."

I want to have a child, Maggie thought. But not this way. Not because Sarah . . . Her mind refused to complete the thought, even silently. "You all have my home and office telephone numbers. If you think of anything that would help the doctors to help Sarah, call me. It doesn't matter how late. Or if there's any problem with Aura."

"We'll be fine, Professor Summer," Maria said as Maggie turned to leave. "Just make sure they take good care of Sarah. Bring her home."

Chapter 5

The Country Doctor. Wood engraving by A. R. Waud, cover of Harper's Weekly, *March 6, 1869. Kindly bearded doctor, saddlebag over his arm, standing next to his horse at the door of a concerned woman, offering her a bottle of tonic or medicine. 10.75 x 15.75 inches. Price: $75.*

Maggie made a mental list as she drove the few miles home from Whitcomb House. Call Dr. Stevens. Check answering machine. Check e-mail. She shivered in the cold, dry November air. Something warm to eat. She should have taken more advantage of the food at the Whitcombs' party. Or—maybe not. She might've ended up like Sarah.

She had two classes to teach tomorrow. "American History to 1865" wouldn't be a problem; she'd summarize economic factors leading up to the Civil War. She was giving an exam Friday, and her students would appreciate the review. But she needed to pull out some Currier and Ives prints to illustrate contradictory views of the frontier for her "Myths in American Culture" class. She should have done that before the party, but instead she'd started matting a new series of Curtis botanicals.

Some of the prints she wanted to use were in her Shadows portfolios; others were reproduced in her reference books. She'd have to find them all tonight.

What she really wanted to do was collapse into bed.

Winslow met her at the back door, mewing and rubbing against her legs. His full name was Winslow Homer, because he was black-and-white and had the same bored expression as the cat in Homer's wood engraving *The Dinner Horn*. About a month ago he'd appeared on the ramp leading up to her study and print room, and when she opened the door, he'd slipped in and established himself. She'd posted "Cat Found" ads in the local supermarket and on lampposts, but no one had claimed Winslow. In the meantime he'd clearly made himself at home. In fact, he now refused to leave the house. Maybe the outside world had been cruel to him.

There was no sign of any previous trauma now, though, as, having had his usual neck scratch, he stood by his food dish and loudly let it be known that dinner was late.

"Relax, Winslow. You're not starving. And your feet haven't been killing you for hours." Maggie kicked off her red heels, pulled off her panty hose, and liberated her sore toes. "Just one more minute." She got out the can opener, and Winslow riveted his attention on the liver-flavored cat food in his dish as she rinsed and filled his water bowl.

She'd promised to call Dr. Stevens, but she hadn't found out anything that would help him. Maybe if she waited a few more minutes before she called he'd have more news about Sarah's condition. Good news. Winslow was eating; now it was her turn.

Usually the kitchen of her 1920s colonial-style home seemed warm and welcoming. She'd hung brass saucepans on one pale yellow wall, arranging them as carefully as she did her antique prints. The warmth of their burnished color reflected light from the small, modern chandelier that hung over the nineteenth-century pine table and usually cheered her even if there were dirty dishes in the sink. Tonight she was too tired and distracted to notice. Even the carefully framed trio of Cassell's lithographed roosters, considered among the finest poultry prints ever made, were not enough to distract her.

She poured low-fat milk into a small pan. Cocoa was what she needed. Maybe the chocolate and caffeine combination would help her to focus on what she had to do. Unless, of course, the calcium made her even sleepier. Maggie wished for a moment she were a child again. A child who could drink cocoa just because it tasted good and made you feel warm and cozy. Analyzing the ingredients of everything you ate didn't make you feel cozy.

As she waited for the milk to heat, she pushed the blinking red button on her answering machine.

"Maggie? This is Gussie. Would it be imposing too much if Jim and I arrived late Wednesday night instead of Thursday? We got inspired by the Arts section of the Sunday *Times* today. We called a couple of theaters and got a wheelchair seat and companion ticket to a Broadway show for Wednesday night. If that won't work for you, though, we can get a room in New York. Call when you can! See you soon."

She and Gussie were both doing the antiques show in Morristown this weekend. Usually Gussie's nephew,

Ben, went with her to antiques shows to help out, but this time her friend Jim was keeping her company and acting as personal porter. One of Jim's old college friends lived in New Jersey, and he and Gussie planned to have dinner with the friend's family Saturday night. Morristown was less than an hour's drive from Maggie's home in Park Glen, so they could all commute from her home to the show during the weekend and save the expense of a motel room. When there were shows to do on Cape Cod, Maggie stayed with Gussie. It all evened out and gave them more time for chatting.

"Maggie, this is Dorothy Whitcomb. Please don't forget to call if you hear anything about Sarah. Oliver and I are so concerned. Call anytime. Thanks."

"Is this the print lady from Shadows antiques? I'm Lucy Standish. Four years ago I bought three prints of dalmatians from you. I saw your name on a list of dealers doing the Morristown show this weekend. If you have any more dalmatian prints, would you bring them with you to the show? I need a fourth to even out my arrangement. Thank you!"

Maggie arranged tomato sauce, cheese, and mushrooms on browned English muffin halves, put them back in the toaster oven, and dialed Gussie's number. Gussie was a night person; she wouldn't be asleep yet. In fact, she must be on her phone; the call went straight to her answering machine.

Just as well. A message would save time. She and Gussie could rarely keep their calls to each other under twenty minutes. "Hi, friend! Wednesday night would be fine. Can't guarantee how awake I'll be, but I'll be here.

I'll expect you around one A.M.—it'll take you about ninety minutes to get from Times Square to Park Glen. Just go through the Lincoln Tunnel, take the New Jersey Turnpike south, and then Route 78 west. You've been here before! As usual, you're more organized than I am. I haven't even packed my van for the show yet. See you and Jim in three days!"

The dalmatian customer she wouldn't worry about; if she had any prints of dogs, they were already matted, and she always took her portfolio of dogs to shows. Customers who didn't normally collect prints would come into her booth to see if one of her engravings or lithographs "looks like our Bowser." At least once during every show she had to explain that breeds had changed in the last hundred years; a German shepherd pictured in 1890 might not look precisely like one today.

It was time. She dialed the hospital and had Dr. Stevens paged. "I checked, and Sarah Anderson's housemates didn't know of any allergies she had. She doesn't smoke, is a light drinker, and wasn't depressed or taking any medications. They all ate the same home-made soup for lunch and the rest of them are fine. How's Sarah doing?"

"Her condition seems to be stabilizing, but hasn't improved. There's nothing to do but wait this out and watch her closely. No one else who was at the Whit-combs' party has come in, so she seems to be the only one affected. It probably isn't food poisoning."

"Can she have visitors tomorrow?"

"She'll still be in intensive care, or at least skilled

nursing. You or Mrs. Whitcomb could stop in briefly. No one else."

"Have the lab reports on her stomach contents come back?"

"I should have preliminary reports within the next hour. I'm hoping they'll help us identify her problem."

"If there are any changes, please call me," Maggie said. "Her little girl needs her."

"Do you know where the child's father is? He should be notified."

"I don't know who he is. But perhaps someone else does. I'll see if I can find out."

"Good. And you're sure she has no family other than her daughter?"

"I'm sure. Would you call me when you get the lab results?"

"As soon as I can."

Maggie left the dishes in the sink and headed for her computer. It was down the hall, in the room the previous owners of this house had called their family room. Maggie used it as a combination library, office, and workroom, where she not only prepared for classes, but also stored her business inventory and matted prints. Bookcases filled with books on art and antiques and American history lined the wall opposite the fireplace, and a wide door at the far end of the room opened onto the ramp she'd installed so she could put her portfolios and cartons on a dolly and roll them down to her van in the driveway.

Had Will e-mailed her? Sometimes he made time when he got into a motel late at night. She clicked on

RECEIVE. An ad for an herb guaranteed to enlarge her penis. Delete. A credit card offer. Delete. A sale at a women's clothing company. Two years ago she'd ordered a red sweater from them. It had never fit. Delete. A note from a student explaining he'd miss Monday's class because his grandfather was ill. Maggie printed it out to put in the student's file.

No note from Will. He was an early riser; she'd no doubt find a message from him in the morning. She hesitated. Should she write to him now? What would she say? A student had become ill; she'd gone with the student to the hospital. It was late; she was tired. She wished he were here. She could use a hug.

Maybe he'd think she was too needy.

Maybe tonight she was.

Maggie turned off the computer and found her Currier & Ives portfolio and books and notes for tomorrow's classes. She had to make up the first-floor guest room for Gussie and Jim. Get some groceries in the house. Maybe pasta with a sauce for Thursday night? Maggie stifled a yawn. She'd figure that out tomorrow.

Last spring she'd redecorated her bedroom, hoping to erase memories of her marriage and make the room her own. Michael's taste had run to grays and browns. She'd painted over the dark colors, papered the walls with a small, light yellow floral print, and hung a series of gold-framed, hand-colored red and yellow Curtis flowers from the 1840s. She'd thrown out Michael's worn leather recliner, which was always covered with dirty socks and underwear, and replaced it with a burgundy reading chair whose color picked up the red of

44

the botanicals. The queen-size brass bed was new, as were the new padded mattress and the soft, hand-loomed wool blanket on the nineteenth-century, pine captain's chest at the foot of the bed.

Tonight the bed looked too inviting to ignore. She'd shower and soak her foot in the morning. It was better already, freed from those torturous shoes. She undressed, smeared some antibiotic ointment on the blister, and nestled under the down comforter. Seconds later Winslow established himself in his usual place on the foot of the bed.

The telephone rang just as she fell asleep.

Three rings later she reconnected to the waking world and picked up the receiver. "Professor Summer? It's Dr. Stevens. I just got the preliminary results of the lab report. I've had to call the police. Your young friend Sarah Anderson swallowed some sort of poison."

"Poison!" Maggie was wide-awake. "What? When?"

"We won't know until the full toxicology screen comes back. If we're lucky, that will be in about twenty-four hours, but it could take longer. In the meantime there's no way of knowing what she took, or whether she took something voluntarily or someone else gave it to her. Which is why we've referred the situation to the police."

"But—police?" Maggie quickly thought through what she knew of Sarah's day. At Whitcomb House, and then at the party. "No one would have any reason to hurt Sarah!"

"That will be up to the police to determine."

Maggie's heart was racing. How could Sarah have

45

been poisoned? Who even knew Sarah, other than the Whitcomb House residents and a few other students and professors at Somerset College? "How is she now?"

"She's holding her own. No changes. I'll keep you informed." The phone clicked.

Maggie pulled the comforter up and hugged her pillow. Poisoned! Should she call Dorothy? She'd wanted to be kept informed. But it was after midnight. Why wake someone else up at this time of the night? She'd call Dorothy tomorrow.

Maggie rolled over and wished Will were there. And prayed Sarah Anderson would still be alive in the morning.

Chapter 6

(Untitled.) Printed instructional example of elaborate Victorian calligraphy. A pen and ink drawing imitates the swirls and loops of handwriting. Two birds, caught in a net of lines that might also be a nest, interwoven with a ribbon that might also be a branch. In the twentieth century artists such as M. C. Escher carried this art of elaborate and sometimes deceptive line drawing into new mathematical dimensions. 8.5 x 11 inches. Price: $60.

The alarm clock went off at the same moment that the telephone rang. Maggie, deep in a dream about swimming through strong currents off the Maine coast, thought at first that she was hearing a foghorn. No, a fire alarm. Could there be a fire in the water? It took another ring for her groggy mind to shake off the fog and a few more seconds for her to turn off the alarm and lift the telephone receiver.

"Have you heard anything? How is Sarah?" It was Dorothy Whitcomb.

She turned her head to see the clock. Six A.M. Monday morning. Sarah Anderson was in the hospital.

Maggie sat up, trying to bring the day into focus. Despite her exhaustion she'd managed to braid her long brown hair the night before, as she always did before going to bed, to keep it from tangling. She brushed a few straggling hairs off her face.

"Maggie, are you there?"

"I'm here, Dorothy."

"Have you heard from Dr. Stevens?"

She was supposed to have called Dorothy if she'd heard anything. Shit. There was no way around this. "He called very late last night. There was no change in her condition, so I didn't want to bother you."

"They still have no idea what caused the coma?"

"They do, actually. It was some kind of poison."

"Poison!" For once, Dorothy was silent. For a moment. "You mean she *was* poisoned? Or that she took it herself, intentionally?"

"One of the two. There's no way of knowing without at least identifying the poison. That's why Dr. Stevens referred the situation to the police."

"No."

Maggie couldn't tell whether the "no" was a comment, a question, or a reaction.

"Will they—the police—be questioning all of us?"

"I'd guess so. Since we were at your house when Sarah got ill."

"Maggie, I need to see you. Privately. Quickly. Now."

"I have a nine-o'clock class."

"It's only six. I need to tell you something, in strictest confidence. And I don't want you to come here." Dorothy hesitated. "I wouldn't want to disturb Oliver. He usually sleeps in. Could you meet me in the parking lot of Christ Episcopal Church? You know where it is— just down the street from the college? No one should be there at this hour."

Maggie hesitated; should she invite Dorothy to her home? Why was it so important they not be seen?

"Give me half an hour to shower and dress. No, make that forty-five minutes."

"I'll meet you there at six forty-five."

Maggie headed for the bathroom, almost tripping over Winslow, who was wishing her a good day in his own way. The hot water revived her, and the smell of her favorite lavender soap brought back a sense of normalcy. Sarah would be all right. Dorothy would calm down. The doctor must be mistaken; no one had tried to hurt Sarah. Aura would be fine, and her mother would come home to her. And Maggie would get something to eat and then have a moment to glance through her day's schedule before meeting Dorothy. What could Dorothy have on her mind that was so secretive it had to be told in a church parking lot at a quarter to seven in the morning?

She bandaged her injured toe, pulled on brown slacks and a white turtleneck, pinned on a rhinestone *M* pin for luck, and was pouring herself a glass of Diet Pepsi (with caffeine) when the doorbell rang. Could Dorothy have changed her mind and come here?

Maggie plugged in her electric kettle just in case she'd need to offer tea or coffee.

But neither of the people standing at her front door holding detectives' badges was Dorothy. One was a young black woman, shorter than Maggie—perhaps five feet four inches tall. Her slightly paunchy partner was a middle-aged white male who looked as though he needed coffee. Badly.

"Professor Summer?"

"Yes."

"We're from the Somerset County detectives unit." Simultaneous flashing of badges. "Sorry to be here so early, but we'd like to ask you a few questions." The man spoke, but the woman was the one with the black notebook. "About Sarah Anderson."

Had Sarah died? Why were the police here? "I talked with Dr. Stevens late last night," said Maggie. "She was still in a coma. Has there been any change?"

"Not that we've heard. May we come in?"

Maggie moved aside. The two detectives walked in, clearly taking mental notes about the state of the house. She wished she'd vacuumed yesterday afternoon, or moved the portfolios. Or done almost anything but what she *had* done: matted prints and then gone to the Whitcombs' party. The party where Sarah had collapsed.

The kettle whistled in the kitchen.

"Would you like some tea, or instant coffee? Sorry I don't have any perked." Maggie headed for the kitchen to turn off the kettle. How long would this visit from the police take? Dorothy didn't deal well with waiting for people. But if Dorothy had wanted a private meeting, then thank goodness she hadn't come here. Maggie grimaced as she wondered what the neighbors would think of her early-morning visit from the police. Had they driven a patrol car? She hadn't noticed.

"No, thanks," said the woman, following Maggie to the kitchen. "I'm Detective Newton, and this is Detective Luciani." Luciani nodded his head as he looked around the kitchen.

Maggie hoped there wasn't anything in the room that could be construed as poison. A bottle of aspirin was lying on the windowsill. Other than an overdose of black pepper or garlic salt, there was nothing else she could see that might be of interest to the detectives. "Won't you sit down?"

Detective Newton took the lead. "How long have you known Ms. Anderson?"

"Since late August. Sarah Anderson lives in Whitcomb House, at Somerset College. I was assigned to be the faculty adviser to the residents of Whitcomb House, and I first met with them at an orientation meeting the week before Labor Day."

"You had access to their records?"

"To their college applications and essays explaining their interest in the Whitcomb House experiment."

"Experiment?"

"That's how the administration thinks of it. Some colleges have tried dorms for single parents, but not many have tied the dorm residences into a full schol-

50

arship program and day care."

"And the program is under your direction?" Detective Newton was asking questions and taking notes; Detective Luciani seemed to be memorizing the pattern of the pots hanging on the wall.

"No. It's under the administration of President Hagfield's office." Why was that? Maggie suddenly wondered. Why hadn't Max delegated the program to someone else? Maybe because of its high visibility. "It's the first year of a new program, and President Hagfield wants to make sure it runs smoothly, so he's keeping a close eye on it."

"How *is* the program going?"

"Of course, we haven't even finished one semester. It will take at least a full year to evaluate the program. But all of the students are completing their class work and seem to be taking the opportunity they've been given seriously. They're conscious of being the first ones in the program."

"So it's a bit of an honor."

Maggie hesitated. "I believe there were several dozen applications for the six positions open. But you'd have to talk to people in Admissions to find out about that. I wasn't involved until the students had been chosen and moved to campus."

"And your job is?"

"To teach American Studies and be adviser to about thirty students. These six students were assigned to me as a group because their needs were seen as a little different from those of our other students. President Hagfield wanted one person to work with all of them in case any problems arose that could be considered group problems, or we were able to identify issues which would require the college to change the program to better meet the needs of these students."

"And have you seen any problems?"

"Not so far. They're a remarkable group of dedicated young parents and students." Maggie hoped they wouldn't ask about Tiffany's grades or Heather's attendance or whether all the children were potty trained. There certainly were no problems in Whitcomb House that could have anything to do with Sarah's being in the hospital.

"What do you know about Sarah Anderson?"

"She was in the foster care system here in New Jersey until she was eighteen. She's been on her own since then. She has a cute little girl, Aura, who is four. Sarah worked as a waitress at a diner before she came to Somerset College." Maggie remembered what Tiffany had said last night. "She wants to teach kindergarten someday."

"Does she have many friends?"

"I only saw her at Whitcomb House and occasionally on campus. The Whitcomb House residents have gotten to know each other well. I don't know if she has any other friends. But it's certainly possible."

"Or family?"

"Or family. But there are no family members listed in her records."

"She made you her daughter's guardian."

How had the police learned that so quickly? Dr. Stevens must have mentioned it to them. She should have kept her mouth shut last night.

"Yes."

"You said you met her at the end of August and had no prior relationship with her." Detective Newton looked down at her notes. "Doesn't it seem unusual that she'd ask you to take such a major role in her daughter's life after knowing you for such a short time?"

"I arrange Monday-night discussion groups at Whitcomb House. Most are led by outside experts. One of the guests was a lawyer. She emphasized that every single parent should have a will and a legal plan designating someone to care for their children if they were no longer able to. I believe after she spoke most of the Whitcomb House residents made out simple wills. That was when Sarah asked me to be Aura's guardian in case of her death or incapacity. She said she had no one else to ask." Sarah had said she wanted Aura to have a strong role model, Maggie remembered. She'd been flattered to have been asked.

"Do you have children, Professor Summer?"

"No."

"Are you married?"

"I'm a widow."

"I see." Detective Newton made another note.

What did she see?

"So President Hagfield was concerned about these young people." Detective Luciani had a voice. A deep one. He was no longer focusing on the copper pans. He was focusing on Maggie.

"Yes."

"Did he have any special interest in the young

women in the group? Or in any particular young woman in the group?"

Maggie looked at him sharply. "I never had that impression. Never. President Hagfield's an excellent administrator. He puts Somerset College first. He would never do anything to tarnish its reputation."

"And last night you and all these single mothers and President Hagfield were at a party at the home of Dorothy and Oliver Whitcomb."

"Yes. And, for the record, one of the residents of Whitcomb House is a single father. He was there, too. Other Somerset students and professors were also at the Whitcombs'. Perhaps forty people in all."

"And you were with Ms. Anderson when she got sick."

"She seemed confused; she said she was dizzy, and then she just collapsed. Someone called 911. Mrs. Whitcomb and I drove to the hospital to see if we could help in any way."

"Mrs. Whitcomb is the person behind the money for this dormitory for unmarried parents?"

Maggie nodded.

"Sounds as though she's pretty involved with the students."

"She cares about the success of the program." Much too involved, Maggie added to herself. She needs a life. But that was Dorothy's issue, not a police problem.

"Before we leave, Professor Summer. Bottom line. Can you think of anyone who would benefit from Sarah Anderson's death?"

"No! She's a dear, sweet girl, and an excellent mother, who's working hard toward making a future for herself and her daughter. There is absolutely no reason I know of for anyone to hurt her."

But, of course, someone had.

Chapter 7

Mr. Phelps as Sir John Falstaff (Number 74). Hand-colored (mainly in shades of green and orange) steel engraving of actor as Falstaff, complete with sword and shield. Published by J. Redington, 73 Hoxton Street, London, about 1830. Small tear mended with archival tape in upper right-hand corner. 6.75 x 8.5 inches. Price: $50.

It took a few more minutes for Maggie to assure Detectives Newton and Luciani there was nothing more she could add to their knowledge about Sarah Anderson.

Maggie wondered about the parents who had deserted Sarah; the many foster families Sarah didn't talk about. What about the last four years, when Sarah had been a struggling single parent with a little girl? There must have been people in her life during those years. There must have been hard times. Could any of those have come back to haunt Sarah now? And Dr. Stevens had asked who Aura's father was. . . . When Sarah had asked Maggie to be Aura's guardian, she'd just said Aura didn't have a father. Did that mean she didn't know who Aura's father was? That the man didn't know he had a daughter? That Aura's father had left them? Or that Sarah, for whatever reason, wanted nothing to do with him?

There was a lot about Sarah Anderson she didn't know. What part of that life had made Sarah a victim yesterday?

The question echoed through Maggie's thoughts as she turned on her computer and piled up her papers for this morning's classes. If she'd known Dorothy's cell phone number, she could have called. But she didn't. She was already late for her 6:45 parking-lot appointment, and Dorothy would just have to wait a few more minutes.

What Maggie needed was a word from someone far away from Somerset College.

That word was waiting in her e-mail in-box.

Good morning, favorite print lady! Ohio is dreary and cold, and I assume our weather is heading east, so put on a heavy sweater before leaving this morning for those salt mines you call a college.

Maggie smiled. Will had been a teacher for years and was now trying to make a living as a full-time antiques dealer specializing in colonial kitchen and fireplace equipment. He couldn't help teasing her about her choice to go the opposite route: to deal in antique prints only on weekends and vacations. She moved Winslow off the keyboard and read the rest of Will's message.

I'm well, but miss you. If you'd been here, I'd have had an excuse to eat a healthier dinner than the burger and beer I had at the bar next to my motel last night. I also might have missed out on the heart-

burn that got me up at 3 A.M. I'm writing to you in the middle of the night, though, so maybe the burger was meant to be. I'm stopping at an auction this morning; their ad in Antique Week *lists an Arts and Crafts set of twisted-column brass andirons and matching fire screen that sound promising. I'll leave a bid if they deserve one, and then head west. Hope your world is calm and sunny. Thinking of you.*

Will

Maggie turned off the computer. Calm and sunny. That's what the world should be, for sure. She checked Winslow's water dish; it was full and he had plenty of dry food. She gave his head an extra scratch for good luck. Luck for all of them. For her. For Will. And for Sarah Anderson.

Dorothy was standing outside the driver's door of her BMW when Maggie pulled up beside her in the church parking lot. The early-November air was dank. Not sunny. And not calm.

"Where have you been? It's after seven. I've been here for almost half an hour!"

Maggie had barely turned off her van's engine, and Dorothy was already questioning her.

"I was held up. Two detectives stopped in to say 'Good morning.'"

"The police? They came to your house?"

"They just left. They were asking questions about Sarah. Dr. Stevens called them when the lab report came back saying she'd been poisoned."

"But—already." Dorothy pushed up the shawl collar on her heavy navy cardigan. It probably kept away some of the cold. It also hid part of her face. "What were they asking?"

"What I knew about Sarah. How long I'd known her. About Whitcomb House and the students there."

"What did you tell them?"

"What I knew, which wasn't much. And that I couldn't think of any reason someone would want to harm Sarah."

"Did they say anything about her condition?"

"So far as they knew it was unchanged."

Dorothy reached into her sweater pocket and pulled out a pack of cigarettes. Maggie had never seen her smoke before.

She lit one, dropped the match, and crushed it with her right foot, grinding small pieces of the paper match into the parking-lot pavement under her polished loafer. Behind her the elegant granite of Christ Episcopal Church's steeple rose into the dim morning light. No other cars were in the parking lot on this early Monday morning.

As she watched Dorothy's measured cigarette ritual, Maggie wondered again why they'd needed to talk immediately. And why in person? And why here?

Dorothy inhaled deeply, then blew smoke and warm air out in a small cloud. Neither she nor Maggie said anything for a few moments.

"Do you think they'll question me?" Dorothy finally asked quietly.

"You funded Whitcomb House, and Sarah was at your

home when she collapsed. I suspect they'll talk with everyone she knows. At least until they learn what it was that poisoned her."

"How is Aura taking all of this?"

"Fine, last night. I'm sure she doesn't realize how sick her mother is. Kayla and Tiffany were going to take Aura to the day-care center this morning. They'll watch out for her while Sarah's in the hospital. They're very concerned."

"They're good girls," said Dorothy. "We chose good mothers—and Kendall—to be in the first Whitcomb House group."

"Yes."

"Did the police ask how we selected them?"

"Not specifically. The police know they're single parents, and I said they'd been chosen out of many applicants."

"Right. That's just right. Maggie, I'm so proud of this program. I wouldn't want any bad publicity to result from Sarah's situation."

"I'm not sure what you're getting at here. You can't stop the press from reporting that one of Somerset College's students may have been poisoned and the police are investigating. They'll get that much from the local police record."

Dorothy dropped the rest of her cigarette. "Hell."

"They have to investigate, Dorothy. They have to find out who tried to hurt Sarah."

"I know. I just don't want anyone getting involved in things that are none of their business. Some parts of life are private. Sarah's life, and other people's lives, too."

Did Dorothy know something? Something that might help the police find whoever had poisoned Sarah?

"We have to cooperate, Dorothy. It wouldn't be fair to Sarah or Aura not to do that." Maggie paused.

"Of course it wouldn't, Maggie." Dorothy set her mouth in a tight smile and patted Maggie's arm. "Of course not, dear. We'll all cooperate. And I'm sure everything will just be fine. No one we know could have hurt Sarah. It was probably just some strange coincidence."

Poison? A coincidence? "Why did you ask me to meet you here, Dorothy? What did you want to tell me?"

Dorothy glanced around nervously, tapping her foot as if she wanted to leave. "It wasn't important. You go on over to the college. You said you had a nine-o'clock class, right?"

"Yes."

"Then you go. I was just nervous this morning; I shouldn't have bothered you. We'll have plenty of time to talk later. I'm going to stop at the hospital to visit Sarah, if I can, and see Dr. Stevens."

"If Sarah's condition changes, or if you hear any-thing—you'll let me know, Dorothy?"

"Of course, Maggie. Just like you called last night to tell me Sarah had been poisoned." The BMW door slammed a little too close to Maggie for comfort, and then Dorothy's car zoomed out of the church lot.

Dorothy knew something. That was clear.

But what was it? Could she know why Sarah was now in a coma and be keeping it to herself?

Maggie's damp and chilly van did nothing to improve

her mood. She wanted to stop at Whitcomb House to check on Aura, but the residents were no doubt busy getting themselves and their children up and fed and dressed for the day. Not a good time to stop in. How had Aura gotten through the night? How had she reacted when she woke up and found her mother wasn't with her?

Maggie had been reading a lot about adoption recently. She wanted to check out every possibility. She'd gotten on the mailing lists of several local and international adoption agencies, and after months of pamphlet-reading she now knew some things about the realities of adoption today.

If Sarah's parents had deserted her as a child, why hadn't she been adopted? She'd been white, she'd no doubt been cute, and she didn't appear to have any physical disabilities. Prospective adoptive parents waited in line for years in hopes of adopting a little girl like that.

Many older children, though, didn't find homes. She didn't know how old Sarah had been when her parents left. Sarah was twenty-three now; what had been the definition of an "older child" when she was a toddler?

Maggie did know that Aura was four and would be missing her mother. She'd stop in at the day-care center to see her. Later in the morning. But first she had to teach her class.

The American wilderness—an Eden offering haven and moral cleansing and an alternative to the corruption and filth of the city? Or a cruel place where savages and beasts roamed, people lived beyond a just world's laws

61

and religions, and nature's ferocity made even survival of the fittest only a possibility?

The theme for her class this morning.

Sarah's survival seemed a much more immediate issue.

Chapter 8

The Snow Storm: Opening Blockaded Roads in the Country. Wood engraving by C. G. Bush in Harper's Weekly, *February 9, 1867. Desolate scene of horses pulling a crude wooden, triangular-shaped platform, somewhat like a pointed sled, which packed the snow down on country roads, making them safe and passable for horses and wagons. Five children sit or stand on the platform to add weight, while a man steadies it from behind. 6 x 9.25 inches. Price: $50.*

"Currier and Ives was among the most successful mid-nineteenth-century American companies," Maggie began. The twenty or so students looked as they often did on Monday mornings . . . as though they hadn't quite woken up. The cups of coffee or tea she saw on nearly every desk would eventually bring them around, she knew from experience. She raised her voice. That might help, too. "The images first produced by Currier and Ives are still a success today, reproduced on calendars, mugs, and T-shirts, giving us a view of America as Americans wanted to think of themselves in the mid and late nineteenth century.

"Lithography, discovered in 1796 in Germany, was

adopted in the first quarter of nineteenth-century America for printing business forms and lettering. Nathaniel Currier was the first to apply the technique to art on a large scale. Beginning in 1835, he produced lithographs of important news events, and then of more general pictures, to decorate the homes of America. His brother-in-law, James Merritt Ives, joined him in 1857, and the firm of Currier and Ives became, indeed, 'print-makers to the American people,' as their slogan claimed."

Maggie took a sip of her Diet Pepsi. Where was Tiffany? She wasn't in class. Again. Single parents didn't have the default excuse of oversleeping. Two-year-old Tyler would definitely have been up at dawn. Maggie made a mental note to talk to Tiffany later. She must be upset about Sarah, of course, but her grades, and her scholarship, depended on her keeping up with class work. Skipping classes wouldn't help with that, no matter what the excuse.

"American culture has grown up embracing contradictory myths. Currier and Ives prints illustrated both sides of the theme we're going to discuss today: the role of the wilderness in American history and myth.

"For some nineteenth-century Americans the wilderness represented freedom and opportunity. Land for all. An untouched Eden; a new world, uncluttered by the corruption of the city, where Americans could make their own future. Life in the country was seen as pure and moral—very different from life in cities. Cities both in Europe and in America had become crowded, dirty, and crime-ridden."

What would the Somerset County of today be considered? Maggie wondered. Frontier? Not anymore. But not a true city, either. Perhaps today's suburban landscape was a classic American compromise. And that compromise bred neither the innocence of the frontier, nor the evils of the city, but something in between.

Maggie removed a print from one of her portfolios and leaned it against an easel.

"This print, *Life in the Country—Evening*, is a Currier and Ives from 1862 which shows a very civilized 'country'—a large house with a trimmed lawn, a European-style fountain and garden, and a gatehouse by the fence that protects the house from the thick woods surrounding it. In this illustration the wilderness is tamed."

She pulled out a second Currier & Ives and placed it on top of the first. "In *The Pioneer's Home—On the Western Frontier*, 1867, the house is a log cabin. But it is similar to the earlier print in that the home is surrounded by a cleared part of the wilderness. The home is full: three small children are clean and well-dressed; chickens and goats are in the yard; and the returning hunters of the family are bringing with them deer, wild turkeys, and pheasants. This wilderness is, like the eastern home, a tamed wilderness, with plenty for all. An Eden of sorts, providing food, comfort, warmth, and community to the family."

One of the students raised his hand.

"Professor Summer, that picture is too perfect! Even the children playing in the dirt yard and the men returning from hunting are wearing clean clothes! Did people really believe the frontier was like that?"

Maggie seized the opportunity to get their attention. "People idealized the frontier, Jason. In the same way many people today believe romance is the way it is in the movies, where couples have simultaneous orgasms and wake up together with perfect makeup, hair in place, and sweet breath."

Two students who had been dozing suddenly sat up. Mission accomplished.

"So, yes, many Americans, especially those who had never been to the frontier, believed in that image. Remember, one of the purposes of these lithographs was to attract people to go West. But now let me show you another view of the American frontier."

Maggie opened a large book of Currier & Ives reproductions to *Prairie Fires of the Great West* and held it up for the class to see. "In this 1871 print the horrors of this same wilderness are clear. Giant flames and clouds of smoke from the prairie fire fill the horizon, threatening both herds of buffalo and the train which transects the scene, symbolizing civilization. The train's billowing smoke blends with the smoke of the fire. This wilderness is uncontrolled and uncontrollable."

Uncontrollable. Was what had happened to Sarah uncontrollable? But how could we prevent what we didn't anticipate? And if it could happen to Sarah, then could it happen to someone else? Maggie hoped fervently that Detectives Luciani and Newton had already found whoever had caused all this pain. Found that person and locked him or her up, far away from civilization.

She turned the book to still another page. "*High Water*

in the Mississippi illustrates another natural danger of the wilderness. The Mississippi has flooded. The large home in the rear of the print is surrounded by water; in the foreground a group of black Americans try to escape the waters by gathering on the roof of a house. Again, as with the fire, the flood has destroyed what men have made; nature is man's enemy, not his friend.

"And here is a final example." Maggie balanced the large book on the desk in front of her. "This 1868 Currier and Ives, *Across the Continent: Westward the Course of Empire Takes Its Way*, takes its theme from a series of paintings Thomas Cole did in 1836 called *The Course of Empire*. Cole's paintings depicted the rise and fall of European civilization: an American reaction to the problems escaped by emigrating.

"By the way, if you'd like to see paintings by Thomas Cole and other American artists of that period, the Montclair Art Museum has an excellent small collection that includes most of the major American artists of the nineteenth century.

"In the Currier and Ives version, 'the course of empire' westward is visualized as a positive, inevitable step in taming the savage wilderness. Instead of Cole's depictions of the crumbling ruins of Europe, here the railroad cuts a dramatic line through the untouched prairie. But civilization has already taken a toll. On one side of the railroad tracks pioneers are resolutely cutting down trees, creating towns and schools, and 'civilizing' the land. On the other side, the Indians on horseback watch near the forests, separated from the white community by the railroad.

"In many ways this print most accurately reflects the way in which Eastern Americans viewed the journey westward in the mid and late nineteenth century."

Maggie closed the large book.

As soon as the bell rang, she could see Aura and find out how Sarah was doing. If she was still alive.

Chapter 9

The Grand Display of Fireworks and Illuminations—At the Opening of the Great Suspension Bridge Between New York and Brooklyn on the Evening of May 24, 1883. *Currier & Ives lithograph. Medium folio. 12 x 17.9 inches. Price: $900.*

"Good morning, Maggie. Although how anyone can call a cloudy, cold day like this good I don't know." Claudia Hall had short, dark hair that varied in curliness depending on the weather. She had been the American Studies department secretary forever and was always ready to provide gossip, chocolates, and a depressing interpretation of life to anyone who came near. This year the department members to whom Claudia offered solicited or unsolicited advice included Maggie, Paul Turk, Linc James, who taught American ethnic studies, and Geoff Boyle, who specialized in American religion and intellectual history.

"Good morning, Claudia. Any messages so far?" Maggie took two chocolate Kisses from the red candy dish on Claudia's desk. Other secretaries let telephone callers leave messages on voice mail. Claudia felt she could provide value-added by answering the calls herself.

"A pile of them. Isn't it awful about Sarah Anderson?" Clearly, the word was out.

"It's very sad. I'm going to check on her later today."

"Then you should return Dr. Stevens's call first," Claudia suggested, shuffling through Maggie's pile of pink slips. "He said it was important. And Mrs. Whitcomb called you. The Whitcombs have to be really upset. I mean, Sarah collapsing at their house and everything! Mr. Whitcomb called Paul Turk this morning. And President Hagfield called and said you shouldn't talk to any reporters. You should only answer direct questions from the police and not volunteer anything." Claudia lowered her voice. "That was just before Evan Connors called from *The Star-Ledger.* President Hagfield must have known he was going to call. He must be awfully worried about Somerset College's reputation. If the word about Sarah gets out—and it will!—then all our students could withdraw, and we could all be unemployed." Claudia's expression implied she had been waiting for just such an event. It was only a matter of time. "And Tiffany Douglass called. She wants to see you. She wouldn't say about what. But I know her grades haven't been so good recently." Claudia looked as though now she had the world organized.

Maggie reached over the desk and took the pile of pink slips. "Thank you, Claudia."

"If there's anything I can do to help, Maggie, I'll be right here. Unless that murderer who tried to kill Sarah Anderson strikes again. I always thought Somerset

County was a safe place to live, but this just shows you can't trust anyone. I've decided to stay close to the office today. I won't even go out for lunch. You never know who might be out there. We all need to be vigilant."

"I'm sure everything will be fine." Maggie opened the door to her office, which Claudia must have unlocked earlier, and a cat streaked out. "Claudia, would you make sure Uncle Sam stays out of my office? He's taken too much of a liking to my snake plant." Dirt from the three-foot-high plant was all over the floor around it, and Maggie sniffed the air. Something else had been added to the large flowerpot in place of the dirt. That was why she didn't have indoor plants at home to tempt Winslow.

"I'll watch him, Maggie."

Uncle Sam was striped, and the biology department would probably have dubbed him Tiger, but the white star on his forehead symbolized something else to the American Studies professors. Sam had been the unofficial departmental cat since he'd appeared in the office two years ago. Claudia was the assigned cat manager, and she took him home on weekends and vacations. They all chipped in for the cat food that was stacked next to the Poland Spring water dispenser. Claudia was also in charge of the litter box behind the copy machine. No wonder she kept letting him into Maggie's office to visit the snake plant.

Maggie's office was small and cluttered. Bookcases to the ceiling overflowed with books stacked horizontally as well as vertically, filling every bit of space between the shelves. The top of the file cabinet in the corner was covered with papers. She stood the Currier & Ives prints she'd used this morning next to the cabinet. Then she unlocked her desk, took her student record books from the lower right-hand file drawer, noted the attendance at this morning's class, including the man who'd left a request for an excused absence on her home computer last night, and locked the record books up again. She must clean out her office. Maybe during Thanksgiving break. In the meantime she looked at the pink message slips, took a deep breath, and picked up the telephone.

Voice mail answered. "Dr. Stevens? This is Maggie Summer, returning your call. I'll be in my office for about half an hour." Maggie checked her watch. She wanted to stop at the day-care center to see Aura. "If you miss that window, then maybe I'll see you at the hospital later this morning when I visit Sarah."

One down. Voice mail was a blessing and a curse. What had Dr. Stevens wanted? She hoped Sarah wasn't any worse.

Max Hagfield's call was clear enough. Don't talk to reporters. As though that would stop reporters from finding someone on campus to talk with. She had other things to do in any case. No call back to *The Star-Ledger.* How had a major New Jersey daily heard so quickly anyway? And Tiffany wanted to see her. About her grades? About Sarah? Tiffany had never expressed any interest in discussing her grades before, despite Maggie's concern.

"Morning, Maggie. You look lovely today." Paul Turk was dressed in what might have been termed *corporate casual* attire in his corporate world. The clothes worked; at about forty (and rumored to have been divorced twice) he still looked like a *Gentlemen's Quarterly* ad as he leaned against Maggie's doorway in pressed Ralph Lauren jeans and a tweed sport jacket over a pale blue shirt unbuttoned just one button too low for corporate decorum. Paul had the office next to Maggie's and often stopped in with questions or comments. Usually she was happy to chat; this morning she had other issues on her mind.

"Just wanted to know how that girl—Sarah—was. Lovely young woman. Such a shock when she collapsed last night."

Maggie nodded.

"You went to the hospital with her, didn't you? I thought of following you, but then I saw Dorothy Whitcomb leave, too."

"Dorothy and I both went to the hospital. The doctors pumped out Sarah's stomach, but she went into a coma. She wasn't allowed any visitors." Maggie thought of Sarah, and of Aura. "I'm going to see her daughter this morning, and then go over to the hospital."

"Would you like company? I don't have a class until after lunch. I'd be glad to go with you."

Why this sudden interest in Sarah? Maybe he was just trying to be helpful. "Thanks, Paul, but that's not necessary. You didn't know her, did you?"

"I've heard about her, of course; I've heard about all the Whitcomb House residents, from Dorothy and Oliver. But, no; I hadn't seen her before last night. I just thought you might like someone with you. Visiting the ICU isn't fun."

71

"No. But I'd rather do it myself." Paul had worked with Oliver Whitcomb in New York, but last night was the first time he'd talked even a little about his relationship with the Whitcombs. Usually he only talked about his current job, and about the plays he still attended regularly in New York. He must be closer to Dorothy and Oliver than she'd realized if he'd heard about individual Whitcomb House residents. And yet—hadn't Claudia said Oliver Whitcomb had called Paul this morning? That must have been how Paul knew Sarah was in intensive care.

"Are you sure? I really wouldn't mind going with you."

Maggie shook her head.

In the past month Paul had asked her to join him for dinner twice, but she'd been busy both times. She'd assumed he was lonely; he'd just moved to the suburbs. Could he be having other thoughts about her? Maggie looked at him again. Paul wasn't a bad-looking man, for sure. And he was intelligent and certainly knew how to dress. If it weren't for Will . . . but she had no commitment to Will. They were friends. Close friends, perhaps, but just friends. In any case, with Sarah in the hospital this wasn't the time to think of anything other than Sarah's condition and prognosis. And about what to do for Aura.

"I'd really rather go to see Aura and Sarah alone," Maggie said. Her telephone rang. "You'll excuse me?"

Paul waved and left the doorway.

"Professor, this is Kayla Martin. The police have been here at Whitcomb House all morning. They said Sarah's been poisoned! They had a search warrant; they went through Sarah's room and really messed it up, and then they went through the rest of the house. Most people were in class, so they haven't spoken with the police. But I have. And—could I see you? I need to talk with someone."

She should have warned the students, Maggie thought. Police arriving first thing in the morning must have been frightening. She was older, with no small children around, and she hadn't been too thrilled when they'd showed up at her house. "I'm going to see Aura at Wee Care and then I'll stop," she said. "Will you be there in"—Maggie checked her watch—"about half an hour? Maybe a little longer. And is Tiffany there?"

"Tiffany left. I assume she's on campus. She took her books and that fancy leather briefcase she always carries. But I'll be here."

"I'll come as soon as I can, Kayla."

Maggie stopped at Claudia's desk on her way out. "If Tiffany Douglass calls again, see if she can stop by my office about four this afternoon. I checked for her at Whitcomb House but she'd already left for the day."

Claudia nodded. "Those poor kids. You just never know what will happen next, do you?" She carefully folded the wrappers from the two chocolate Kisses she had just put in her mouth and dropped them squarely in her wastebasket. "A person could die just from the fright of it all."

73

Chapter 10

Hawk Owl (found in northern Europe and North America). Hand-colored engraving from the Reverend F. O. Morris's Natural History of British Birds, one of the most successful and most often reprinted of all illustrated bird books. It was issued in sections, monthly, from 1851 until 1857. 4.5 x 7.25 inches. Price: $60.

The Somerset College Wee Care Center, a day-care center for the children of students and members of the college staff, was a small, bright green building near the gym. Its grassy playground, now browned by November cold, was surrounded by a high fence, giving it the appearance of a secure army base, with swings and slides added for attempted camouflage. Inside the rooms were warm and bright, the walls painted in primary colors and covered by children's crayoned drawings.

Maggie gave her name at the reception desk just inside the front door. Her college identification card got her inside, but she knew it wouldn't be enough to let her take Aura home. Each parent had on file a limited list of people who could, after showing their identification and signing, take their children out of the building. The parents at Whitcomb House had made arrangements so that any of them could drop off or pick up any of their children. Other than that, pickups were limited to biological parents and perhaps one trusted neighbor or older sibling. Too many national newspaper reports of kidnapped or missing children had resulted in security here being far tighter than anywhere else on campus. Too bad security hadn't been as heavy as this at the Whitcombs' house last night.

"Professor Summer? Welcome. Aura is in the Bunny Room, on the left, but most of the children there are taking naps now. Let me check with one of the aides."

Maggie nodded, looking at the rows of brightly painted lockers that lined the hallway, their owners' names pasted in large block letters on colored poster board. Aura's locker was red, with her name in yellow. A small, pink fleece jacket hung inside it.

The receptionist was back in a few minutes, holding Aura by the hand. Kayla and Tiffany had done their job well. Aura was dressed neatly in denim overalls with a long-sleeved, orange T-shirt. Her curly hair was mussed, as though she'd been rolling on it.

"Look who wasn't sleeping after all! Aura, do you remember Professor Summer?"

Aura nodded. "Hi."

"Hi, Aura." Maggie knelt down so that she and Aura were on the same level. Aura smelled of baby shampoo and breakfast cereal. Maggie resisted the impulse to smooth her unruly curls. Aura was a beautiful child. And one with a bigger problem than any four-year-old could imagine.

"Did you come to take me to Mommy? Kayla said Mommy was sick."

"Yes. She is sick, Aura. But the doctors are taking care of her. I can't take you to see her right now. I promise to tell her that I saw you and that you have a beautiful smile."

Aura smiled a little back. "When can I see Mommy? When can Mommy come home?"

"Soon, I hope, Aura. Very soon. But Kayla and Tiffany and the other people at your house will be with you after school."

A tear straggled down Aura's face. "I don't want them. I want Mommy."

Maggie reached out, and Aura stepped into her arms. "I know, Aura. I know. And Mommy wants to come home to you, too. But she has to get better first. It's going to take time."

The girl's arms around her neck felt warm and trusting. Maggie wanted to hold her forever, to keep anything else from hurting her.

Aura stepped back. "Mommy misses me, I think. She always misses me when she's away, even when the away is just a little."

"I'm sure she does. But you have to be big and brave for her and know she loves you, even if she isn't here to tell you herself." Maggie felt her eyes filling. It wouldn't help for Aura to see her crying. She stood up.

"That's what Kayla said. That I should be brave."

"Kayla was right. Now, you go and take your nap with the other boys and girls, and I'll do everything I can to bring your mommy home." If only she could. How could anyone have done something to separate this little girl and her mother who had only each other? Maggie's anger almost took over her voice. "I promise."

"I'm going to lie down, then. Mommy's lying down,

too, isn't she? Because she's sick."

"Yes. She's resting so she'll get better." I hope, Maggie added to herself. How could you let a child know her mother might not come home? But it was still way too early to think about that. Sarah might be fine. Please, please be fine, Sarah.

The aide took Aura's hand. "After your nap maybe you'd like to draw a picture for your mommy, Aura. A picture of how happy you'll be when she's home again."

"Yes!" The smile was back.

"Good-bye, Aura." Maggie stood and watched as the heavy door closed on the classroom. There was nothing she could do medically to help Sarah recover. But she could try to find out why someone had been targeting her. Maggie had a sudden chill. Whatever reason that person had, she hoped it didn't extend to Aura.

Kayla and Sarah had been friends; maybe she knew something that would help.

In the meantime, Aura was as safe here at the Wee Care Center as she would be anywhere.

Kayla opened the door at Whitcomb House. She was twenty-two, but looked older. Her black family hadn't approved of her marriage to a white man, but her daughter, Katie, was a stunning and exuberant combination of brown skin and wavy black hair. Now Kayla's husband was her ex-husband, an army corporal stationed in North Carolina. He paid child support occasionally, Maggie knew, and sent postcards to Katie. Kayla was one of the few single parents in the house in touch with their child's other parent, although she made it no secret that she was actively looking for a new father for Katie, and a new husband for herself. She was wearing jeans and a form-fitting top today, but her clothing style was not as provocative as Tiffany's.

Kayla's cup of coffee was on the kitchen table. "Would you like some coffee, Professor Summer? Or I can heat water if you'd like tea. Or cocoa? The kids love it, so we have boxes full. Mrs. Whitcomb is always bringing us more."

The practical Formica-topped table was large, piled with books and papers and several boxes of cereal that must have been out for breakfast. Most of the cabinet doors were open; two drawers of silverware and kitchen tools were dumped on the counter. A pile of dirty dishes filled the sink. "Cocoa sounds great," Maggie agreed.

Kayla turned on the kettle while she pulled a box of instant cocoa packets from a cabinet.

Maggie noted that the dozen hand-colored 1840s steel engravings of apples, pears, and plums that Dorothy had carefully selected from Maggie's collection and framed for Whitcomb House's kitchen were now almost totally covered by crayoned children's drawings taped on the glass. Crayoned drawings also covered the refrigerator and most of the kitchen cabinets. With six small people proud of their work, there was never enough space to display it all.

Would her kitchen someday sacrifice her favorite Cassell roosters to drawings of purple houses and people without legs? Maggie smiled to herself. She could live with that.

"I stopped at Wee Care on the way here. Aura looked

fine, but she's upset that her mother's not home."

"Of course she is. And so are we." Kayla sat down to wait for the kettle to come to a boil. "We talked late last night, after you left." She hesitated. "People were pretty nervous. Someone had to have given her something that made her sick. But we couldn't think of a reason why she'd be a target." Kayla paused. "Now we know for sure that she was poisoned. But it all seems unreal."

"Could someone she knew before she came here want to hurt her?"

"No one anyone of us knew about. And even if there were someone like that, how could it have happened? She was here all day yesterday until we went to the Whitcombs' together. No one at the party had any reason to be angry at her."

Kayla was right; who would have had both motive and opportunity to poison Sarah? And based on what Dr. Stevens had said, the poison had worked quickly. So the source must have been here, at the house, or at the Whitcombs'.

"The police went all through the house . . ." Maggie suddenly connected that the open cabinets and piled-up food might not have been left that way on a typical Monday morning. "They dumped Sarah's room, and the study area and bathroom she shares with Tiffany. They took Sarah's address book, her calendar, and some papers from her desk. I overheard one of them say so. They told me to stay in the living room while they searched. I felt so stupid, not to be able to help. Or to stop them from touching everything."

Kayla wiped her eyes and turned to pour the now

steaming water from the kettle into the cocoa powder in Maggie's cup. "Sarah likes her things to be neat. I picked up some of her clothes and remade her bed, but her room is still a mess. I would have cleaned more"—she waved her arm to indicate the mess in the kitchen—"but then I saw this morning's paper, and I couldn't concentrate on cleaning. I had to talk with you." A rumpled copy of *The Star-Ledger* was on the table.

Maggie picked it up. The article's headline was "Unwed Mother Poisoned at Somerset College Affair." Maggie winced. How had the newspaper gotten the information about the poisoning so quickly? There had to be a direct line from the police station to the news bureau. No wonder President Hagfield had told her not to talk to reporters.

She was sure Max was wincing at the "unwed mother" line, too. "Single parent" he could cope with, but . . .

"It makes all of us seem awful," said Kayla. "Immoral. Some of us weren't 'unwed' when we had our babies! And the police said they were going to check the backgrounds of everyone Sarah knew. Will they do that? Do they have the right?"

"Until they find the person who hurt her." Kayla was the second person today who had implied she didn't want to be investigated. Maggie understood the desire for privacy, but couldn't think of anything in her own life that would be unearthed by any inquiry. I must have a boring life, she thought to herself. Nothing to hide. Dorothy, though, and now Kayla . . .

"I don't have anything horrible in my past except a

bad marriage," Kayla continued. "And my family's being embarrassed to know me. Nothing the police could dig up that would look like a motive to hurt Sarah. But that's not true for everyone."

"The other people in Whitcomb House?"

"We've all had some problems. I know some things, but I think you'd better ask the others yourself. Or the police will. But Sarah . . ."

"Yes? You and Sarah are close, aren't you?"

"Sarah isn't really close to anyone. Of course, she knew Tiffany before she came here. But she doesn't talk that much even to Tiff. She doesn't share a lot."

"She knew Tiffany before she came to Somerset College?"

"They shared an apartment last summer for a couple of months. Tips weren't good at the diner where Sarah worked, so she advertised for a roommate. She knew she'd be coming here in late August. I think Tiffany found out about Whitcomb House from her. Neither of them talk about it much. I got to know Sarah more because Aura and Katie became such pals." Kayla smiled. "They're so alike—so full of energy and fantasies—yet so different."

"Like two wonderful four-year-olds should be," agreed Maggie. "You and Sarah are good mothers to them."

"Katie has a father, too. Even if he isn't here a lot."

Maggie remembered Dr. Stevens's question. "What about Aura's father, Kayla? Did Sarah ever say anything about him?"

Kayla hesitated. "Not by name. I got the impression

he was older. Maybe married. Remember that lawyer you brought in to talk to us about parental rights and obligations?"

The lawyer had emphasized that *both* parents had moral and legal responsibility for their children. That even if the father or mother of your child had taken off, they should accept some of the financial burden. One parent should not have to shoulder that alone.

"Some of us were talking after that. Maria said Tony's father, Eric, might settle down and come back to them. You know she's always believed that?"

Maggie shook her head. She hadn't ever heard Maria mention Tony's father. "Tiffany said she was definitely going to sue Tyler's father for child support. But that it would be better to find a new father for him. Or a more consistent source of money."

"What did Sarah say?"

"That she didn't want Aura to ever know who her father was. That he was pond scum, and he could stay in the pond."

"So she knows who he is."

"It sounded that way. Definitely. Knows who he is and wants Aura as far away from him as possible. But that's why I called you this morning. I remembered something else."

"What?"

"About a month later I was in Sarah's room, getting Katie so I could give her a bath. Aura and Katie had been playing together. They were coloring all over papers they'd found in Sarah's wastebasket." Kayla hesitated. "This may mean nothing, Professor Summer.

82

But I picked up the papers and put them back in the wastebasket before I took Katie to our room. One of them was a fancy envelope addressed to Sarah here at the college. The return address sounded like one of those ritzy law firms—lots of names one after the other. The return address was somewhere in Princeton. I noticed it because most of the other mail was the usual college notices and ads."

"Was there anything in the envelope?"

Kayla shook her head. "I shouldn't have looked, but I did. It was empty. I put it back in the wastebasket. I was just surprised Sarah would get a letter from a place like that."

"Maybe it was junk mail. Sometimes those letters look pretty official."

"Maybe. But Sarah lived in Princeton once, you know. With her last foster family. She used to joke about how she had 'gone to Princeton.' She meant she'd gone to live there." Kayla shrugged. "Maybe it doesn't mean anything. But I thought I should tell someone. And the police would probably think I was paranoid. Or, worse, making it up. They don't seem to think too highly of us."

Maggie reached out and touched Kayla's hand. "You're not crazy. Maybe it doesn't mean anything, but I'm glad you told me."

They both sat silently for a few minutes. Suddenly Maggie remembered something. "Just before Sarah passed out last night she mumbled a few words. I thought I heard her say 'Simon.' Has she ever mentioned anyone with that name?"

Kayla shook her head. "I don't think so. I wish I knew more that would help!"

"You're doing fine. If you think of anything else, make sure you let me know. Or the police."

"Okay. You know, Maria's going to be really pissed when she gets home this afternoon," added Kayla. "The police took her gun."

Chapter 11

Passiflora (passionflower). Hand-colored engraving from A. B. Strong's American Flora, *1846. 6.5 x 9.5 inches. Price: $50.*

"Her gun? Maria had a gun here at Whitcomb House?" Maggie was appalled. "In a house with all these children? Aside from the fact that guns are never allowed in the dormitories!"

"It was okay." Kayla realized her mistake in telling Maggie. "Maria kept it unloaded and hid the bullets somewhere else. The gun was on a really high shelf in her closet. None of the kids could reach it."

Maggie thought of Heather's son, Mikey, who was tall for six. "Why did she have a gun?"

"For protection, she said. Professor Summer, I shouldn't have told you. It's just that Maria's going to blame me when she gets home and finds out the police took it."

"Maria could be thrown out of the college for having a gun! Have you any idea how crazy it is to have a gun around all these kids?"

Kayla looked down. "I shouldn't have told you."

"Well, you did. But I don't think you or I will have to do anything about it. The police will do that." That was just the kind of additional publicity President Hagfield would be thrilled about: one of his students had a gun in her room. In a house where six children lived. "Has Maria ever used the gun?"

"No! At least not that I know of. She just had it . . . in case."

It was clear Kayla wasn't going to say anything else.

Maggie left Whitcomb House and headed for the hospital. Maybe Sarah was better. Maybe the doctors would know more about the poison.

Dorothy Whitcomb was at the hospital ahead of Maggie, sitting on a straight chair in the waiting room reserved for families of those in intensive care. "I'm glad you're finally here, Maggie," she said. "Dr. Stevens says Sarah can have one or two visitors for five minutes every hour. I get nervous going in alone. She's so still."

"Has there been any change?"

Dorothy shook her head. "She doesn't respond at all when I speak to her. But they say sometimes people in comas can hear things even when they seem to be unconscious."

"I've read that."

"So I think someone should be with her as often as possible."

"If Dr. Stevens feels that's best."

"He should be back soon."

Maggie sat on the blue vinyl couch next to Dorothy's

chair. A selection of well-worn six-month-old *Field and Stream* and *People* magazines littered a laminated wooden table in front of them. This waiting room had no TV. Maggie squared her shoulders. "Dorothy, you called me this morning, after we met."

"I just wanted to see if you'd heard anything else, Maggie. The students trust you."

"I haven't heard anything new." Maggie thought about the police finding Maria's gun. But that had nothing to do with Sarah; Sarah had been poisoned, not shot. Why tell Dorothy something that would upset her and wasn't directly related to the current situation? "I didn't learn anything about Sarah. But the police searched Whitcomb House this morning and questioned Kayla Martin, who was the only one there at the time. They left the place pretty messed up."

"Those poor young people! Coping with Sarah's illness, and now this." Dorothy looked at Maggie. "Do you think they'll want to search my house, too?"

"I don't know. Maybe. That's where Sarah collapsed." It could be the crime scene, Maggie thought. "I don't know exactly what they're looking for. Has Dr. Stevens found out what kind of poison Sarah took?"

Dorothy shook her head. "I don't think so."

A tall nurse with short brown hair under her cap joined them. "You're here to see Sarah Anderson? You can go in now, for a brief visit."

Sarah was lying in a small alcove curtained by off-white sheets. Her body was connected by an assortment of wires and tubes to several softly beeping monitors. Her face and hands were pale even above the white sheet covering her. Her uncombed light red hair was the only splash of color in the room.

"Sarah," Dorothy said quietly, "it's Dorothy and Professor Summer. We're here to see you. We care about you. Please try to wake up and talk to us."

Sarah didn't move.

Maggie tried. "Sarah, I went to see Aura this morning. Kayla and the others at Whitcomb House are taking good care of her. She looks fine, but she misses you. She's going to draw a picture for you. Next time I come I'll try to bring it with me. Aura's fine, Sarah, but she needs you."

The nurse indicated they should go. The visit had been brief, but it had been long enough to scare Maggie.

What if Sarah didn't recover? What if she came out of this brain-damaged?

I'm Aura's guardian, Maggie thought. I have to start thinking about what it would mean to have her move in with me. To be a second mother to her.

She'd been thinking about making a home for a child who had no one. What changes it would make in her life; how it would work for both her and her child; how she could change her guest room into a child's room. But all of a sudden that time seemed as if it might be frighteningly close at hand.

Maggie shook her head. She couldn't let herself think about this. Not even a little. She wanted so much to be a mother, to have a child to love and care for and to prepare to go out into the world. But not this way.

Lost in her own thoughts, Maggie suddenly realized that Dorothy was crying.

Chapter 12

Undine. Lithograph by Arthur Rackham of the main character in the book Undine. *A girl stands, terrified, in the dark of a forest, surrounded by dead tree branches that appear to be reaching out for her. A raven is above her; a castle is high on a distant hill, bathed in pink skylight. 1909. 5 x 7.25 inches, with larger printed mat. Price: $75.*

"Dorothy, what's wrong?" Maggie sat next to her on the hard waiting-room couch. They were the only people in the waiting room. The beeps and buzzes and footsteps and intercom announcements of the hospital continued in the background.

"I don't know what to do, Maggie," she sobbed. "I just don't know how I'll cope if Sarah dies."

Sarah's being poisoned and falling into a coma was horrible, to be sure. It was catastrophic to Sarah and Aura. It was of great concern to those who knew Sarah and cared about her. It could be a source of embarrassment for Somerset College.

But, even given all of that, Dorothy was overreacting. Was her life so empty that the students at Whitcomb House meant everything to her?

"You've created a wonderful program, bringing young parents together and sponsoring their scholarships and living arrangements. I don't know what's happened to Sarah, but, whatever it is, you will go on, and Whitcomb House will go on." Maggie reached out and put her hand over Dorothy's. "It's an awful situation, I know, but you can't let yourself get so distraught. Students have problems; sometimes they're involved in tragic situations. But the school will still be here, and I'm sure the work you've started with Whitcomb House will go on. Somerset has already received inquiries from other schools; the program you've started may turn out to be a model for other colleges."

"You don't understand, Maggie." Dorothy reached into her brown leather Coach pocketbook and pulled out a handful of tissues. "I planned Whitcomb House around Sarah and Aura. If they don't benefit from it, then Whitcomb House will be a failure."

"You planned Whitcomb House around the needs of a wide variety of single parents in Somerset County. I listened to your proposal, and so did the rest of the community. Giving young single parents the opportunity to live in a supportive environment was a wonderful idea. You made it possible for them to prove themselves. Now they can get two years of community college behind them and be in a position to get better jobs. They'll be better able to support their families, or even to go on to a four-year college and get their bachelor's degrees. And helping the parents also helps their children. Whitcomb House was your idea, and it will leave a lasting legacy."

Dorothy nodded as she blew her nose and wiped the tears from her face. "I said all that, didn't I?"

"And you worked with a consultant to prepare all the facts and figures to prove your theory. It was very persuasive, Dorothy. The only doubt anyone had was where the money would come from to begin such a program, and you provided that. In fact, not only did you provide the money, but you provided the dormitory and the furnishings, and the funding to support this first group of scholarship students. You made it happen."

Maggie kept her voice low and calm. Dorothy was clearly distraught. "There was never a promise that every one of the students would make it. That would have been an unrealistic expectation, and you knew that. You allowed for it in your planning. And you did a darn good job of convincing everyone around, from the Board of Trustees to the local media, that your idea was going to work. Something has happened to Sarah Anderson; that's sad. It's tragic. But it's not the end of your program."

Unless the media runs away with this story, Maggie thought to herself. Unless there's any connection between Sarah's poisoning and the college. Unless the college is forced into a position of defending the program in the press and chooses not to do that.

Dorothy blew her nose again. Her face, usually so composed and immaculately made up, was red and blotchy, and lines of mascara were under her eyes. "Maggie, I need to tell you something. I need to tell someone, and you've always been so organized and calm and so good with the students."

Dorothy had clearly never seen Maggie during an exam period when she also had an antique show to attend. Did she really want to listen to Dorothy's confidences? Dorothy was on the Board of Trustees; Maggie was a professor. Would this change their working relationship? But if what Dorothy was about to say would provide information that might help Sarah and Aura . . .

"Of course, Dorothy. You can talk to me."

"You have to promise to keep what I'm going to tell you a secret. You can't tell anyone. Not the police. Not Oliver. Not anyone."

"I can't promise that, Dorothy. I can promise not to volunteer any information. But if the police ask me something directly, then I won't lie."

Dorothy looked at her. "I don't think anyone will ask you this, Maggie. No one knows enough to ask."

"Then we'll be like the army. If no one asks, I won't tell." Maggie smiled slightly. This conversation was making her uncomfortable. But, for Sarah's sake . . .

Dorothy seemed satisfied with her answer. "The story starts a long time ago. Over twenty years ago. I was living with my parents, here in Somerset County. But not in a big house like the one Oliver and I have now. I was a nobody who lived in a little house in Somerville with a father who worked for the post office and a mother who stayed home. And I fell in love. I thought he was handsome and charming and kind and he would take me out of Somerville and into a new life. His name was Larry." Dorothy smiled at the memory and dabbed at her damp face with tissues. "Larry wasn't much older than I was. But he went to Rutgers. I worked as a supermarket cashier. I wasn't smart enough to get a scholarship, and my family didn't expect it. No one in my family had ever been to college."

"Did your family like Larry?"

"At first I didn't tell them about him. I'd met him at a

91

bar near the campus, and I didn't want them to know my girlfriends and I sometimes went to bars. We were underage, and my father would have killed me. But after I'd been seeing Larry for a couple of months I finally introduced him to my mother, and then my father, and they seemed to like him." Dorothy sat back for a moment and smiled quietly, as though to herself. "I don't think I've ever been happier than I was in those next few months, Maggie. Larry and I loved each other; my parents were pleased. Everything was going so well. Larry and I talked about getting married. He was a junior then. I saved every dime I could, putting it away to pay for an apartment and furniture someday."

"And what happened?"

"The world ended. That's all. It came crashing down, and nothing was ever the same again. On his way from my house back to his dorm one March Saturday night, Larry's car was sideswiped by some drunk kids in a truck. His car flipped over and hit a tree. The police said he was killed instantly. He didn't have a chance."

Maggie could feel her heart beating faster. Her parents had been killed in a car accident, and so had Michael. She knew what that telephone call from the police, or from Larry's family, must have been like.

"Dorothy, I'm so sorry."

"But that wasn't all. A couple of weeks later, when I got myself out of bed and washed my face and knew I had to start over again, I realized I was pregnant. At first I didn't want to believe it. But it was true. The baby was Larry's, of course, and I wanted to keep it, although I didn't know how I could support a baby. I didn't tell my parents; my mother would have wanted me to have an abortion. I didn't think my father could have dealt with the situation at all. So I didn't tell anyone. I kept saving my money and thinking it was for my baby and me. That I had a little part of Larry left, and that would help me go on."

Maggie sat, listening. So Dorothy had been a single parent herself. No wonder she had felt so strongly about founding Whitcomb House.

"After a few months I couldn't hide my pregnancy anymore. My parents were furious. They said they wouldn't support an unwed mother or her child. That I was a disgrace to them." Dorothy blew her nose again. "I knew there were other girls who managed to keep their babies, who left their parents and went on welfare, or found apartments. But I'd never lived away from home. I didn't know what to do. I'd always depended on my parents for advice. And I needed love and support then, Maggie. I needed it more than anything else."

Maggie nodded. It must have been a horrible time for the young Dorothy.

"When my time came, I went to the hospital alone. My mother wouldn't even go with me. But I had a beautiful little girl. It was all arranged; the social worker came to have me sign the papers and take my baby away and find a family for her. But I couldn't sign. I panicked. I didn't want to give her up; I wanted to take her home with me. But my parents would never have allowed that."

Maggie handed Dorothy another tissue.

"The social worker told me the best thing for my

daughter would be to release her for adoption, that she was a beautiful baby and there were lots of families waiting for a little girl like her. But she was my baby. All I had left of Larry. I just couldn't give her up and turn my back. So the social worker said they would put her in foster care until I could offer her a home."

"And you went back to your parents'."

Dorothy nodded. "They thought I'd given the baby up for adoption. They never even asked whether it was a boy or a girl. They didn't want to know. I went back to work at the supermarket. But I wasn't the same after that. I was afraid I'd never be able to do everything necessary to get my little girl back. Every time I saw a baby her age, I'd start to cry."

"Did you call the social worker?"

"All the time. Until she said not to call her again until I had a plan for my future. But she sent me pictures of the baby and said she was in a good home. And every few months I could visit her for an hour or two. She was such a beautiful little girl, Maggie, and so happy! Every time I saw her I wanted even more to take her home with me. But I knew I'd never make enough money as a supermarket cashier to support myself and a baby. Everything was so expensive and seemed so impossible. And then I met Ed."

Dorothy paused, as though remembering. "Ed worked for a construction company in Bridgewater. A big guy, with sort of a red face, but nice. He used to buy his lunch at the supermarket where I worked. We talked, and flirted a little, and he asked me out. He was almost thirty and had his own apartment. I thought maybe this was the way. If I married Ed, I'd have a place to live, and a place for the baby, and I could offer her a real home. I knew Ed loved kids—he said so, all the time—but I didn't tell him about my baby." Dorothy looked at Maggie as though asking for forgiveness. "I should have told him, I know. But I was scared that if he knew there'd been another man in my life, he wouldn't want me. So I waited until we were married to tell him about my daughter."

"And?"

"He blew up. Said I'd married him on false pretenses; he wasn't going to take care of another man's kid. That's about the time I realized he was drinking too much. After that he started drinking a lot too much. Maggie, understand, my dad was a pretty good drinker, too, so the drinking in itself didn't bother me. My dad would come home and pick up a couple of six-packs of beer and sit in his chair by the TV and drink until he'd go to sleep every night. Most mornings my mother would have to wake him up and get him to shower and shave and get dressed to go to work. But my dad never yelled at anyone. He never hit anyone."

"And Ed did."

Dorothy nodded. "I knew I couldn't stay; life with him wouldn't be good for my little girl even if he'd wanted her. By that time she was four years old. I saw her once in a while. Supervised visits, they called them. But then the social worker said I'd had long enough to get my life together. The Division of Youth and Family Services was going to take me to court to take away my parental rights, so they could place her in a permanent home."

Maggie thought of all the prospective adoptive parents waiting for a four-year-old girl. The social worker had done what she was trained to do: given the biological parent a fair amount of time to provide a home for her child before finding a permanent home for the child.

"I gave up," Dorothy continued. "I felt I'd never get off the bottom, do you know? No, you probably don't. But I knew I couldn't stay with Ed, and my parents wouldn't want my little girl, and I still couldn't support her by myself. The social workers were right. She needed to be with a family who would love her and provide for her. I hadn't been able to do that." Dorothy sagged deeper into the hard couch.

Dorothy herself must have felt very unsafe and unloved then, Maggie thought. It must have been nightmarish. "So you relinquished custody of your daughter. Did you stay with Ed?"

"For a few more months. Then I got up enough courage to leave him. I went home for a few weeks, but my parents said I was grown-up and I couldn't even keep a husband, so I needed to find out what it was like to live on my own. To see how hard it was to deal with the real world." Dorothy paused. "The next years were pretty rough. At first I shared an apartment with an older woman I worked with at the supermarket who had just gone through a divorce. She had furniture, and I paid half the rent, so that was all right. But I wasn't really making it on my own. I was depending on her for things I'd depended on my parents for. Plus I had no privacy. I couldn't invite friends over without checking with her, and she liked the apartment to be quiet."

Dorothy paused for a moment. "I must be boring you, Maggie. I'm going on and on. But I've never told anyone. No one."

"It's all right, Dorothy. I'm here. And I do care." As she said the words, Maggie realized they were true. She did care about the young Dorothy who had felt trapped and limited by circumstances. Her own family situation had been far from perfect, but she'd been able to get a college scholarship so she could leave home and make a new life. She hadn't had to depend on her mother and father. No wonder Dorothy wanted to help young single parents. Their plights were all too real to her.

"Then I married for the second time. I was in my late twenties by then, and Fred was a nice man. He had a job at the local bank, and he wasn't aiming at being its president. All he wanted was a wife to love him, and a small home in the suburbs, and children. He wanted children more than anything. He'd been an only child, and he wanted his children to have lots of brothers and sisters."

"That must have been a great relief . . . to be with someone who loved children, as you did."

Dorothy nodded. "Yes. Of course, I didn't tell him I already had a child. He would never have understood my giving her up. And it wouldn't have made a difference; she was living with her adoptive family by then. Fred and I planned to have our own children. But life is ironic, Maggie. That's a word I probably didn't know when I was eighteen, but I sure know it now. Ironic. Because Fred and I couldn't have children. And it was all my fault. We both had all the tests, and he was fine. But I had endometrial adhesions that were blocking my fallopian tubes. I couldn't conceive. The doctor said the condition was too far advanced for surgery to help. That I had been very lucky to have a child when I was so young, before the condition had progressed. Because I'd never have another child."

"Oh, Dorothy." Maggie could see the pain in her eyes as she told her story.

"Fred said that a marriage wasn't a real marriage unless there were children. So he divorced me, and I was alone again. He married a friend of mine. Last time I heard they had four children. By then my parents had died, and I'd gotten a little money after the divorce. I decided that marriage and children were not to be my life. Can you believe, Maggie? I came here, to Somerset College, and got my associate's degree, and then went on to Rutgers. Just like Larry had."

"How wonderful, Dorothy! You pulled your life together."

"After I graduated I got a job down on Wall Street. I was an 'administrative assistant'—really a glorified secretary—but I was finally earning enough to support myself and to buy some nice clothes and have my hair done." Dorothy smiled almost shyly at Maggie. "That's where I met Oliver. He was married when I first met him, but his wife had breast cancer. We all felt so sorry for him. And about a year after his wife died he asked me to have dinner with him and . . . here I am."

"Have you ever told Oliver about your baby?"

"No. Never. That was so long ago. And Oliver had two children with his first wife and didn't want any more. It didn't bother him that I couldn't have children.

I don't think it ever occurred to him that once I might have been able to."

"But you found a way to help single parents who were struggling as you had. That's a wonderful story, Dorothy."

"Not quite that wonderful, Maggie. I did have the idea of creating a dorm for single parents and their children. But the more I thought about it and started talking to people about it, the more I thought about my own daughter. So I hired a private detective to find her."

"And?" Maggie suddenly had the feeling she knew where all this was leading.

Dorothy raised her head and looked straight into Maggie's eyes. "Sarah Anderson is my daughter, Maggie. Aura is my granddaughter. And now Sarah may die before I really get a chance to know her." The tears started again. "I finally found my daughter, and now I may have lost her."

Chapter 13

The Course of a True Love Letter Runs Smoothest when written with one of C. Brandauer and Co.'s circular pointed pens. *Full-page advertisement, wood engraving, from* The Illustrated London News, *September 25, 1886, showing an elegant young woman sitting with pen in hand, gazing romantically into the distance . . . ignoring the five little cupids perched on her shoulder, desk, and in the sky behind her. 11 x 16 inches. Price: $70.*

Dorothy was Sarah's biological mother. As Dorothy had

told her complicated story, Maggie had started to wonder . . . but now she knew for sure. Dorothy and Sarah both had slightly red hair. And Aura, too. Three generations. Now that Dorothy had told her, the connections seemed obvious. "Does Sarah know you're her mother?"

Dorothy looked up from her tissues. Her expression became almost threatening. "No! And no one must ever tell her." She paused. "But you need to understand, Maggie, that if Sarah dies, then I *will* take custody of Aura. She's my granddaughter, and she's the same age Sarah was when she was taken from me for the last time."

Maggie moved back in her chair. This was all going too fast. Sarah was very sick, but it was not certain that she would die. And, should she die, she had left custody of Aura to Maggie. Not to Dorothy. Aura should be with the person her mother had named in her will.

Besides, Dorothy was obviously used to getting her own way and might not be able to give Aura the freedom she would need to grow up. Grow up to be herself—not a replacement for another little girl who was no longer there.

"Dorothy, Sarah made me Aura's guardian. And although I never dreamed that this situation would come up, I did promise Sarah that I'd love Aura and care for her as though she were born to me."

"You can't, Maggie. That's why I told you my story. She's *my* flesh and blood."

"But unless you can prove that—which means everyone will know Sarah was your daughter—then

100

you have no legal right to question Sarah's will."

"But you'll do the right thing, Maggie. You'll relinquish custody of Aura to Oliver and me. You're not married; you work two jobs; you have no time for a child. I'll make sure any needs you have are met. Oliver and I can give Aura everything she would ever want. For Aura's sake, you *will* give her to me."

Maggie stood up. "Sarah's not going to die. I can't have this conversation. We mustn't even think of anything but how to get Sarah well again."

Neither of them noticed Dr. Stevens approaching until he spoke. "I'm glad both of you are here. I just saw Sarah again, and there's been no change. But it hasn't even been twenty-four hours. We have to wait this out. At least there's been no change for the worse."

"There is no way of predicting?" said Dorothy. The only sign of her earlier emotional story was her slightly swollen face and a trace of black mascara smudged beneath her left eye.

"We may know more when we identify what poison she swallowed. I'm hoping those test results arrive very soon. Now we can just monitor her closely and hope for the best." Dr. Stevens was clearly sticking to a middle ground. He was neither holding out hope nor accepting defeat. "I'll let you know as soon as I learn something."

"I should be home by midafternoon." Maggie glanced at her watch. "Right now I need to get back to campus. I have a class at one o'clock."

"Remember what I said." Dorothy reached out her hand as though to stop Maggie, but Maggie kept walking.

"I'll remember."

There was no chance of her forgetting, Maggie thought as she drove back to campus. She swerved around the remains of several smashed pumpkins. What was Dorothy really asking—or telling? Did she expect Maggie to hand Aura over to her on the basis of a story that, much as it sounded credible, was at this point just a story? Would that even be legal? And was Dorothy offering to bribe her?

Maggie still hadn't sorted the situation out when she reached her office and picked up her classroom notes. Social, political, and economic reasons for the American Civil War. She had given that lecture often enough that she didn't need to prepare for it. Which really isn't fair to the students, she thought guiltily as she gathered up her notes and shooed Uncle Sam out from under her desk. Claudia must have left her office door open again.

She had ten minutes before class.

She sat down at her computer and started typing a note to Will. She hadn't answered this morning's e-mail, and she needed to communicate with someone who was not involved in this whole mess. But she couldn't say anything about Aura, or about Dorothy's confession. Not only had she promised Dorothy she wouldn't tell anyone, but Will had made it clear that he didn't want to have children. How would he react if Maggie suddenly had custody of Aura? Would fulfilling her dream of becoming a mother move her away from the one man she cared about?

Maggie looked down at her right hand. She'd once

mentioned to Will that she'd always loved nineteenth-century "posy" or "poesie" rings, but had never had one. Will had given her one—in friendship, they both stressed—when they last saw each other, at an antiques show in Philadelphia. He'd bought it from an estate jewelry dealer at a show in Rochester. She'd hesitated about the symbolism of a ring, but it was so lovely, and clearly chosen for her, that she couldn't say no.

Posy rings were simple Victorian gold bands inlaid with a series of small stones that spelled out words or names. The most common were called regard rings because, like the ring Will had given her, their inlaid stones were a tiny *r*uby, *e*merald, *g*arnet, *a*methyst, *r*uby, and *d*iamond. Her friend Gussie had a "dearest" that her former husband had given her, and Maggie was secretly thankful that the one Will had found was a "regard." It was the perfect word for where they were in their relationship.

And it was a beautiful ring. She smiled and held her hand out under the desk lamp to admire it.

Even so, she deleted her note to Will. She couldn't tell him all that was happening, and she didn't want to tell him only part.

It was easier to say nothing. She turned off her computer, picked up her notes, and headed for her "American History to 1865" class. What good was a relationship where you couldn't share everything that was important to you?

As she walked, Maggie realized she was also thinking of the relationship she'd had with her former husband. She hadn't shared her desire to have children; he hadn't shared his doubts about the marriage. Maybe he'd shared that with his other women.

And now, knowing Will had no desire to be a father, she was again keeping her thoughts to herself. Could there ever be a relationship in which you could be truly honest and open? She'd never had one. But that didn't mean she'd given up hope.

The causes of the American Civil War were simple compared to the causes why relationships succeeded. Or failed.

Chapter 14

Mandan Foot Warriors in Counsel. Lithograph by George Catlin, from his Indians of North America, *1841. Catlin was the first white person to travel throughout the American West and live with and draw Native Americans. Although in later years his portfolios and oil paintings were highly valued, this, his first book, was of no interest to North Americans at the time, and Catlin self-published it in London. 6 x 10 inches. Price: $65.*

"Professor Summer, you have another pile of messages." Claudia popped one of her omnipresent chocolate Kisses into her mouth and handed Maggie several pieces of pink message paper. No piles awaited other teachers.

"Am I the only one lucky enough to be in the line of fire today?"

"No, Professor Summer. Mr. Turk"—Maggie smiled

at the use of the *Mr.* Paul had just reregistered at New York University to complete the doctoral program he had dropped out of ten years ago to go into the business world, and Claudia saved the term *professor* for those who had already earned their doctorates—"Mr. Turk's been in and out all day. He has all his messages. He was looking for you, too. I think you have a message from him."

Maggie looked down. Sure enough. *Dinner, tonight? Paul.*

"I've heard he takes people to really nice restaurants," whispered Claudia. "Usually in New York. Most of his women call to say thank-you the next day."

"I see," said Maggie. Most of his women. So Paul's charms were spread thin.

"He went out for coffee, but he'll be back soon. Professor James is in class, and Professor Boyle is in his office."

"Thank you, Claudia."

"Professor Summer? Is there any news about Sarah Anderson's condition? I heard she was a total vegetable, just hooked up to wires and tubes and everything."

Where was this information coming from? "Sarah's in a coma. Some people are in comas for a few hours or days, come out of it, and are fine. I talked with her doctor a couple of hours ago and he was optimistic." Well, at least not pessimistic. "So if you hear any rumors like that, squelch them, please! Sarah's going to be fine."

"I'm glad. I keep thinking of that poor little girl of hers. She's so pretty. And she has no one but her mother. It's so sad." Claudia pulled a tissue from the box on her desk and blew her nose loudly. "Oh, and Tiffany Douglass called again. I told her four o'clock would be okay with you. She'll be here then."

It was three-thirty. Maggie's office was as cluttered as always. She cleared a space on the desk and put down the papers from her class. Luckily she had already prepared Friday's exam.

Paul's message was on top of the "call back" slips. He had asked her out before, but never so persistently as today. Could his sudden interest have anything to do with Sarah, or with his friendship with the Whitcombs? She put his message aside.

Her dentist had called, reminding her it was time to have her teeth cleaned. Rah.

A student was going to miss Friday's class because he had to attend a business conference. He wondered if he could take the exam early. That would be a change, Maggie thought. Usually in such circumstances people asked to take the exam later. In fact, based on her students' requests, she suspected exams coincided with a fair percentage of the illnesses, deaths, and business commitments of the population of Somerset County.

An antique show promoter in Pennsylvania asked if she could do a show in Allentown this weekend—another dealer had canceled at the last moment and the show could really use a print specialist like Maggie. Too bad, but she was committed to doing the Morristown show. The promoter must be frantic to fill the space at this short notice.

And finally, a message from Heather Farelli. Would

Maggie call her at Whitcomb House as soon as she got in?

Maggie dialed the number, and Kendall picked up the telephone.

"I'm glad you called, Professor. We're all here—well, most of us are. The police left the house a wreck. And then they took each of us out of our classes and questioned us. But let me get Heather. She's the one who called you."

Heather came from a large Italian family and used most of her emotional energy, aside from that spent chasing six-year-old Mikey, trying to separate herself from that family. It had been a great relief to her to get the Whitcomb House scholarship. At twenty-four, after three years of attending part-time, she had managed to accumulate one year's worth of credits at Somerset College. Living on campus with a scholarship meant she could finish her associate's degree in relative comfort, away from her family, and then apply to a state four-year college. In one of the Monday-night seminars Heather had been clear about her goal: "I got screwed over once in my life, by Mikey's father, and I'm making sure it don't happen again. I'm going to be a lawyer. That way no one can put anything over on me again. Or over anyone I can help."

Maggie smiled, remembering. Heather's tattoo would stand out in a courtroom, but if anyone could make it work, it would be Heather. She had definite ideas about almost everything. And she hadn't separated totally from her close-knit family. Wasn't it Heather's mother who had made the minestrone everyone at Whitcomb

House had eaten for lunch yesterday? Yesterday.

"Professor Summer? This is Heather. You're the only one who'll give us a straight story. There's a lot going on. The police messed up the house, reporters are following us around, and our families and friends are driving us crazy. And we don't know what to say to anyone! We don't know what's happening." Maggie heard a child crying in the background. It sounded like one of the little ones, Josette or Tony. "First of all, how is Sarah? Really? We're hearing all sorts of rumors."

"Sarah's holding her own, Heather. She's still in a coma, and as of about two hours ago they still didn't know what poison had caused it. But she's hanging on, and the doctor has hopes she'll recover."

"Then she isn't dead?" Heather put her hand over the receiver. But her muffled voice was still clear. "Hey, guys, Professor Summer says Sarah's not dead." Maggie heard assorted voices in the background. What rumors were going around campus? Or had something happened to Sarah that she didn't know about?

"I promised you all I'd let you know anything as soon as I heard it," Maggie said, "and I will. No word from me means the situation hasn't changed." And I'll call Dr. Stevens as soon as I get off the phone, she told herself. I have to make sure what I'm telling people is accurate.

"Okay. That's good. Now, I won't say we aren't all pretty pissed off about our property being dumped by those cops, but we know they were trying to help. Did they find anything that would tell them what happened to Sarah? Or who tried to kill her?"

"Not that I know of, Heather. But I haven't talked with either of the detectives this afternoon. Again, if I hear anything, I'll let you know."

"Okay. I'll tell everyone. We're pretty nervous. We were with Sarah the whole time yesterday—all day and at the party. I mean, some people might even think one of us gave Sarah that poison. The other students on campus, and even some of the professors, looked at us funny today because we're 'those Whitcomb House people.'"

Maggie felt her blood pressure rising. Stay calm. "It's going to be all right, Heather. Sarah lived with you, and the detectives are crossing off possibilities. She was poisoned, after all! There's going to be talk."

"That's for sure! President Hagfield even called here!"

Max called Whitcomb House? "He called to say he was sorry about what happened to Sarah?"

"Not exactly. He just muttered about how none of us should talk with anyone in the media. He asked to speak to each one of us and just kept repeating the same thing. 'Don't talk.' He must think we're idiots."

"I'm sure that's not true. He's just upset. So he talked to everyone?" That didn't sound typical of Max. Usually he avoided talking to students directly when there was any kind of problem. He left confrontations up to people like Maggie.

"Everyone except Tiffany. She must still be on campus. He seemed aggravated at that, too. He asked to speak to her first, and then asked each of us where she was. And his tone of voice made it sound as though he thought one of us had poisoned Sarah!"

"He probably just wanted to make sure he'd talked with you all."

"Maybe so. But no other dorms were searched today, and detectives aren't wandering over campus asking about any of the other students."

"Let's hope this is all settled quickly, Sarah will be fine, and we can all go back to living our own lives," said Maggie. And, she added to herself, let's hope the police find whoever did this to Sarah and make sure he or she disappears. Permanently.

"What should we do about people calling for Sarah?"

Calling for Sarah? By now everyone in the world seemed to know what had happened to Sarah. "She's been getting calls?"

"A man called earlier, a couple of times. Finally Kendall told him Sarah was in the hospital. That was okay, right?"

"I'm sure it was. Do you know who it was?"

"He didn't leave a name. But Sarah doesn't get many calls, so it was a little weird."

"I'm sure you all handled it well. Anyone in New Jersey could have read *The Star-Ledger* today and known that Sarah is in the hospital. But if she has any other calls, try to get a name. Sarah might have friends or acquaintances none of us know about."

Or enemies, Maggie thought.

Chapter 15

Orrin, Make Haste, I Am Perishing! *Wood engraving, story illustration by American artist Winslow Homer (1836–1910), printed in* The Galaxy, *August 1867. Fully dressed young woman in deep water desperately clutching a post under a bridge. 4.5 x 6.75 inches. Price: $125.*

Maggie took a long sip from one of the cans of soda she kept in the bottom right-hand drawer of her desk. There wasn't time to get to the campus cafeteria every time she was thirsty, and warm Diet Pepsi was better than no Diet Pepsi.

"You look like a lady who could use a stronger drink, and a sympathetic ear." Paul stepped into Maggie's office and offered her a selection from a box of chocolates. "Not to speak of some instant energy. I hear chocolate-covered cherries go well with diet soda."

Maggie couldn't help grinning. Paul was sweet, and he was trying to fit into the Somerset College staff. Besides, chocolate-covered cherries were her favorite. She reached out and took one and then, when the box didn't waver, another. "You'll spoil me, Paul Turk." The sweet cream filling and cherry tartness on her tongue filled her taste buds as the chocolate began to melt. "Mmmmm."

For a moment neither of them said anything; she savored the treat, and Paul grinned at her and then went over to look at the Currier & Ives *Maggie* hung on the wall next to her door. She'd recently moved it here from her home office. "I don't know much about Curriers. Who was Maggie? Other than you, of course."

"Maggie's no one in particular. N. Currier and then Currier and Ives printed a wide selection of hand-colored lithographs featuring portraits of young ladies. Some are full figures, and some are just heads. They're all labeled with names popular in the nineteenth century. Maggie was one of them. They were designed to be given to women who had those names, and they still make wonderful gifts. Although today there aren't as many Cornelias and Agneses as there were then."

"How wonderful that you found a Maggie."

"It was the very first antique print I bought. I was still in college. It started me down a long road." Maggie smiled at the memory, and at his interest. "Unfortunately, they didn't do a similar series of prints for men, or I'd look for a Paul for you. Although I think there was a Pauline."

"Somehow I don't think Pauline would be quite right for my office," he said. "Mind if I sit a moment?"

"Go ahead. I'm taking a deep breath. I have an appointment with a student at four."

Paul looked at his watch. "Then I'll come right to the point. I'd like some advice on capturing student interest in class, and I've heard you're one of the campus experts at doing that. I'd like to buy you dinner, give you a chance to take another deep breath, and talk about the business of student management."

Maggie laughed out loud. "'Student management'?

When you figure that out, let me know. I'll buy a copy of your book!"

"Seriously."

"Seriously." Maggie thought a moment. "I have a lot on my plate just now, Paul, and I have to pack my van for an antique show this Saturday."

"It's only Monday." Paul looked so eager, and so enthusiastic. So attractive.

"On the other hand, I do have to eat." The calm in Paul's eyes and manner was definitely appealing, especially on a stress-filled day like this one.

"Then an early dinner, very local—Enrico's in Somerville? It's not far, and pasta can be comfort food. We could eat as early as five-thirty if you want to. I skipped lunch."

"Now that I think of it, so did I," agreed Maggie. "Can we make it five forty-five and meet there? I have a few things to do after my next student appointment."

"I'll see you at Enrico's, then." Paul stood up. His wavy brown hair was slightly tousled in a way that was somehow sophisticated as well as casual. He winked at Maggie. "Until five forty-five." He left, his aftershave lingering a moment.

Paul was so different from Will. Will was a big man; his body would have filled the doorway. And Will's graying beard was not so kempt as Paul's tousled hair. Will's blue eyes were striking, yet comforting; very different from Paul's dark eyes, which seemed to take in every detail of a room, and of the person he was talking to. Maggie shivered a bit. What would Paul think about her situation with Sarah and Aura? She found herself wondering and shook her head. An early dinner. That was all she was committing to.

Not a date. Just a meeting of colleagues to discuss business.

"Professor Summer?"

Maggie jumped slightly. She had been far away. Tiffany Douglass was at the door. Tiffany was almost six feet tall, but she carried the height well. Her blonde hair looked professionally streaked, but Maggie suspected Tiffany had perfected that technique herself. While most students wore jeans and sweatshirts or sweaters, Tiffany's slacks or skirts, although usually polyester, matched her stylish tops. Today she was dressed in shades of beige, from her eye shadow to her stockings. Her gold mesh belt and the gold knot earrings were the only exceptions. When Tiffany's parents had named her, they had unknowingly anticipated her style. Tiffany Douglass was far from rich, but Tiffany Douglass was definitely as polished as she could be considering her budget and circumstances. Her long, pull-on chiffon skirt looked a little light for a November day. That skirt would be great for an antique show. If only Tiff spent as much time coordinating Tyler's outfits. Unfortunately, at two, Tyler usually wore something either too big for him, or too small. And his hair sometimes looked as though it hadn't had recent contact with shampoo.

"Sorry to bother you when you've got so much on your mind." Tiffany put her pile of books and her brown leather briefcase next to Maggie's guest chair and sat down.

"Not a problem. I've been wanting to talk to you, too."

"You have?" Tiffany's straight back scrunched down a little.

"Your grades have been slipping, Tiffany, at least in my class. I haven't had a chance to check with your other professors. But you've also been missing some classes. Like your 'Myths in American Culture' seminar—both last Friday and this morning."

"Tyler's had a cold, Professor Summer. I've been busy. I won't skip any more classes. I promise."

"Try not to, Tiffany." Maggie didn't remember any of the Whitcomb House kids having been sick recently, but children did catch colds easily. And hadn't Kayla said she was the only one at the house this morning? Still, she'd give Tiffany the benefit of the doubt. This time. At least until she checked with colleagues to see how Tiffany was doing in her other classes. "I wouldn't want to see you lose your scholarship."

"Oh, I won't," Tiffany said, sitting up straight again. "I know Oliver and Dorothy Whitcomb have faith in me, and I won't let them down."

"You wanted to see me about something else, then?"

"About Sarah. I didn't want to say too much to the cops. I don't know what they're looking for, but I don't appreciate being pulled out of math class and grilled in front of the whole student body."

"In front of . . . ?"

"In front of the Student Union, actually. And everyone knew they were cops. Cops aren't exactly my favorite people, Professor Summer."

"Those detectives are trying to find out who poisoned Sarah. They're doing their jobs. You need to cooperate with them, Tiffany."

"I don't know anything that would help them!"

"They're the ones to decide that."

"I guess. But no way do I like their style. That's why I came to you."

"Me?"

"I figured you'd know what I should say. And I'd rather talk to you than them anyway."

"Telling me something won't mean you can avoid telling the police, Tiffany."

"But maybe you can tell me what's important for them to know, and what's just my business or Sarah's business and has nothing to do with them." Tiffany paused. "One cop said they searched our rooms today!"

"I heard."

"What happened to our right to privacy?"

"I assume they had a search warrant. And they're trying to figure out what happened to Sarah's right to live a safe life."

Tiffany's shoulders fell. "You're right. But will you talk with me?"

"Of course I'll talk with you. But if you know something that would be helpful to the police, even if it's something that seems very minor, then you need to talk to them, too."

"Okay, okay. I'll talk to the cops. If they ask me again."

Maggie waited. Tiffany pushed up the sleeves on her sweater, recrossed her legs, then began. "Sarah's my roommate, you know, and that's worked out fine. I have a lot to do"—Maggie translated that as *I'm not around a lot*—"and Sarah is good with Tyler." *Sarah took care of Tyler as often as Tiffany did.* "Sarah doesn't talk a lot about her childhood. I guess it was rough, growing up in foster care, and then finally being placed for adoption and having your parents divorce and you ending up back in the system."

"Sarah never told me she'd been adopted."

"Oh, yeah. Or pre-adoption, or something. Her bio parents signed papers so she could be adopted when she was about four, and she was placed with a family almost immediately. An infertile couple."

The first choice for adoptive placements, Maggie thought. Of course. "I thought she had grown up in foster care."

"She did. Most of it." Tiffany shook her head. "She never actually laid out a timeline for me, or anything, but I know she was in foster care before she was placed for adoption. Anderson was the name of those parents. They wouldn't tell her what her birth family's name had been, if they knew. She was with them for a couple of years, I think, but they got divorced just before the adoption was supposed to be finalized. A real mess. Her mom and dad both swore they loved her, but neither of them wanted her after they separated. Terrific people. For some reason she kept their last name when she went back into foster care. Courts can't make parents love their kids. I think she had four or five different families after that."

"That must have been hard on her."

"It was. She hated most of the foster families." Tiffany hesitated. "I think she was abused by an older foster brother when she was about twelve. And then she was moved to a family that was very strict and religious, and they said she was sinful. She jokes sometimes about the devil in her. And there were bad problems in her last foster home. I don't know exactly what they were, but Sarah left as soon as she could and once told me she never wanted to drive through Princeton. She was afraid she'd see him again."

"Him?"

"Her foster father, I guess. All I know is that when we first met each other—you know we lived together for a couple of months before we came here? Well, we were with a friend who wanted to do an errand in Princeton, and Sarah refused to go. She said no way she'd go near there. Not even to pick up dry cleaning!"

"How did you and Sarah meet?"

"She was a waitress at a diner in Somerville. I used to work down near Atlantic City, at a supermarket. Then I was transferred up here, and I needed an apartment. She'd put an ad up on the bulletin board at the diner asking for a roommate to share with a single parent and her daughter. I answered the ad and—that was it!"

"You both ended up here."

"Sarah told me about the Whitcomb House program. One of the customers in the diner told her about it, and she'd applied and been accepted. After she told me, I figured I'd apply, too. It seemed a perfect way to get a new start. We were lucky both of us got interviews and were accepted."

"Tiffany, Sarah's doctor asked me if anyone knew who Aura's father was. Perhaps he should be notified. Do you know who he is?"

"No way. She was really bitter about him. She didn't want him in her life. I tried to get her to call him, to tell him she'd sue for child support. She and Aura deserve that. I'm suing Tyler's father now. He was my boss at the supermarket. He helped Tyler and me for a while, but then his wife found out about it and the checks stopped and he had me transferred to Somerset County. As far away from him as he could manage. He gave me some money for moving expenses. He wanted me gone from the area. Out of his sight. And his wife's sight. But I'm not going to let him forget he has a son. No way. Tyler is his kid, and he's going to support him. I have a lawyer working on it."

"But Sarah didn't want to do that."

"No chance. I thought at first she'd do it. I even gave her the name of my attorney. Not the woman you brought in to tell us to have wills made out, and powers of attorney, and that stuff. A real high-powered lawyer. The kind who advertises on TV and promises results. But Sarah wimped out. She wouldn't go through with it. Even though I told her it would be good for Aura. She'd have more money, and Aura'd know who her father was. That could be important to her someday."

"Where is your lawyer, Tiffany?"

"Princeton."

The envelope Kayla had seen in Sarah's wastebasket had been from a law firm in Princeton. "Just before

119

Sarah passed out she said the name Simon. Does that name mean anything to you?"

Tiffany shook her head slowly. "No. Nothing."

"The police think Sarah was poisoned. Do you have any idea who would do such a thing to her?"

"I haven't thought of anyone. She wasn't like me, you know? She never made trouble. She always did what she was supposed to do. She was a good mother. And she'd made it totally on her own. Aura's father was never part of the picture, from the time she was pregnant. She told me she'd taken off as soon as she knew she was pregnant. Must have been rough for her. At least I had a family to live with for a while, and then Tyler's dad gave us some money. Sarah never had any help. She wants to teach kindergarten, and that takes a four-year degree and certification. It's not easy. Sarah should go after Aura's father."

"You're sure she didn't contact that lawyer."

"She said she wouldn't do that with the last breath in her body." Tiffany paused. "She will be all right, won't she? I mean, everyone at Whitcomb House has some problem in their past. Or even their present—like Maria, who's always following that idiot photographer around, hoping he'll drop his new girlfriend and go back to her. And the guy I'm suing so Tyler can get some money. That guy's pretty mad, you can believe." Tiffany smiled confidently. "But I'm not like Sarah. I'm not going to sit still and let life kick me around. There are people who do, and people who don't, Professor Summer. And I'm one of the doers. Sarah is someone people do things to."

Chapter 16

Large eggs, untitled. German lithograph by A. Reichgert; pattern of twenty-one brown-and-gray-speckled life-size birds' eggs, all identified (in German) by species. 11 x 15 inches. Price: $75.

Enrico's was a small restaurant with a classically stereo-typical Italian decor, including large, gaudily framed color photographs of Mount Vesuvius and the Colosseum, a selection of Italian wines in the window, and red-and-white tablecloths with candles in Chianti bottles on the small tables that would have been appropriate for an outdoor café or piazza. The walls could have been improved by hanging some large eighteenth- or nineteenth-century etchings or engravings instead of the travel posters, but the heady aroma of garlic and oil and cheeses emerging from the kitchen was definitely tempting.

Paul was at the bar when Maggie got there. Had he come directly here after they'd talked? In any case, their table was waiting, in a quiet corner as far as possible from either the kitchen or the bar.

"You must try some of their house wine; it's really an amazing valpolicella." Paul smiled at Maggie over their menus.

"Remember, I have to work tonight."

"What difference can a little wine make? Loading a van is physical work; you'll be more relaxed after a glass or two, and the work will go much faster." He gestured at the waiter. "Bring us a bottle of the house red, please! Now I won't force you to drink it, Maggie, but you do have to taste it."

Maggie fought the impulse to override his order and ask the waiter for a diet soda. But maybe a little wine would be relaxing. She was exhausted, between not sleeping much last night and a stressful day. She'd called Dr. Stevens before she'd left her office. He'd called her back from his home. Sarah's condition hadn't changed, and he hadn't gotten back the toxicology report yet.

Paul raised his glass to Maggie. "To new friends."

She touched her glass to his. "New friends." He'd been right; the wine was better than most house wines. She took a second sip and smiled.

"See? The wine is already working its magic. You're not frowning anymore."

"Was I frowning?"

"You were looking troubled. I know you must have Sarah Anderson on your mind. I can't believe I moved to Somerset County from New York City, where I never personally encountered any violence, and only weeks after I arrive in New Jersey someone is poisoned at a cocktail party I'm attending." Paul signaled to their waiter again and ordered an appetizer of fried calamari with a spicy tomato sauce for them to share.

"Have you bought a home out here?" she asked. He hadn't asked if she liked calamari, but it was one of her favorites.

"Just an apartment so far. Since my divorce."

Maggie recalled hearing Paul had been divorced at least twice.

"I don't want to commit a lot of money for more room than I need. I'm a typical bachelor. I eat out. I have friends in the city. I don't entertain much. Why would I need a house?"

Paul poured himself another glass of wine and added some to Maggie's glass.

Why, indeed, would a bachelor need a house? Although Maggie was now single, and she seemed to have no trouble filling her four-bedroom home. "Have you been divorced long?"

"About a year." Paul hesitated, as if he wasn't certain how much he wanted to share. "She left me. It was a complicated situation. It's over, and we both have our freedom." He returned the question. "I heard your husband died about a year ago."

"Last December. Right after Christmas."

"Then the holidays may be difficult for you. Perhaps we could spend more time together then?"

Was Paul pushing? Or was he just being considerate? "I have lots of friends, and I don't mind being alone," she countered, knowing that sounded a bit prim. But how candid about her personal life should she be with a colleague? She ordered fettuccine; he ordered spaghetti. "You wanted some advice about teaching."

"Your students seem so excited about learning, and I heard there's already a waiting list for one of your spring courses. In my classes I have students falling asleep. What kind of magic do you work?"

Maggie took another sip of wine and another piece of calamari. The wine was definitely bold. So, she decided, was Paul. She just hadn't decided whether she liked his style. "No magic. Talk loud; balance lectures with discussions. And call on students whether they're prepared or not. They learn to be prepared."

"I've heard you show pictures in your classes."

"When it makes sense, I use prints to illustrate eighteenth- and nineteenth-century ideas or events. I sometimes play music, too. Adult audiovisuals. Some students seem to understand more, and retain more, when they see something, others when they hear it. So if we're talking about the jazz age, I play jazz. If we're talking about myths of the American frontier, I show prints of the frontier. And I have my students give short oral reports on different topics. They'd rather listen to each other than to me. And that's one way to bring the classroom information into their world. For example, when discussing the Civil War I might assign one student to be a Charleston cotton broker; one a plantation owner; one a Boston slave trader; one a London cotton-mill owner; one a slave on a plantation; one a member of Congress from Pennsylvania. Then I have them debate slavery, presenting only the perspectives of whoever they are."

"And they do it?" Paul poured himself another glass. Maggie's was still almost full.

"Some are shy; and some do more research than others. But, especially in the smaller classes, it often works better than my presenting a lecture on economic issues of the 1850s. The debate is more memorable for the students; they internalize the information as they hear it discussed."

"Fascinating. I've been staying up nights preparing

long lectures and was disappointed that my students looked bored," Paul said sincerely. "Maybe what I need to do is relax and turn more class time over to the students."

Maggie took a bite of her fettuccine Alfredo. Sinfully rich, but delicious. She nodded to the hovering waiter to add some freshly ground pepper. "Try consciously varying your voice level, too. And don't read your lectures. Break them up. Read a quotation in the voice of the writer or speaker. Ask questions. Walk around. Do anything but just talk at the students. Especially the students in evening classes. Most of them have full-time jobs; they've already worked a full day, and they're tired. They're here because they want to learn, they want to get a degree, and they want to apply what they learn at college in their workplaces. So if you can connect nineteenth-century White House political maneuvering to today's office politics, or make your students think about what decisions they themselves would have made at a particular point in history, then your topic will mean more to them."

"You make it sound so simple, Maggie. I was separating my life in business from my life teaching. Based on what you've said, maybe I could use some of my corporate experiences to illustrate points I'm trying to make." Paul smiled and raised his glass to her. "Oliver was right when he said I should talk with you."

"Oliver suggested you talk with me?"

"I hope you don't mind. He and I have known each other for years."

"I'd heard rumors that he helped you get your job

here." Was she going too far? But Maggie was curious, and the wine was having an effect. With Paul refilling her glass occasionally she must have had two glasses by now. At least. Certainly enough to feel warm and relaxed.

Paul nodded and took another bite of his spaghetti puttanesca. "He introduced me to Max Hagfield, and the rest, as they say, is history. I was bored with corporate life—long hours, stress, and the feeling I wasn't contributing anything to society but a decimal point in a bottom line. I had a master's in history and a few courses toward my doctorate as well as an MBA. Oliver knew there was an opening here. And—voilà! But knowing a little about a subject is very different from teaching it."

"If you understand that, then you've taken a major step toward being an excellent teacher." Paul might be full of lines and stories, but he was trying to fit into the college community, and she wanted to help him. "How do you like your new life so far?"

"Very much. I miss New York, and my friends there, although I do visit on weekends. And I haven't quite gotten the hang of this teaching thing yet. But with time, your help, and a little patience from my students, I'm sure I'll be able to do it. The students are remarkable. Most of them are here because they want to learn."

"That's one of the wonderful things about a community college. Few students attend because their parents packed them off and told them to achieve. They're here because they decided on their own that they want a degree. And that they were willing to work for it."

"If they can learn to be good students, then I can learn to be a better teacher. I've always been a fast learner." Paul picked up the now empty bottle of wine. "Another bottle?"

She hoped he wasn't planning to drive far. His voice was beginning to have that blur that said "too much."

"I don't think so. I have to get home. And load my van, remember?"

"Waiter! Two Sambucas, please."

Maggie frowned.

"You don't have to drink it. Just sip."

How much had Paul had to drink before she had arrived? He *had* been sitting at the bar when she'd arrived. Maggie left her glass on the table as Paul raised his Sambuca in her direction.

His voice was slightly slurred. "Sometime I must go to one of your antique shows. The walls in my apartment are embarrassingly empty. My ex-wife took most of our artwork."

Ex-wives were not a topic Maggie wanted to pursue. "It must be strange, having known Oliver at work in New York, to see him at home here."

"I didn't see him in his office too often. I saw him in the gym and then, sometimes, in social milieus." His slight smirk suggested he wasn't talking about trips to the opera.

Maggie choked a bit. "Social milieus?"

"You know. Places outside the usual spots he and Dorothy are seen here in Jersey." Paul lowered his voice. "Many men have, shall we say, *interests* outside their families? And sometimes maintaining those—*interests*—requires that there be someone else, known to the family, who they can go places with. Or—not."

"In other words, you gave Oliver an alibi." Maggie was more amused by Paul's not-so-subtle description than she was shocked. Oliver had worked long hours in New York City, and Dorothy had mentioned how glad she was when he retired and could be at home more. Those long hours in New York had sometimes required he use a company suite in a hotel instead of coming home to New Jersey. It had been clear to Maggie then, if not to Dorothy, that a company suite could be used for a multitude of purposes.

"And he's a fair man. Turn and turn alike!" Paul actually winked at her.

Was this his idea of a suave gentleman having a discussion with a colleague? Maggie had the distinct feeling that she was on Paul's ex-wife's side of whatever disagreements had led up to his divorce. "New Jersey must seem very tame to you after all that excitement."

"Oh, New Jersey isn't all that boring, really." Paul glanced around all too obviously and lowered his voice. No one at nearby tables was paying any attention. "Oliver has his interests here, too."

"Why are you telling me all this?" Maggie suddenly felt uncomfortable. Oliver Whitcomb was a Somerset College trustee; his wife was someone who trusted Maggie enough to confide in her. She did not want to know things about their life together that would make it awkward for her to work with either of them in the future. "Oliver Whitcomb's personal life is his personal business."

"I've never told anyone, Maggie. I'm discreet." Paul raised his glass and downed the rest of his Sambuca. "But you care about your students. And maybe someone should know about Oliver's . . . interests."

"I do care about my students. But I really don't care about Oliver's interests. They're his business. And his wife's." Maggie hesitated. Was this just gossip? Or could Paul be saying something she needed to understand? "Unless his interests have to do with my students?"

"Haven't you ever wondered why Oliver is so supportive of those single mothers at Whitcomb House?"

"Whitcomb House is Dorothy's project." And just today she'd heard a great deal about why Dorothy Whitcomb had chosen that particular charitable endeavor.

"Oliver's pretty interested in it, too, Maggie. After all, it's his money Dorothy is spending on those students."

"He's always been very enthusiastic about the project." Maggie tried to keep her voice steady.

"Think about why a mature, educated, wealthy man like Oliver Whitcomb might be so interested in that group of young women, Maggie. Think about motives. Not all motives are altruistic, you know. Not even in the suburbs." The waitress dropped their bill on the table and Paul fumbled with his wallet before pulling out a gold card. Maggie decided she wouldn't fight for the bill. "I won't tell anyone anything. I've promised not to. Oliver helped me to get my job. But someone needs to ask some questions. Before anyone else gets hurt." For a moment Paul looked at her directly. In that second he appeared completely sober.

Before anyone else gets hurt! Oliver was interested in "that group" of young women? Was another student in danger? Maggie swallowed deeply. Could Oliver Whitcomb have been involved with Sarah? His wife's daughter? "Who should be doing the questioning, Paul? Dorothy?" Maggie hesitated. "The police?"

"I've already said too much. You're a smart woman, Maggie. You'll figure it out."

As they walked into the parking lot, Paul stayed close to Maggie, their shoulders almost touching. She moved a bit away. Whatever scent he used was attractive. It was somehow mellow and spicy at the same time. She enjoyed the totally unimportant exercise of analyzing it as they walked toward their cars. It took her mind away from what she had just heard.

Their steps crunched through the dry red and brown leaves in the parking lot. The air was cooler than it had been earlier today. Somewhere nearby a solitary cricket was chirping November time. As they got to Maggie's van, Paul turned her around gently and she let the kiss happen. His lips were gentle, and his arms felt strong around her. For a moment Maggie relaxed. She wanted so much to be able to lean on someone.

Then reality hit, like a chill breeze. This man was a colleague. He clearly had relationships with many women. She was involved with Will. Maggie stepped back, pushing Paul away. Besides, he was at least a little drunk.

"No. I'm sorry. No." She got into her van and closed

the door, not waiting for a response.

He stepped back, shaking his head slowly at her.

She wished she couldn't still feel his lips on hers or smell the light, intoxicating scent of his cologne.

Chapter 17

Presented to . . . *Steel-engraved Plate VI in Gaskell's Compendium of Forms, 1882; beautifully drawn dove demonstrating calligraphy techniques. Above the quotation (also in calligraphy): " 'The schoolmaster is abroad! I trust more to him, armed with his primer, than I do to the soldier in full military array.' —Lord Brougham, in 1860." Lord Henry Peter Brougham (1778–1868) was a Scots-born lawyer and liberal leader in the House of Commons who proposed educational reforms and was a founder of the University of London. 8 x 10.5 inches. Price: $60.*

Maggie shook off thoughts of Paul that were anything but businesslike and headed her van toward the hospital.

But Dr. Stevens wasn't there, and Sarah's condition appeared the same.

"Mrs. Whitcomb's been here most of the day," said the intensive care nurse. "She left about seven; you just missed her."

Maggie glanced at her watch. It was seven-thirty.

"A man called here, asking about Sarah. I told him she couldn't have visitors and gave him Dr. Stevens's number."

Could that have been the same man who'd tried to reach Sarah at Whitcomb House? What man could be asking about Sarah? "Did you get his name?"

"No. I just talked with him briefly." The nurse hesitated. "Should I have found out who he was? Was that important? I know Ms. Anderson is involved in a police matter."

"I don't know. But it might have been."

"Maybe Dr. Stevens would know."

"Would you have him call me?" He should have gotten the toxicology reports back by now, too.

Maggie's home was only a five-minute drive from the hospital, in a section of Park Glen that had been built up in the early 1920s after the train line from Hoboken was extended, making it possible to commute to New York via train and the Hoboken ferry across the Hudson. Houses in Park Glen were larger and better made than those built later, in the housing boom after World War II, but they were set close together. Maggie's neighbors were teachers and small-business owners and middle-management executives. The town where Oliver and Dorothy lived insisted on five-acre zoning and attracted investment bankers and the horsey set. That neighborhood was far beyond Maggie's means.

She and Michael had bought their house when they were first married, with the help of a loan from his parents. The house needed a lot of repairs, but they'd had two incomes and thought it was a bargain. Since then most of the houses on their street had been restored, and taxes had gone up with the appearance of the area. Maggie'd thought of selling and moving last spring, but she loved the house too much, and some of her neighbors were now her friends. Jerome and Ian next door kept an eye on her house when she was away doing antique shows or on vacation. And the Cushmans across the street included her whenever they entertained, even after Michael's death, when her presence meant an uneven number of guests. Suburban social life was like Noah's ark: everyone two by two. The number of social invitations Maggie received had dropped dramatically in the past year. For the most part, she didn't care. Between teaching and running her business she didn't have a lot of unscheduled time. But there were moments when she missed dressing up for dinner parties and seeing people she didn't work with.

Dorothy and Oliver, for example, could be busy every night if they chose to be. But tonight, while she and Paul were having dinner, Dorothy had been with Sarah. Maggie wondered where Oliver was. How credible were Paul's implications that Oliver was involved with the women of Whitcomb House? Were Paul's hints the result of his having too much to drink? Or was he drinking to get up enough courage to say something important?

She sighed deeply as she unlocked her back door. It had been a long day.

Winslow ran to greet her, meowing a welcome and rubbing himself against her legs, clearly letting her know she was late and his dinner bowl was empty. She filled the dish with tuna and made a decision.

"I will not sit down or listen to my messages or check

e-mail," Maggie told Winslow. "Not until I've packed the van." Winslow was concentrating on the tuna and didn't appear to have an opinion on the matter.

She stowed her day's pile of students' papers, lecture notes, and lists of tomorrow's appointments on the kitchen counter and put on her old red L.L. Bean field jacket. The November evening was now decidedly chilly.

Packing her van for an antique show was both a physical and intellectual chore. For the next hour she blocked out all thoughts about Sarah, Aura, Dorothy, Oliver, Paul, or anyone else connected with Somerset Community College.

She'd contracted with the Morristown show promoter to provide four eight-foot tables for her booth; she packed two light five-foot folding tables in her van to use in front of the heavier tables that would border her booth. She needed six table covers, and Peg-Boards to clamp to the backs of the tables to provide space for prints to be displayed above the tabletops. A deep display easel would hold an assortment of her larger prints.

First she packed the heavy tools of her trade: the furniture, including a folding ladder to be used during setup, her bag of tools, and a separate bag of tapes—duct tape, masking tapes of different widths, transparent tape, archival tape—to attach matted prints to backgrounds, or to repair prints or mats that required maintenance during a show.

She packed her large portfolios next. Some of them held a hundred prints. Every January Maggie went through her portfolios, replacing those that were worn.

But it was now November and many of the portfolios were missing handles or had torn sides or even bottoms. By this time of the show season she had liberally applied tape to repair torn seams on almost every one of her dozens of portfolios. Maggie made a mental note to stop at the local office supply store and order new portfolios, and then to set aside one day of Thanksgiving vacation to make new labels (Nests and Eggs; Winslow Homer Civil War; Human Anatomy; Nursery Rhymes) and transfer the prints into the new containers.

In the meantime she carried most portfolios by cradling them in her arms. Like mothers would carry children, she thought wryly. Maggie's paper children. A broken portfolio could drop hundreds, or even thousands of dollars' worth of prints on a sidewalk or floor. And if that sidewalk should be wet . . . Maggie had insurance, but her premiums would have gone through the roof if she'd put in claims for every print that had been damaged by rain or snow when she was moving prints in and out of antique shows. She hoped this weekend the weather would be clear. Dampness was the enemy of paper.

She stood her largest portfolios up and stored them vertically across the back of her van, carefully alternating framed prints between portfolios to cushion the glass from abrupt stops or hard surfaces. Then she stacked medium-size portfolios in back of the large ones, finally piling her small portfolios in rows.

The bulkiest things she had to pack were the many plastic and wooden racks and holders she used to showcase the prints. Some holders had been designed as kitchen storage pieces; some had been intended to hold greeting cards or posters at book or art stores. Maggie had made the wooden racks when she'd started Shadows fifteen years ago.

She'd been only twenty-three then, and working on her doctorate, much younger than most people entering the world of antiques. She was looking for a way to have fun, make some money, and ensure that she didn't spend the rest of her life in libraries. She and Michael hadn't even met then.

Starting the business had been an adventure: searching antique shows, flea markets, antiquarian-book fairs, paper shows, and auctions for bargains. Matting the treasures she found and then designing her booths. As Maggie carefully fit her racks above and between her portfolios, she smiled to herself as she thought of those first shows. In those days she'd designed the placement of items on the walls before she left for the venue, ensuring that she had enough inventory to fill the booth—and enough equipment to display it well. Many of the racks and display techniques she used today she'd created then.

Now she never had enough booth space for everything she'd like to display. Should she take fish and shells and maritime prints to an inland location? Wall Street prints to Cape Cod? For Morristown she packed Christmas prints, and engravings of New Jersey and Manhattan. She had dozens of nineteenth-century wood and steel engravings depicting scenes in North America and Europe, but most customers wanted pictures of local sites. Maggie did shows throughout the Northeast, but she had a backlog of Colorado and California views.

Maybe some summer she'd travel and do shows in other areas of the country. Nashville had a great show, she'd heard. And St. Louis. Of course, traveling would be more difficult if she had a child . . .

By the time the van was packed, Maggie was exhausted. Dinner with Paul seemed hours ago.

She hung her jacket on one of the hooks behind the kitchen door, thought of soda, then of cocoa, and took out one of the Edinburgh Crystal cut-glass brandy snifters she'd paid too much for at a show last year and poured in a small amount of Courvoisier.

She walked to her bedroom, kicked off her shoes, curled up in her reading chair, and breathed in the aroma of the cognac. As she savored the feel of the heavy crystal, she warmed the glass with her hands.

A worn iron horseshoe hung above her bedroom door. It was upside down, of course, so her luck wouldn't fall out. Tonight she felt as though she needed every bit of that luck.

Then the telephone rang.

Chapter 18

Tobacco. *Lithograph of the tobacco plant in bloom. First used by Native Americans, then imported to Europe, it is now cultivated in every part of the globe with an appropriate climate. From* The Grocer's Encyclopedia, *compiled by Artemas Ward, New York, 1911. Quotation from the* Encyclopedia: *"We cannot honestly say more against tobacco than*

137

can be urged against any other luxury. It is innocuous as compared with alcohol; it does infinitely less harm than opium and is in no sense worse than tea." 8 x 11 inches. Price: $65.

Maggie put down her cognac and reached for the telephone.

"Professor Summer? Dr. Stevens."

"How is Sarah?"

"The same. No changes. The good news is that she hasn't gotten any worse. But I called because we got back the preliminary toxicology report."

"Yes?"

"I called the police immediately, but then I had an emergency. Sorry not to have gotten to you earlier."

"So there was definitely poison?"

"Sarah swallowed an overdose of nicotine."

"Nicotine? But she didn't smoke!"

"Which would make her even more vulnerable to nicotine poisoning."

Maggie remembered: Sarah's breath had smelled like cigarettes. "But even if she didn't smoke . . . I've never heard of anyone going into a coma from experimenting with a cigarette!"

"I don't think she smoked a cigarette. Or even two or three. That might have made her dizzy or nauseated since she wasn't used to it, but it wouldn't have sent her into a coma."

"Then?" How could anyone get nicotine poisoning without smoking?

"It could have entered her system in one of several

138

ways. It could have been through wearing several nicotine patches—the kind designed for people trying to stop smoking. Or it could have been through ingestion."

"Ingestion? Why would anyone eat tobacco?"

"It doesn't make sense, does it? Usually we see nicotine poisoning only in children or pets who have chewed cigarettes or chewing tobacco or snuff, or even a nicotine patch or gum. Nicotine is highly toxic, especially to people whose systems are not used to it. As little as two to five milligrams can cause nausea, and ingesting forty to sixty milligrams can kill someone. There was a case in Florida a couple of years ago where a woman murdered a man who was mentally ill by forcing him to eat two tins of snuff. Children have been poisoned by biting into a nicotine patch, or chewing a piece of nicotine gum."

"I can't imagine Sarah eating snuff or chewing a nicotine patch!"

"Which is why she appears to have been poisoned. Perhaps by drinking something that had liquid nicotine, which is very potent, mixed in it. She isn't a big woman, and she didn't smoke. She would have been affected quickly."

"How much do you think she drank?"

"We can't tell exactly. But I'd guess at least thirty-five milligrams to put her in the coma. Keep in mind there are fifteen to twenty milligrams of nicotine in a cigarette, but drinking liquid nicotine is much more dangerous than inhaling it."

"Wouldn't it taste awful?"

"Perhaps it was mixed with food or drink that was

highly spiced and the spices partially covered the taste and smell. That's up to the police to figure out. I passed the information on to them, and knew you wanted to hear, too."

"One more question, Doctor. How long would it take for the effects of liquid nicotine poisoning to begin?"

"It would happen very quickly. Depending on the size of the person and the amount ingested, liquid nicotine can take effect in as little as one or two minutes. In a smoker it would take longer."

"One or two minutes!"

"She probably ingested the nicotine immediately before her collapse. Dizziness, nausea, weakness, and then coma. That's all consistent with her condition immediately before and just after her arrival at the emergency room."

"Yes." Maggie paused. There was no doubt, then: Sarah had been poisoned at the Whitcombs' party. Where she had been in full view of everyone. "Will knowing that nicotine poisoning is the reason for her coma mean you can help Sarah more?"

"We're hoping so. I'm not an expert on poisoning, but we've contacted some people at the regional poison control center who are. The good news is that we haven't done anything contraindicated by nicotine poisoning. We just need to find out if there is anything additional we can try."

"I hope so, Dr. Stevens."

"I do, too. Shall I continue to call you if there are any changes in her condition?"

"Please. I'll stop at the hospital first thing in the morning in any case. And—one more question? Sarah's nurse said a man had called asking about her, and she'd referred him to you. Do you know who he was?"

"I did talk with someone briefly today. He said he was a relative, and I told him her condition was critical and she couldn't have any visitors. Should I have gotten his name?"

"If he calls again, would you, please? We didn't know Sarah had any relatives. It could be important."

"I'm sorry I didn't question him."

"You've helped Sarah. That's what's important."

"Ask one of the nurses to call me if you have questions in the morning." Dr. Stevens paused. "Will Mrs. Whitcomb be with you?"

"I don't know."

"She spent a good part of today at the hospital and seemed very upset. It might be good for her to have a friend nearby. You'll tell her about the nicotine?"

"I'll tell her."

She sat back in the armchair and sipped her cognac. Nicotine poisoning.

Maggie thought back to the party. Sarah had been talking to Dorothy. She had seemed fine then. Maggie had recommended the roast beef . . . but she had eaten that, too, and she wasn't ill. Sarah had been drinking nothing but Bloody Mary mix.

The Bloody Mary mix! It had been a full pitcher, and it would have been spicy. Could it have covered the smell of liquid nicotine? Had anyone else seen Sarah drinking it? Who had access to the bar?

Oliver had organized the bottles. Paul had helped him. But what possible reason would Oliver or Paul have had to poison Sarah? Even if there was a relationship between Oliver and Sarah . . . How would he have known she would drink the Bloody Mary mix? Anyone there could have helped themselves. Anyone could have been poisoned. Maggie shuddered. She liked Virgin Marys herself. She could have been the one in the hospital.

Oliver might have less-than-ideal moral standards, but he wasn't stupid. Even if he'd wanted to hurt Sarah, why would he have done it in his own home, where he would be the logical person to have mixed the drinks?

Paul? But he didn't even know Sarah! Or so he'd said.

Maggie felt surrounded by hazy clouds of information. She was exhausted. She needed to call Dorothy. No matter what the consequences, she didn't want Dorothy to think she was hiding something.

Maggie looked at her watch. It was after eleven. No matter; she had promised to call.

Oliver answered.

"I'm sorry to call so late, Oliver. It's Maggie Summer. Is Dorothy there?"

"She's here, Maggie, but neither of us can talk now. The police are here. Dorothy's with the detectives."

Chapter 19

T-Tiger; U-Unicorn; V-Vampire. Lithographed alphabet page from Walter Crane's New Toy Book. Picture shows a tiger, a bat, and, interestingly, not a unicorn but another one-horned creature—a rhinoceros. Walter Crane (1845–1915) was an English designer, illustrator, and painter, grouped with the Pre-Raphaelites but remembered for his illustrations of books for children. He, like William Morris, tried to bring art to the home through the design of textiles, windows, and tapestries. c. 1880. 7 x 9.5 inches. Price: $60.

The police must have gone directly to the Whitcombs' after hearing about the nicotine.

How awful for Dorothy to know for certain that Sarah had been poisoned in her home. Everyone at that party was a potential suspect. Even the caterers, Maggie realized. And, of course, Dorothy and Oliver would be on the list.

Dorothy wouldn't have killed Sarah; Sarah was her daughter. But the police didn't know that, and neither did Oliver. Could the detectives have found out that Dorothy had given a child up for adoption and connected that child to Sarah?

Not likely, with sealed adoption records. But someone could have seen Oliver and Sarah together and suspected Dorothy of jealousy. Or Oliver could have been trying to cover up an affair.

Anything was possible.

Maggie took another sip of her cognac, and then another. If any day called for cognac, this was it. She looked down at the telephone in her lap and realized she hadn't even checked her answering machine. It was probably too late now to return calls.

But in the morning she'd be focused on getting to the hospital to see Sarah as quickly as possible, before her ten o'clock class. Thank goodness she'd packed the van tonight. Tomorrow was Tuesday. She'd have to stop at the grocery and then make up a bed in one of the guest rooms for Gussie and Jim.

The house should be dusted and vacuumed; the dishes in the kitchen sink washed. No matter how tired she was, she had to do something now. She was a night person, not a morning person, she reminded herself. She was exhausted, but if she did the work, she could sleep in a little tomorrow.

She finished her cognac, considered pouring some more, reconsidered, and then went to the kitchen and washed the crystal under running water. No matter how tired she was, crystal had to be washed by hand. She rinsed the dishes she'd left in the sink yesterday and put them in the dishwasher. Already she felt more organized. At least if the police came back, they wouldn't find dirty dishes in the sink.

She grimaced. They had no reason to come back to her home. Not that she could think of. But they probably had a search warrant for the Whitcombs' house. Did a house where someone was poisoned qualify as a crime scene? She wasn't sure of the legalities. But as long as Sarah was alive, at least it wasn't a murder scene.

As Maggie straightened her study, replacing the portfolios she hadn't packed, and piling her unmatted prints near her paper cutter, her mind kept returning to one question: Who poisoned Sarah? Who had a motive? No matter how much she scrutinized the people who'd been at Sunday afternoon's gathering, she couldn't imagine anyone who had a reason to hurt Sarah.

Sarah's housemates all had different backgrounds and interests. Dorothy said she was Sarah's mother. She wanted custody of Aura should Sarah die. But would Dorothy kill Sarah to get custody of Aura? Improbable.

Paul had insinuated that Oliver might have a relationship with Sarah. But would he try to kill her?

Who else at the party even knew Sarah? President Hagfield had met Sarah at other receptions. Paul knew of her, but said he'd never met her. She must have classes with other professors who were there besides Maggie.

It just didn't make sense.

I should write to Will, she suddenly thought. She felt a surge of guilt. He wrote to her every day, and she'd had dinner with Paul . . . and the computer was right here in the study.

Dear Will,
Life has been more hectic than usual here. One of my Whitcomb House girls is in the hospital, and she doesn't have any family, so I've been visiting her between classes and getting ready for the show this

weekend. But the van is finally packed! You know
what a relief that is. Gussie and Jim are driving
down from Massachusetts and should be here late
Wednesday night. I hope you've found wonderful
bargains and that both our shows this weekend are
fantastic. I'm weary—you can tell by when I'm
writing this—way past my usual bedtime. Wish you
were here. I could use a shoulder to lean on.
Although if I did, I'd probably just fall asleep on it.
Fair skies and clear roads, and know I'm thinking
of you.

Maggie

Short, but she'd let him know she was still here. And
caring about him.

The answering machine was in the kitchen. One more
task before she gave up for the night.

"Maggie, it's Gussie. Got your message, and Jim and
I are almost packed and ready to go. We'll drive down
Wednesday, and see you in the early hours of Thursday
morning, after the theater. Don't bother having food for
us; we have reservations to eat in New York before the
play starts. Looking forward to seeing you!"

Good, Maggie thought. That means I don't have to hit
the grocery store until Wednesday. It would be good to
see Gussie. Gussie could sometimes see solutions
where Maggie saw only puzzle pieces.

There were two hang-up calls before "Professor
Summer? It's Tiffany. I forgot something. I need to see
you again. Soon. I'm going to be out for a while this
evening, so could I meet you at your office first thing in

the morning? I'll call tomorrow to confirm. Thanks!"

What could that be about? Had Tiffany thought of something that might help Sarah? Darn. If she'd checked her messages earlier, maybe she could have called Tiffany back tonight. But not this late. Whatever it was would have to wait until tomorrow.

"Is this Maggie Summer? I'm Martha Graves. I live down the street from you. David George, next door, said you were an antique-print dealer. I've been cleaning out my mother's attic and I found a whole box of *Godey's Lady's Book* fashion prints. Would you be interested in buying them? Please call."

Godey's! Maggie could always use more early fashion prints, especially if they were the double-size ones that had folded into the magazines. Those were getting harder and harder to find, and if those were in good condition . . . people hung them in bedrooms or bathrooms or hallways and liked the light touch of the elegant Victorian fashions. Especially when the scenes included children or animals or men. Or brides. Brides were the hardest to find, and the fastest to sell. They made wonderful shower or wedding or anniversary gifts. But it was too late to call Martha Graves tonight.

Maggie wrote down her number and yawned. Enough was enough. Sleep called.

Too late for the *Godey's*, too late to call Tiffany. Too late.

Chapter 20

Les Modes Parisiennes: Peterson's Magazine. February 1891. Five slender, elegantly dressed women in a hand-colored steel-engraved (by Illman Brothers) fashion print. Two of the women are dressed in blue; two in tan; one in gold. A young girl, also elegantly dressed, peeks from behind their skirts, as does a small terrier. Originally a centerfold in Peterson's, *a monthly magazine for women. Fold still visible. Small tears in left margin covered by mat. 9.5 x 11.5 inches. Price: $50.*

For the second morning in a row Maggie's dreams were interrupted by the persistent ringing of her bedside telephone. She tried to focus on the illuminated dial of her clock radio: 5:34.

"Professor Summer! We called 911 and the police came. But we knew you'd want to be here."

Maggie struggled to sit up and identify the tearful voice. She'd been in bed less than five hours. "Kayla?"

"Yes, it's Kayla. It's awful. I can't believe this nightmare. Maria is talking about leaving right now and dropping out of college and moving back to her parents' house. Kendall's trying to talk her into staying." Maggie heard sobbing in the background. "Heather is crying, and I just don't know how we're going to explain it to the kids. They're all awake and they know something awful happened."

"Whoa, Kayla. Slow down. What did happen?"

Maggie was definitely awake now. She picked up the pencil near her telephone pad, in case she needed to write down anything.

"I'm sorry. It's just so awful . . . and I don't know how it could have happened! Aura woke up early this morning. She was probably missing her mother, but I put her in her own bed last night, because she and Katie didn't get much sleep Sunday night."

Could something have happened to Aura? Maggie felt her heart take a leap. "What happened, Kayla? Is Aura all right?"

"She's in shock, I guess. She was crying at first. But now she's just sitting on the floor in the corner of the kitchen holding her teddy bear."

"But what *happened?* You said you'd called 911. The police were there!"

"Yes. But it's not Aura. It's Tiffany."

"Tiffany!"

"Aura found her on the kitchen floor. She looked awful. Professor Summer, she's dead!" Kayla began to sob, and Maggie missed her next muffled words. ". . . came in late last night, I guess. We must all have been in bed. She was lying just inside the kitchen door, sort of stretched out, on her back. Kendall and I heard Aura scream, and we both got there at about the same time. We found Tiffany on the floor. Aura was sitting next to her, stroking her hair and sobbing. Tiffany looked awful. Her lips and mouth were swollen, and dark, and her blouse was stained, as though she'd thrown up. We knew right away that she was dead."

"And you called 911?"

"Oh, yes! We kept thinking about Sarah, and that the police had just been here this morning—I mean yesterday morning—and we got really scared."

"And the police came?"

"They came, and they wouldn't let us use the phone right away. Not until they'd talked with us. That's why I didn't call until now. They just took Tiffany away. They've taped off part of the kitchen with that yellow crime-scene tape, like you see on TV, and one of the detectives is in the living room right now trying to talk to Heather." Kayla paused for a moment and Maggie realized she was holding back her sobs. "But she's kind of hysterical. I was sure you'd want to know what was happening."

"Hang on, Kayla. I'll be right over."

"Thank you, Professor Summer! Heather and Maria and I . . . we're scared. Maybe it's just a coincidence, but Sarah and Tiffany, both."

"Sarah's not dead, Kayla. This must be some sort of horrible coincidence. Try to keep calm, for the children's sake. Tell the police whatever you can. None of you have anything to hide." Maggie wished she believed that was true. But Tiffany had left a message last night saying she'd forgotten to tell Maggie something. Could it be a coincidence that she was dead only hours later? "I'll be there as soon as I can."

Chapter 21

Penitentiary, Philadelphia. Steel engraving drawn by C. Burton, New York, engraved and printed by Fenner, Sears & Company, published in London, 1831, by Hinton & Simpkin & Marshall. High-walled, turreted stone building across a walkway from a lawn. Man and horse with a pull-cart in foreground. 4 x 6 inches. Price: $60.

Maggie pulled on a comfortable pair of navy slacks and a navy-and-white sweater, quickly rebraided her hair, and pinned it up in a crown. "You look a lot older than thirty-eight," she said to her pale reflection in the bathroom mirror. She added lipstick and shrugged. "But who cares this morning. At least you're alive." A grim thought. She pinned on one of her brass *M* pins for luck. Her horseshoe alone didn't seem to be doing the trick.

She picked up her classroom papers and pocketbook to leave and then stopped. She must call Dorothy.

Although it was Tiffany who was dead, not Sarah, Dorothy would want to know. Better for Maggie to deliver the news than for the police to do it.

"Dorothy? It's Maggie. There's another situation at Whitcomb House."

"Another situation?" Dorothy was beginning to wake up and focus.

Winslow jumped onto the bed and rubbed against Maggie's arm. She pushed him back onto the floor. No time for cats this morning. "Kayla called me half an hour ago. Tiffany's dead. They found her body on the floor of the kitchen early this morning and called the police. They've already taken her away. Probably to do an autopsy."

"Tiffany? Autopsy? What happened, Maggie?"

"I don't know. I'm on my way over there right now. Kayla said Tiffany looked as though she'd thrown up; her blouse and face were stained."

"Stained with blood? Could she have had a hemorrhage of some sort? How could she have just died? She was so young!"

"I don't know. Kayla was upset, and the children were crying. When I find out more, I'll let you know. The police will have to figure it out."

"How awful. Two of the girls in fluke accidents in the same week! It's a nightmare."

As she put down the phone, Maggie realized she had better make one more call. To Max Hagfield. If she was lucky, she'd reach him before the police did.

He answered on the first ring.

"Max? Good morning, this is Maggie Summer."

"It's just after six! I call that dawn, not morning! Couldn't whatever this is wait until I'm in my office?"

"I'm sorry, but, no, Max."

"Is it the Anderson girl? Has she died?" Max's voice quavered. "That's all I need. The murder of one of my best students in the Whitcomb experimental program, in the home of one of Somerset College's trustees."

Maggie's temper flared. Should she apologize for Sarah's rude behavior? If Sarah was going to be poisoned, why couldn't she have arranged to do it somewhere other than at the Whitcombs'! Clearly, in Max's mind, she had been inconsiderate, to say the least. "No; it's not Sarah. So far as I know her condition is unchanged."

Unchanged. In a coma. With a little daughter who was now doubly traumatized: her mother was ill and had seemingly left her, and the woman she had shared rooms with was dead. "It's Tiffany Douglass. She's dead."

The line was silent for a long moment. "Dead?" Max's voice was low and deliberate. "Dead? Are you sure?"

"Kayla just called me from Whitcomb House. They found Tiffany's body in the kitchen early this morning. The police have been there, and I assume they're looking into all possibilities, because of Sarah's poisoning."

"How could this be happening to Somerset College?" Max's voice trembled. "What are we going to tell *The Star-Ledger*?"

Maggie couldn't believe his first thought was of publicity. "Just tell the press you don't know anything pending the result of the police investigation. That as soon as you do know something, you'll announce it. That the Somerset College community expresses its deepest sympathy, to Tiffany Douglass's family, and, especially, to her young son."

"Do the police think she was murdered?"

"I don't know, Max. But it doesn't sound good right now. The Somerset College students are going to need you to provide as many answers as you can."

There was silence on the end of the telephone.

"Maybe you should increase security on campus." Why was she telling him how to do his job?

But he jumped at the suggestion. "Yes. We could do that. Increased security. I'll talk to our people, and to the police. They should all be working together." Max had somewhat recovered his voice and control. "We made a major mistake in letting those single parents live on campus, Maggie. A major mistake. Many of them have led unstable lives. Who knows what criminals they're attracting to our campus? We've already seen the result. But bringing them here is a mistake that can be corrected."

"Don't do anything drastic, Max. Maybe there's an explanation. Don't give up on the students. They're frightened and they need to be reassured. I'm going over to Whitcomb House now."

"That's good, Maggie. And, Maggie, we've got to keep anything else from happening. I'm counting on you, Maggie. Remember—I'm counting on you."

Chapter 22

Meriwether Lewis, Esq. *Drawn by St. Manum Pine and engraved by Strictland for the* Analectic Magazine and Naval Chronicle, *1815. Early engraving of Meriwether Lewis (1774–1809), wearing a fur hat and fringed, military-style jacket, holding his powder horn and musket. Lewis was stationed in various frontier posts and learned the language and customs of the Indians.*

Under the sponsorship of President Jefferson he led an expedition to the source of the Missouri River with his fellow officer William Clark, making a portage overland through the Rockies, and reaching the Pacific Ocean. His early death was controversial; it was either murder or suicide. Some light foxing. 5 x 8 inches. Price: $55.

Maggie didn't bother to knock; despite the November chill Whitcomb House's front door was open, and although police cars were parked outside, no crime-scene tape prevented her entrance. She walked into the familiar front hall. The house looked like a scene in a TV crime drama.

The kitchen was covered with dust—for finger-printing, Maggie assumed—and a photographer was carefully focusing on every detail in the room. Detectives Luciani and Newton were sitting on the living room couch, bent low over a notebook on the coffee table in front of them. They probably hadn't had much sleep lately. Newton's hair needed combing, and Luciani looked as though he hadn't shaved in a couple of days.

Yesterday morning they were in my kitchen, Maggie thought. Yesterday was a long time ago.

"Professor Summer?" Luciani looked up from his seat on the couch. He got up quickly and walked toward her. "What are you doing here?"

"The students asked me to come. I'm their adviser."

"We don't need any more people in this house," he said, backing her against the wall in the hallway. "There are already enough fingerprints in here to keep the FBI busy for weeks."

"Not quite," Newton said from the living room. "And you're on the list of people we need to talk to. Since you're here, you might as well stay. But come into the living room, please."

Luciani backed up, watching Maggie closely. She stepped by him. "Where are the students? And the children?"

"Upstairs. We had them take the kids and get them dressed and calmed down. And away from the porch and kitchen. We've searched the upstairs already."

"I'd like to see them." Maggie heard footsteps upstairs. How were they all coping?

"In a few minutes." Newton gestured for Maggie to sit on the couch in the spot recently vacated by Luciani. The binder on the table was closed, but Newton had her small black notebook out and pencil poised. Luciani sat on the chair opposite her.

Maggie'd sat in that room on so many Monday evenings, enjoying the chaos and joy of the six adults and six children who lived here. This Tuesday morning the blocks and dolls and trucks piled in the corner were untouched. The television was off. No music from upstairs broke the silence. Whitcomb House had always felt so full of life and laughter. Now, with two of the young women gone, it seemed ghostlike. Although Sarah wasn't really gone, Maggie corrected herself. Sarah would be back. She hoped.

"I know we talked with you yesterday morning, but that investigation centered on Sarah Anderson."

Detective Newton's question brought her back to the moment.

Maggie nodded.

"I assume that you've already heard we're here in response to a call from the residents reporting the death of Tiffany Douglass."

"Kayla called to let me know."

"Because you're their adviser."

"And, I hope, also their friend." They could use friends this week, Maggie thought. A lot of friends.

"You told us yesterday what you knew about Sarah Anderson. Could you tell us something about Tiffany Douglass? Or anything that might help us see if there's a link between the crimes?"

"It's definite, then, that Tiffany was murdered?"

The detectives looked at each other. Luciani shrugged. "We'll know for certain after the medical examiner has taken a look at her. But the dark stains on her lips and mouth and the vomit make it look like some, possibly caustic, substance was involved." He hesitated. "I'm sorry. I'm tired. I'd appreciate your not sharing that information. It isn't official in any case. Not until the medical examiner has seen her."

"The students are pretty sharp. They seem to have figured it out even before we got here," Newton said.

"Of course, they were probably thinking of Sarah, too. Two young women poisoned in two days . . . are any of the other students in danger?" Maggie had to ask.

Newton didn't smile. "We don't know. At the moment everyone here is a suspect, and anything is possible. Have there been any threats to Whitcomb House or its residents that you've heard? From inside the house or outside?"

Maggie shook her head. "Never. In fact, the house has gotten some very positive publicity and, so far as I know, has been accepted by the campus community and the town itself. Everyone who lived here seemed to get along."

"What about President Hagfield? Has he had any negative feedback about the house?"

"You'd have to ask him. I don't know of any." The only negative comments Maggie had heard about Whitcomb House had come from Max himself, this morning. The police could find that out themselves.

"We understand the two victims shared a suite here with their children. We're assuming they were close friends. They might also have shared thoughts? Shared acquaintances?"

"You'll have to ask the other students about that. I do know they met before they came to Somerset College. They shared an apartment last summer. So they certainly knew each other. How many confidences or friends they shared, I don't know." Sarah was so quiet, Maggie thought. So different from Tiffany. And Tiffany wasn't around that much. What had Tiffany been doing?

"They came from different parts of New Jersey," continued Newton. She stretched a bit, pulling down her navy jacket. Dark circles were under her eyes.

Being a detective is a rough job, thought Maggie sympathetically. She told them what she knew. "Tiffany used to live in South Jersey. Outside of Atlantic City somewhere. She worked at a grocery store, I think she said, and the chain transferred her up here." She paused. "Sarah might know more, of course."

"If—when—she comes out of her coma, we'll be sure to talk with her. But in the meantime, any information you have would be helpful." There was a small crash upstairs and a child's wail. Detective Newton listened for a moment and smiled. "Six children living here with their parents! There must be some interesting days. I have trouble coping with one husband and one child."

Detective Luciani looked at her as though she had just mentioned landing on the moon. "We've got work to do. Today."

Maggie continued, "Tiffany lived here, and she was in one of my classes, but I didn't know her as well as I do some of the other Whitcomb House residents. She seemed to have an active life, many friends. She wasn't always here." Or in class, Maggie added to herself.

"Do you know any of her friends? Outside Whitcomb House."

"No, I don't."

"She has a little boy."

"Tyler is two."

"And his father? Do you know anything about him?"

"No," Maggie started. And then she remembered what Tiffany had said yesterday afternoon. "I believe he worked with her, or maybe he was her boss, at the supermarket where she worked in South Jersey. She told me he was married, and that she was asking him for child support for Tyler." She had said suing him, actually.

"Was that a problem?"

"I don't know. Just yesterday she told me she had a lawyer. Located in Princeton, she said."

"Do you know the name of Tyler's father, or of Tiffany's lawyer?"

"She didn't say." Tiffany had suggested Sarah should ask for child support, too, thought Maggie.

"So you talked with Tiffany Douglass yesterday?"

"She made an appointment to see me at my office yesterday afternoon. You could check with my secretary, Claudia Hall, at the college. I think it was four o'clock."

"She came to the appointment on time?"

"Yes. She was upset about Sarah's illness. She talked about Sarah during most of the time she was with me."

"Did she seem concerned for her own safety?"

"No. Nothing like that. She was just worried about Sarah. And about Aura. She didn't indicate any concern for herself."

"So she didn't seem to think whatever had happened to Sarah would happen to her?"

"She never even hinted at that. And she had no ideas about who might have wanted to hurt Sarah. Tiffany seemed very capable of taking care of herself, not worried or afraid." Unlike Kayla, on the telephone this morning, or Maria, who had been talking about leaving Whitcomb House and going home. Maggie needed to talk with them both. And with Heather and Kendall, too. "I really don't have anything else to tell you. May I go and talk with the students now, please?" Maggie looked at her watch. Almost seven-thirty. "Most of them have classes this morning, and they need to get the children to day care." Kayla was looking after Aura, but that was, they all hoped, a temporary situation. Who would watch Tyler now? What would happen to him? Would his married father from South Jersey get involved? Not likely.

Chapter 23

Beetles in a Flood. c. 1885. Chromolithograph of dozens of multicolored beetles of various sorts crawling up the stems and leaves of grasses and twigs, the bottoms of which have been submerged, perhaps by a heavy rain; water covers the meadow. Not all the beetles are safe . . . a hungry frog sits on a branch in the water, watching them climb above him. 6.5 x 10 inches, including margin. Price: $55.

Maggie found the four remaining adult occupants of Whitcomb House sitting on the second floor near the top of the stairs, clearly listening to what was happening downstairs. She looked around. "Where are the children?"

"A miracle. They're all asleep in Kayla's room. The past two days have been exhausting, and with all the excitement today they were up early," Maria said. Maggie wondered whether she wore her nose ring twenty-four hours a day. It was in place this morning.

"That *is* a miracle. How are they coping?"

"Tyler is too little to understand about his mom; Aura's taking it pretty hard. Her mother not here, and then finding Tiffany this morning. Mikey fell asleep out of pure exhaustion. He's been asking questions nonstop since yesterday. Same for Katie. The two little ones probably won't sleep for long. They know something's different; they can sense how we're reacting to everything, but they don't understand enough of what's happening to be upset about anything specific," Kayla said.

"What *is* happening, Professor Summer?" Kendall asked. "Are we in danger? Are the kids? Who's doing this?"

"We've already decided not to leave here today," said Maria. "Not even to take the kids to day care or go to classes. We feel safe here. The police are in and out. And we trust each other."

Kayla nodded.

Maggie sighed. "One day probably won't make a difference to your grades or classes. Certainly your teachers will understand. If they don't, you come and see me. But you can't hide here forever." And you're all suspects, too, she added to herself. Maybe Whitcomb House is the most dangerous place of all.

"We've been trying to put it together," said Kayla. "Trying to think of anyone who really hated Sarah, or Tiffany, or both of them. Trying to figure out why they were poisoned."

"If they were poisoned," said Kendall.

"We know Sarah was," said Heather. "And that dark color on Tiffany's lips, and on her sweater . . . I'm sure she was poisoned, too, but she threw up some of it."

"Why didn't I hear her? I usually hear when someone comes in. If she had called for help, I'd have come." Kendall paced the small upstairs hall. "I'm a light sleeper. Anyone with a baby is. I heard the kitchen door open around two this morning. I assumed Tiffany was coming in—she comes in late all the time. I didn't hear anything more, so I fell back to sleep."

"Kendall, you heard the door close at about two. And you and Kayla found Tiffany at about three-thirty, after Aura started crying, right?" Maggie wanted to make sure she had the time sequence correct.

Kendall nodded and sat down on the floor again with the others.

Kayla put her hand on his. "It's all right, Kendall. She came in late so many nights. How could you have known this time she was in trouble?"

"Tiffany was always trouble," said Maria. "That would have been nothing new."

Maggie sat on the top step. "Why was Tiffany trouble?"

The residents looked at each other, waiting for one of them to say something.

"I know Tiffany skipped classes sometimes. I know she missed about half our Monday-night meetings." Maggie took a guess: "I assumed she had a pretty active social life."

"If that's what you want to call it," said Kayla.

"What do you mean?"

"We might as well tell her what we know. It doesn't matter anymore. We've covered up for her enough times." Kayla looked at the others, some of whom slowly nodded. "It might make a difference for us, or for Sarah. We've got to let people know!"

"Know what?" Maggie asked.

"Tiffany had friends," said Kayla. "Older, male friends. She used to get telephone calls from a man who wouldn't leave his name. He'd just say, 'Tiffany will know who this is.' "

"Usually the calls were telling her to be someplace, at some time," Maria said. "Usually at night."

Maggie listened. "Was she a call girl? Is that what you're saying?"

Maria shook her head. "I don't think so. Nothing that organized. There was only one man—well, maybe two men—who called. And she did go out several evenings every week. As I say it, that might sound like she had a pimp. But she didn't seem to have a lot of money or anything. And although she wore makeup and dressed up a bit, she didn't look . . . well, not like a hooker, anyway. Or at least not what I think of as a hooker. I've never known one."

"I asked her about the calls once. She said she was making a life for herself and Tyler. That she was investing for the future," Heather said.

" 'Investing for her future'? It didn't look as though she was dating a stockbroker or anything," said Kendall. "Whoever this guy was, he wasn't giving her advice on the market. Although he did give her that fancy briefcase she carried her school papers in. Like she thought she was an executive or something!"

"That's all I ever saw that he gave her," said Kayla. "Pretty weird gift from a guy, if you ask me. Why not give her jewelry, or even a nice pocketbook? And there's something else." Kayla paused. "I saw her in the bathroom once . . . Katie opened the door, the way little kids do, and Tiffany was in the shower. She had bad bruises on her wrists and legs and back. Not on any part you'd see. But those bruises were dark."

"Did you ask her about them?" Maggie said. "Did she say she was being abused?"

"She yelled at me to shut the door fast. I asked her later, but she said nothing was wrong; she wasn't hurt, and it was none of my business. She said it was 'just part of the deal' and she was taking care of it."

"Didn't sound like a deal she should be making," said Kendall. "We all watched out for her. Tiffany was a big woman. She looked like she could take care of herself. But sometimes she didn't think things through all the way. We were scared someday she'd get herself in big trouble. And now . . ."

"You all knew she was being abused?"

All four of them nodded.

"I couldn't keep that a secret," Kayla said. "I was worried about her, so I told everyone else. I thought if we all knew what to look out for, maybe we could find out what was happening. And stop it."

"None of you know who this man, or men, was?"

"She used to be picked up in a black car," Maria said. "A big black car. I saw it once down at the corner. Tiffany walked in that direction, looked around, and then got in."

"I saw her get in a black car once, too, over on the other side of campus," Heather said. "But I couldn't see who was in it."

"What model car was it? Did either of you get a license plate number?" Maggie asked.

They shook their heads. "We were concerned, but we weren't playing detective or anything, Professor

Summer. We didn't know she was going to be killed. We just thought she was dating someone who was rough."

"And probably married," said Maria. "I asked her why she didn't bring him here for dinner sometime, the way the rest of us do if we've gone out with someone a few times. She said she couldn't; he had other commitments. I figured he had a wife."

Maggie suddenly thought of something. "You said you thought she'd been poisoned because of the dark marks on her mouth and on her shirt . . . were the stains wet or dry?"

Kayla answered. "They were dry, I think. It looked like it was dark vomit. Sort of grainy. I didn't touch it though." She shuddered.

"I agree; the stains looked dry," said Kendall. "Nothing was dripping."

"Then she probably came in at two, when you heard her, and fell to the floor, already poisoned. She wasn't poisoned here. It happened too fast." Maggie couldn't believe Tiffany had been poisoned by anyone at Whitcomb House, although clearly the detectives were exploring that possibility.

"I would have heard her if she'd fallen," said Kendall. "I've been thinking about that. She is—was—a big woman. I heard the door shut. If she was well enough to close the door, could she have gotten sick that fast, to have collapsed right inside the door?"

Clearly they'd already discussed this. The others were nodding.

"We're pretty sure," Kayla said, "that someone killed her somewhere else, and then opened the door, maybe with her key, and left her there on the floor. Left her dead."

They sat in silence.

"Where were all of you last night?" asked Maggie quietly.

"You think one of us poisoned Tiffany?" said Kayla. "How could you think that?"

"I don't," said Maggie. "But the police are going to ask."

"Tiffany left at about eight last night," said Kendall. "The rest of us were here all evening. We can vouch for each other."

They nodded, around the circle.

"I believe you," said Maggie. "I just needed to hear you say it."

"There's something else," Maria said quietly. "I don't know who Tiffany's lover was, but I think she was blackmailing him."

Chapter 24

Ring a-round a rosie, a pocket full of posies . . . Jessie Willcox Martin (1863–1935) lithograph, illustration for The Jessie Willcox Mother Goose. *1914. Children dancing in a circle to the familiar tune. This nursery rhyme was originally sung to remind people of the Great Plague, which began with a red rash on the skin and resulted in death within days. 7.25 x 11 inches. Price: $65.*

"What?" All heads turned toward Maria.

"Are you sure, Maria?" said Maggie. "If Tiffany were blackmailing someone, that could give him a motive for murder!" At least Tiffany's murder . . . no one was thinking about Sarah now. Maggie had planned to stop at the hospital before her first class. She glanced at her watch. She could still do that; her first class wasn't until ten. This was a critical conversation.

"I don't know for sure, you understand," Maria said quickly. "Tony's father, Eric, is a photographer. A few weeks ago Tiffany asked me for his telephone number. She said she needed some pictures taken. At first I thought she meant photographs of Tyler—studio baby photos—but she laughed and said that the photos she had in mind couldn't be taken in a studio. Then she asked if Eric had a long telephoto lens, or one of those miniature cameras like spies use. I told her I didn't know, but I didn't think it would be good for her to call Eric. I've had trouble with him. He wasn't supporting Tony, and I didn't want him having any connections to this house, or excuses to come here." Maria hesitated, and her eyes got a little damp. "I still love him. But he's got a real temper. And a new girlfriend."

Kendall reached over and gave Maria a brief hug.

Maggie suspected conversations about Maria's exboyfriend were frequent. And she was the one who'd hidden a gun in her room. How hot was Eric's temper? Did Maria have problems that were in any way related to those of Tiffany and Sarah? Could Eric have anything to do with Sarah's illness or Tiffany's death?

"Just because she wanted to find a photographer

doesn't mean she was going to blackmail someone!" said Kayla.

"Maybe not," replied Maria. "But she wanted those pictures bad. She said if I didn't give her Eric's number, then she'd find someone else herself. She said, 'Soon I'll have some real money,' if she could get someone to help her."

They were all quiet.

"Do any of you know if Tiffany found a photographer?" Maggie asked.

Silence.

"When the police were searching here yesterday, did they take anything from Tiffany's room?" Maggie tried to think of what evidence might have been at Whitcomb House.

"I was the only one here when they searched," said Kayla. "Except for Maria's gun, and the papers they took from Sarah's room, I don't think they took anything." Maria gave her an aggravated look. "But they might have. I couldn't watch every minute. They made me stay downstairs while they searched our rooms."

"And totally messed them up," groused Heather. "My drawers look as though they pawed through every piece of my underwear!"

"At least it wasn't sexist, Heather. My underwear drawer was the same way," said Kendall. "They were doing their job. But I don't know what they could've found. No drugs hidden in the diaper bags, and no dirty pictures that I know of!"

"Unless Tiffany had some incriminating photographs," Maggie said.

169

"If she did, she wouldn't have left them around, would she? At least I hope not, if they were pictures designed to embarrass a husband," Heather said. "I wouldn't want Mikey to see anything like that!"

"She'd have put them in a safe-deposit box, maybe," agreed Maria. "Someplace locked and secure. Someplace no one could get them."

"Maria, you should tell the police what you've told us," Maggie said. "It may be important. I need to go and see Sarah, and then get to class."

"I'll tell them," said Maria. "At first I thought it was awful, and embarrassing, and maybe I was dreaming the whole thing, but with all we've been talking about, I do think the police need to know. I want them to catch whoever hurt Tiffany. No matter what she was doing, she didn't deserve to be beat up, or to die."

"And then there's Sarah," said Kayla. "Although Sarah wasn't like Tiffany. I can't see the connection between them, but both of them being poisoned is just too weird. It can't be chance."

Maggie stood up. "Just be sure to tell the police everything you've told me. They need all the help we can give them." She hesitated. "And Tyler? Tiffany's parents are in South Jersey, right?"

Kayla nodded. "We gave the police their names and number. Tiffany had the information on her bulletin board, in case of an emergency. The police said they'd notify them, and I guess they'll come and get Tyler. For now we'll watch out for him."

A little boy with no father in his life who had just lost his mother.

And Aura was still here. A little girl who had no father, a mother who was very ill, and a secret grandmother who wanted custody of her. And me, thought Maggie. Aura doesn't know it, but she has me.

Maggie got up to go.

"Wait!" Kayla said. "I have something for you." She went into her room and was back in a moment, holding a piece of paper. "Professor Summer, if you're going to see Sarah, would you give her this? Aura drew it for her."

The crayoned drawing was of a tall person with arms, but no legs, standing next to a small person. Both figures had red hair. And a big red heart was in the sky, with rays like the sun, above them. Maggie's eyes filled. "I'll make sure Sarah gets it, Kayla. Thank you."

Her old blue van felt like home, crammed with antique prints, as she headed for the hospital to check on Sarah.

Two other people were in the intensive care waiting room: a balding short man in his midforties wearing a bright yellow shirt and reading a rumpled copy of *The Star-Ledger*, and an elderly man with a walker. No Dorothy. Maggie checked in at the nurses' station with the same dark-haired nurse who'd been working Monday morning.

"Sarah Anderson?" She looked down at a sheet of paper in front of her. "Yes, Professor Summer, your name is here; you may see her. Her condition hasn't changed. Dr. Stevens saw her an hour ago, but none of the critical measures have varied much since yesterday. He said he'd be back later."

"Has Mrs. Whitcomb been in this morning?"

"No. Not yet." The nurse leaned toward Maggie and lowered her voice. "There is a man here to see Sarah Anderson, though. He arrived after Dr. Stevens left, and I wouldn't let him in, because he isn't on the approved list. Dr. Stevens told us she had no relatives, and only you and Mrs. Whitcomb were approved visitors. That it could be dangerous to let anyone else in to see her. The man said he'd wait to see the doctor; he'd stay all day if he needed to, but he had a right to see Sarah." The nurse lowered her voice even further. "He said he's her father."

"But her father is dead," Maggie blurted without thinking. Assuming Dorothy's story was correct. And why would Dorothy lie about giving up a child for adoption? If she hadn't lied, then Sarah's father died in an accident before she was born.

The nurse nodded. "Dr. Stevens said the only living relative she had was her little girl." She lowered her voice. "I don't think it's safe for Sarah to be here without protection. What if he's the one who tried to poison her?"

"I don't remember seeing him at the Whitcombs' party, and that's where it happened." Maggie kept her voice low, too.

If he was trying to kill Sarah, why would he ask to see her and then wait in the waiting room? Wouldn't he find a way to sneak into her room? And yet—who was he?

"I called Dr. Stevens to ask what we should do about him, but the doctor hasn't checked back yet. He's on an emergency case."

"Is the man who's waiting for Sarah the one with the walker?" That would make the possibility of his attacking Sarah considerably less likely. Assuming he really needed the walker.

"No! That's Mr. Chambers. His wife's in the room next to Sarah's. It's that other man; the one wearing the yellow shirt. He said he'd driven all the way from Princeton to see her."

Maggie started. Princeton! The town Sarah wouldn't even drive through. Where Tiffany's lawyer practiced. The lawyer she had recommended to Sarah. Could this man be her lawyer? Maybe Sarah had contacted someone without telling Tiffany. But certainly a lawyer would announce himself as her lawyer. Not as her father. Or—could this be the person Sarah had never wanted to see again? If so, how long had he been in the area? And why would he say he was Sarah's father? Unless that was just a ploy: declare himself a relative so he could gain access to her room.

Maggie suddenly felt a chill. "Sarah should be protected by the police." The door to Sarah's room was only feet from the nurses' station. But the nurses had other patients. Anyone could walk into the room where Sarah was lying, immobile and vulnerable.

"This is Somerset County, New Jersey, not New York City. The police don't have a guard here. They do call every few hours to see how she is. I think they're hoping she's going to open her eyes and tell them all about the person who poisoned her. You're right—they should have someone here."

"I don't know who he is or why he's here. But you

were right not to let him bother Sarah." Maggie hesitated. "I think I'll go in to see her for a moment now."

Sarah, and the room she was in, and the monitors she was connected to, hadn't changed since yesterday. Maggie touched her hand. "Sarah, Aura misses you. So does everyone at Whitcomb House, and at the college." Maggie didn't mention that Sarah's roommate was now dead, and that both Whitcomb House and, she assumed, the Whitcombs' home were sites of police investigations. Or that a strange man was in the waiting room asking to see her.

She tacked the picture Aura had drawn up on a small bulletin board that Sarah would be able to see when—if—she woke up.

"Aura drew this for you. She wanted you to look at it and know she loves you. She wants you to get well and come home." Maggie wiped away a tear. "Come back to all of us, Sarah." Maggie squeezed Sarah's hand one more time. She waited another moment, hoping against hope that Sarah would open her eyes and blink and tell her what to do. Tell her about the man in the waiting room; tell her what to do for Aura.

When Maggie walked past the nurses' station on her way out, the nurse had vanished; probably caring for another patient. That's why Sarah should have police protection, thought Maggie. Anyone could get into her room. And in the meantime someone should talk to that man in the yellow shirt. But there was no one else; that someone had to be Maggie.

"Excuse me," she said to him politely. "The nurse mentioned that you were here to see Sarah Anderson.

I'm her college adviser." Maggie held out her hand in greeting.

The man looked at Maggie's outstretched hand for a moment and then took it. "So you know my Sarah." His hands were rough, but his grip was weaker than she expected.

"Yes. She's a very special young woman." She sat down next to him, prepared to play as dumb as necessary to find out more. "I've only known her since August, though. Have you known her long?"

"Yes." He turned back to his newspaper.

Clearly he had no desire to chat. Perhaps the direct approach would work better. "How do you know her?"

The man looked at her. "Not that it's any of your business, lady. But I'm Sarah's father."

"Her father? That's strange. I was sure she'd told me her father was dead." Then Maggie realized there was another possibility. "Or—maybe you're Sarah's adoptive father—Mr. Anderson?" The Andersons had relinquished custody of Sarah, but Mr. Anderson had been her father during the years she'd lived with them.

"No. I'm not Mr. Anderson. Not that it makes any difference to you." The man cracked his knuckles. They were red and callused. Clearly he worked with his hands. "I'm Sarah's foster father. Haven't seen her since she ran away four or five years ago. The wife saw in the paper how Sarah'd been hurt and was in the hospital. Figured as how we ought to get reacquainted; she might decide she needs her family after all."

"How—kind—of you," said Maggie. Four or five years ago. Aura was four now. Had Sarah been pregnant

175

when she had left this man's family? Could he possibly be Aura's father? That would explain why Sarah had left her foster family so suddenly. "Then you haven't been in touch with her in all those years?"

"Didn't know where she was. She just dropped out of sight. She was old enough to do that, you know. Legally. There wasn't nothing we could do about it. If she didn't want us, that was her choice. But the wife's been worried, you know. All these years. We've had lots of foster kids, but most of 'em stay in touch. At least a Christmas card or something. And then we saw the story in *The Star-Ledger.* Thought maybe she would've been home by now—papers will say anything to sell copies—but I called the place the article said she lived, and they said she was here."

A man had called Sarah at Whitcomb House, Maggie thought.

"My wife would've come too, except for the arthritis. It's getting pretty bad now, and car trips wear her out. I had to take a day off from work to come here, and these people won't even let me in to see the girl."

"She's very sick," said Maggie.

"So it said in the paper. It also said she had a daughter. I don't suppose you'd know about how old the little girl'd be?"

If he was Aura's father, then he didn't know it. Or he didn't know it for sure. But if Sarah had wanted him to know, he would have, Maggie was sure. Tiffany had said Sarah didn't want to have any contact with Aura's father. "I'm just her adviser at the college. I don't know anything about her personal life."

176

"I was just wondering. It said in the paper she was a single parent. The wife said I should find out. If she's really that sick and all, then maybe she needs us to take care of her baby."

Aura wasn't a baby. Maybe this man didn't know any more than the paper had printed.

"I believe arrangements have been made to take care of her child."

"Couldn't be with relatives, though, could it? The wife and I are the closest thing Sarah Anderson ever had to real relatives." He stood up and stretched. "I don't see no one at the nurses' station now. I think I'll just go in and say hello to my little girl." He looked down at Maggie. "No one's going to tell me I can't see my Sarah, are they?"

"She's very ill," Maggie said firmly as she rose. "She can't have visitors."

"So? I wouldn't hurt her. I just want to see her. Make sure she's the same Sarah Anderson as used to live with us in Princeton."

"Princeton? I don't think Sarah ever mentioned Princeton. I thought she said she was from Pennsylvania."

"Oh? You sure?" The man looked at her. "Well, she might not have said." He looked down the hall, then at Maggie again, and hesitated. "I guess I'll wait for that doctor. He's supposed to be here soon." He sat down again, heavily.

Maggie glanced at the clock on the waiting room wall. It was after nine-thirty. She had to get to campus; her class started at ten. But should she leave this man alone?

177

The nurse appeared in the doorway. "Professor Summer? I have a call for you at my desk."

The man looked at her. "You get calls at the hospital?"

Maggie shrugged. But who could it be? She followed the nurse, who handed her a telephone.

Maggie just heard a dial tone. The nurse talked quickly. "You don't have a call. I got worried after what you said, so I paged Dr. Stevens, and he told me to call the police. They're sending someone over to talk to that man now. And they're going to post a guard outside Sarah's room. I wanted you to know."

"Thank you," Maggie said. "He says he was Sarah's foster father, but I know she didn't want to see anyone she lived with in foster care. I don't know if he would physically hurt her, but she shouldn't be told he's here."

"Got it!" whispered the nurse. "You can trust us here at the hospital. We'll keep her safe."

"Good. And Mrs. Whitcomb will probably come in later. I think it would be best if she didn't know about this man's interest in Sarah." Dorothy didn't need to know that someone was claiming to be Sarah's father.

And the man could be dangerous. What if he was Aura's father and didn't want his wife, or the Division of Youth and Family Services, to know he'd sexually molested Sarah? On the other hand—what if he wanted custody of Aura? Maggie shuddered.

As she turned toward the waiting room, she saw a policeman heading their way.

Chapter 25

A Tobacco Mart in Lynchburg, Virginia. *Wood engraving from sketches by F. H. Taylor, published in* Harper's Weekly, *May 3, 1879. Six scenes in Virginia showing black and white men and women working together, from "Auction of Leaf Tobacco" to an assembly line, "Twisting Plug Tobacco" to "Tobacco Wagons and Market" to "Pressing Bales of Smoking Tobacco." 11 x 15.5-inch page, including header. Price: $65.*

By the time Maggie got to the campus there was only time for a quick stop at the soda machine before her class began. Luckily she'd taken her lecture notes with her when she'd left campus last night, and her portfolio of Black Americana prints was in her van. The prints were going to Morristown with her Friday.

There's never enough time, she thought as she took off her coat and arranged her materials on the table in front of the classroom. Gussie and Jim are arriving tomorrow night, I have no decent food in the house, and I never even turned on my computer this morning to see if Will e-mailed me late last night or this morning. She looked down at his ring. What would she say in her next note? She didn't want him to worry about her. But all she could think about was who could be poisoning young women at the college.

She also needed to return calls to that show promoter who wanted her to do Allentown, and to the woman

179

who wanted to sell *Godey's* fashion prints. Maybe after class she could find a free half hour to catch up with her life.

Once each semester she and Linc James, who taught ethnic studies, exchanged a day's classes and perspectives. He was going to teach her "Myths in American Culture" course Friday morning, concentrating on the contributions of racial minorities to America's perspectives about itself and its peoples. And, coincidentally, giving her a little more time to prepare for the Morristown show. Today it was her turn to take his "African-American History and Culture" class.

Clearly news of Tiffany's death had already spread. She heard "Tiffany" and "Whitcomb House" and then "Sarah" whispered within clusters of students around the classroom. By this afternoon the news would have hit the media, and no doubt television, radio, and newspaper reporters would be interviewing students in the quadrangle. Publicity. But not the sort Max would value.

Where was Max? And Dorothy and Oliver Whitcomb? Dorothy hadn't been at the hospital. Although with Sarah's foster father waiting to see her, it was probably just as well if Dorothy had other commitments this morning.

The students broke off their conversations and filled in the seats as Maggie introduced herself. "I'm Professor Summer from the American Studies department, and I'm also an antique-print dealer. Professor James and I are exchanging our class periods this week. This morning I'm going to share some visual perspectives of

African-Americans in nineteenth-century America. The prints I'm going to show you are from my business or are reproductions of prints I wish were from my business!"

There were a few smiles in the classroom. Maggie was glad this would be one of her show-and-tell lectures; the students were distracted by the events on campus, and visuals might keep them focused on what she had to say and not on what had happened during the last two days. And today's subject was an interesting one—at least to her. Her task was to share that excitement with students who probably had little background in either nineteenth-century art or nineteenth-century popular culture.

"Relatively few engravings of any kind done in America until the middle of the nineteenth century included black Americans, slave or free. But that in itself is not a commentary on America's view of African-Americans. Until the middle of the nineteenth century, when lithography made printmaking easier and more accessible, there were very few prints made of *any* Americans unless they were famous. And, not surprisingly, those who were famous were, for the most part, white men. Newspapers rarely contained illustrations. Book illustrations were either wood engravings in children's primers, steel engravings of scenic views, or hand-colored engravings in natural-history books. And many of those, despite being of American subjects, were actually printed in Europe, usually by publishers in London or Edinburgh.

"However, by the 1850s Nathaniel Currier and his

partner and brother-in-law, James Ives, had declared their intention to become 'printmakers to the American people,' and *Harper's Weekly* in New York and *Ballou's Pictorial* in Boston, among other newspapers that featured wood engravings, were bringing illustrations of current events to their readers. Both Currier and Ives prints and those in the periodicals included pictures of black Americans.

"Some of the pictures we're going to look at are what we today consider racist. During the mid-nineteenth century stereotypical views of racial or ethnic groups were common, especially when the subjects were black Americans, Irish Americans, or, a little later in the century, Chinese Americans."

A student in the first row raised her hand. "Did publications in the American South reflect the same views of black Americans as the ones you mentioned that were in the Northeast?"

"Good question. Southern periodicals tended to ignore black Americans rather than depict them negatively. And newspapers in the South such as *The Charleston Mercury* were, for an assortment of reasons, not distributed as widely as, say, *Harper's Weekly*. Their influence was therefore more limited." Maggie paused. "Since we're talking about geographic differences, the *Illustrated London News* was one of the few publications anywhere that included illustrations of slave ships and slave sales in America.

"The first Currier and Ives prints of blacks, pre–Civil War, showed them as realistic, individual people, but usually as background figures in both city and country scenes. For example, several lithographs of George Washington show Washington speaking with or being attended by his slaves. As the abolitionist movement grew in popularity, some depictions of blacks illustrated the horrors of slavery. In this 1845 print, *Branding Slaves on the Coast of Africa Previous to Embarkation*, Currier shows a white sailor who is smoking a pipe, and, at the same time, casually branding the back of a chained black man. It's the strongest antislavery print Currier ever published.

"On the other hand, during and after the Civil War, Currier and Ives went back to largely picturing blacks in dependent, stereotypical roles.

"Currier and Ives were trying to appeal to the largest possible audience. At that time opinions on the status and possible future of blacks in America varied greatly. Some Northerners blamed slaves for the Civil War. The intelligence level of black Americans was still being debated. Ironically, after the Civil War, racist jokes became more popular.

"Reflecting that popularity, between the mid-1870s and the 1890s racism clearly appeared in two different series: the Darktown series of cartoons drawn by Thomas Worth, 1834 to 1917, and published by Currier and Ives, and the Blackville series of wood engravings by Sol Eytinge, which appeared in *Harper's Weekly*. In both of these series black Americans are depicted in overtly racist ways. They're doing everyday things—celebrating holidays, racing horses, having picnics, getting married—but they're drawn with stereotypical looks and are shown behaving and dressing in ways that emphasize their ineptitude. For example, blacks in this series were illustrated dressed in formal hunting attire, but riding donkeys backward and falling off, in imitation of formal British hunting scenes featuring whites. Some critics say these pictures are parodies of hunting prints of the period, that they're designed to make fun of the habits of upper-class whites. But, whatever their intent, they clearly imply that blacks could not compete in such 'white' pastimes.

"But in the same postwar period, to appeal to those who valued black contributions to American life, Currier and Ives and *Harper's Weekly* both published lithographs and wood engravings that showed black Americans engaged in real, respected activities. *The Gallant Charge of the Fifty-fourth Massachusetts (Colored) Regiment*, issued in 1863, was reissued by Currier and Ives in 1888 on the twenty-fifth anniversary of that regiment's famous attack on the rebel stronghold on Morris Island, near Charleston. The lithograph was clearly designed to show the valued role black soldiers played in the Civil War. And as part of its series of portraits of beautiful women, Currier and Ives included *The Young African* and *The Colored Beauty*.

"A number of *Harper's Weekly* illustrations by such artists as Winslow Homer and S. G. McCutcheon also showed black Americans as 'real people,' not stereotypes, as did the work of William Ludwell Sheppard, an officer in the Army of the Confederacy who illustrated the Southern side of the Civil War.

"Here is one of my personal favorites." Maggie picked up a print from the desk. "*A Lesson in History—*

Decoration Day, 1881, by McCutcheon. A schoolhouse is in the background, and in the foreground an old black man is sitting on a stone wall outside a cemetery, pointing at a grave decorated by a laurel wreath and an American flag, telling three black children carrying slates and books about the black contribution to the Civil War.

"In short, during the second half of the nineteenth century we can find examples in popular art of a variety of views of the black experience. And since in the same publications we can find both views that today we see as racist and views that are respectful and complimentary, it appears the editors were trying to market to audiences with a variety of thoughts and opinions. I will add that Thomas Nast, the great political cartoonist of the late nineteenth century, who lived here in New Jersey, was an abolitionist who believed in the worth of black Americans, and he frequently depicted their detractors in unflattering poses in his cartoons."

Maggie went on, covering other artists, and other series. As often happened when she talked about prints, she could sense some of the students catching her excitement. Many of them had never seen actual nineteenth-century views of black Americans.

"You said the prints you've been showing us are from your business," said a bearded young man who stopped to speak with Maggie after class. "Is it easy to find prints like that?"

"Challenging, but not impossible," said Maggie. "Paper printed over one hundred years ago has to have been well cared for to have lasted until now. But there are people who collect old newspapers or prints. You can find the prints at antique shows, where dealers like me exhibit, or at 'paper shows,' which are showcases for dealers in all sorts of paper ephemera, from newspapers and magazines to advertisements to postcards to books."

"I'd really like my father to see some of your prints," the student said.

"I'll be doing an antique show in Morristown this weekend." She handed him two discount admission cards to the show. "Give these to your father, and if he's able to come, be sure to tell him to introduce himself to me."

Maggie packed up her prints and notes and headed for her office. Today's lecture had gone well, despite the thoughts of Sarah and Tiffany that kept filling her mind. She loved her prints and loved introducing students to them. Her lectures were a success if students at least became aware of nineteenth-century American prints as a way to see the nineteenth century as it had seen itself. Shadows of the past . . .

But this week her world was full of other kinds of shadows. Had there been any sort of confrontation between the police and Sarah's foster father at the hospital? Did they have any suspects in Tiffany's murder? Had Maria kept her promise and told the police her suspicion that Tiffany had been trying to blackmail someone?

Someone had to pay for what had happened. Someone *would* pay. And she would do all she could to make that happen.

Chapter 26

The Praying Mantis. *Tipped-in lithograph illus-*
trating Fabre's Book of Insects, *illustrated by E. J.*
Detmold, 1921, New York. The delicately colored
mantid, or mantis, holds out its front legs gracefully
in an upraised position suggestive of prayer while it
is lying in wait for its prey. For that reason the
Greeks named it mantis, *or "prophet." Often the*
female devours the male after mating. 5.75 x 6.75
inches. Price: $75.

Maggie picked up the pile of pink slips waiting for her
on Claudia's desk. Uncle Sam was curled up on
Claudia's chair; Claudia must be having lunch. Sam
looked up at Maggie, yawned widely, and put his head
down again. Clearly he was the only one on campus not
concerned about Sarah, Tiffany, or his own safety. And
Claudia hadn't unlocked Maggie's office this morning,
so he hadn't been playing bravest cat in the jungle with
her snake plant. One positive point for today.

Linc had planned to take the day off since Maggie was
handling his class, so his door was closed, too. She
heard voices inside Paul's office. Probably he was with
a student. Good. She needed some quiet time to get
caught up. And she didn't want to think about last night.

Maggie searched the depths of her pocketbook for her
keys. She always dropped them on top. How did they
manage to maneuver their way to the bottom and camouflage themselves, hiding themselves next to the loose

change, pens, tissues, single aspirin, business cards, magnifying glass, credit cards, and . . . there they were. Maggie unlocked her office door.

She put the portfolio on the visitor's chair and turned to sit at the desk. Then she turned back. Something was different. She saw it at once: Tiffany's briefcase was on the floor next to the visitor's chair. She must have left it there yesterday afternoon.

Could Tiffany have been trying to blackmail someone? If so, since there was no trace of photographs in her room at Whitcomb House, then she might have had them with her. Maggie took a deep breath, picked up the briefcase, and tried to open it. Locked. Of course. If Tiffany was carrying something valuable, then she would have locked it.

Should she call the police? They'd be able to break the lock. Or pick it.

But maybe Maria was mistaken about the blackmail. Tiffany was dead, but she still deserved some privacy. But her killer didn't deserve any protection. Maggie sat at her desk and held the smooth leather Coach briefcase on her lap. With its rich, soft leather and burnished hardware, it was not the sort of accessory a typical supermarket cashier would have.

Kendall had said one of Tiffany's gentleman friends had given it to her. Maybe the man she was supposedly blackmailing?

That would be ironic, Maggie thought. To carry materials that could destroy someone in the briefcase he had given you.

Paul's words last night came back to her: "Oliver is

interested in the young women of Whitcomb House." Could he have been the person she was going to blackmail?

Maggie unlocked the large file drawer on the right side of her desk where she kept records of student grades. She slipped the briefcase inside and relocked the drawer. She needed to think.

Oliver certainly had money. Enough money to be worth blackmailing. He was married. Tiffany had implied to Maria that the man she was seeing was married. But the bruises . . . Could Oliver have been abusive? Maggie shook her head in confusion. Oliver was a big man, but he had always seemed so gentle. Maybe not in business. But Dorothy certainly didn't seem afraid of him. And people who were abusive were consistently abusive, weren't they? Oliver didn't look or act like a brute. Yet . . . there had been opportunity. He had met the women of Whitcomb House often enough. And Oliver wouldn't have wanted Dorothy to know if he was having an affair.

Maggie stood up and looked out the window of her office, over the campus, toward Whitcomb House. Michael had cheated on her, and she hadn't known until after he'd died. Wives didn't always know. Or at least know for sure.

She and Michael had had such separate lives; he was often on the road during the week for his insurance business; she was away at antique shows or auctions over the weekends. There had been lots of opportunities for Michael to have cheated and for her not to have known. She could have cheated, too, she thought. But adultery had never been even a remote possibility for her. She'd naively believed everything in her marriage was going well.

Was that the way Dorothy felt? Since Oliver had retired, they spent a great deal of time together. Even their separate projects—his gymnasium, her Whitcomb House—were both on the same campus, only a mile or so from their home. Maggie had never sensed any problem between them. Oliver was openly affectionate with Dorothy and quietly amused with her foibles, such as his going along with her not wanting a bartender Sunday night. A small thing, Maggie thought, but a telling one. Oliver enjoyed spending the money he'd earned, and enjoyed watching Dorothy spend it.

Did any of this mean he wouldn't have an affair with a younger woman? Tiffany was attractive and flirtatious. Maggie had seen her in action.

Would a man like Oliver risk a marriage he seemed happy in, and his reputation in the community, for an affair with Tiffany? It didn't make sense to Maggie. But, then, adultery hit a little too close to home for her to be rational about it.

What about Sarah? She had collapsed in Oliver's home; she had been poisoned there. What did she have to do with this? Tiffany might have had an affair with Oliver. Maggie granted that. She appeared to have had an affair with someone, and Oliver fit the picture: older, married, wealthy. But Sarah? Could she have been having an affair with Oliver as well? She was his step-daughter, but he didn't know that. Paul had said Oliver and the *women* of Whitcomb House. Did he really mean more than one woman? Or possibly even more than two? Could Kayla or Maria or Heather be involved? At first they had been reluctant to share information about Tiffany. But now it felt as though everything they knew was out in the open.

Maggie needed to talk to Paul. She needed to find out exactly what he'd meant last night. For now she'd keep Tiffany's briefcase under lock and key.

And cope with immediate issues. She called back the Pennsylvania promoter; no, she couldn't do his antique show this weekend. Sorry; yes, he could keep her on his waiting list for other shows. The woman with the *Godey's* prints didn't answer.

The first new message was from President Hagfield. Would she please make an appointment to see him? As soon as possible. Maggie sighed. Clearly, when the man at the top of the pyramid called, it was a priority. She dialed his number without looking at the other messages.

"He really wants to see you," his assistant said. Jennifer was a former student of Maggie's. "But he's at lunch right now. Could you come by in about an hour?"

"Do you know what he wanted to talk about?"

"I'm not sure, Maggie, but it had to do with Whitcomb House. He's very upset."

"It's sad, isn't it?"

"It is. But to tell the truth, Maggie, Max seems more upset about what the reporters will write about the college than he does about what happened to Sarah Anderson or Tiffany Douglass. Although I'm sure he cares about them."

"Of course. And it's part of his job to keep up the public image of Somerset College."

"The newspapers keep calling him. And someone from ABC. Do you think we might be on CNN, too?" Jennifer's voice implied that being on CNN might make it all worthwhile.

"I have no idea. I just know that the faster Tiffany's killer is found, the better things will be for all of us."

"And the safer," Jennifer said. "A lot of professors and students have been calling to ask if we're going to close the school for a few days. Asking if it's safe to be on campus."

"What are you telling them?"

"That we're all saddened by these tragedies, but that Sarah and Tiffany would have wanted us to continue operating Somerset College, keeping the light of learning alive." Jennifer stumbled a bit on the last *l* sound.

"Who wrote that for you?"

"President Hagfield. He even typed it out himself. It sounds good, doesn't it? Really professional. Like CNN."

"Absolutely, Jennifer. Just like CNN. I'll be over in an hour, then. In the meantime, I think I'll go and get some lunch myself."

Maggie did a quick calculation. She needed food in the house for her impending houseguests. She could just about make it to a supermarket, pick up the basics, drop them at home, and be back in an hour. Bread and cheese to eat in the car would be her lunch.

She left a note for Claudia. "Gone to lunch, then to see

Max at 1:30. Back after that." That should cover any questions that came in while she was gone.

She made a mental list as she put the Black Americana portfolio back in the van with her other prints. Diet Pepsi. Orange juice. Milk. She drank skim, but she remembered Gussie liked 1%. What about Jim? He'd have to drink what they did. Wheat bread—enough so they could make sandwiches to eat at the show this weekend if sales weren't high enough to splurge on lunch. Ham and cheese for the sandwiches. Honey mustard. Romaine. And breakfasts: marmalade, she thought, and maybe some strawberry jam. Eggs. Bacon, despite the fat content. Maybe turkey bacon. And she'd make lasagna to have after setup Friday night, when they were all tired. Lasagna noodles, ricotta, mozzarella, spinach, sausage, onions, mushrooms, garlic, tomatoes . . . By the time she'd reached the supermarket she had the weekend meals figured out. If she was lucky, they'd do well enough at the show to eat out Sunday night, and Gussie and Jim were eating with friends Saturday night. But, if plans changed, she'd have options covered. Bless a mind that could multitask. She added a hard roll and some soft blue cheese for her lunch today and pushed her cart toward the checkout line.

The headline on today's local newspaper was bold and three columns: "Somerset College Coed Found Dead in Single-Parent Dorm!" Maggie cringed. No wonder Max wanted to see her. It had been her assignment to ensure that Whitcomb House and its students were an asset to the campus community. That, if anything, they provided positive publicity for Somerset College. She picked up a copy of the paper and scanned the article.

Nothing was included that she didn't already know. But the article didn't miss the possible connection to Sarah's poisoning Sunday night. Or that Oliver and Dorothy Whitcomb had donated Whitcomb House to the college, and that Sarah had collapsed at their home.

"It couldn't be Oliver," Maggie thought. "At least not with Sarah. Even if he would consider poisoning someone . . . how could he do it in his own home and expect to get away with it?" And yet no one had been arrested as far as she knew. It just didn't make sense.

She dropped off the groceries at home, stopping only to make sure anything needing refrigeration was put away, and to give Winslow a special scratch and a bite of salmon. She'd straighten the kitchen later.

Two blocks from her house she saw a large HOUSE SALE sign. Today she really didn't have time . . . but once in a while they were worthwhile. She deserved ten minutes of possibilities, no matter what. This was for her business.

The sale was in the garage and family room of the house. She glanced through cartons of books. There were a lot of children's books. Maybe she should start collecting some . . . No. It was too early. She hadn't officially decided about adoption yet. But these were in great condition. She hated to leave them. Maggie hesitated and then picked out half a dozen picture books for the children at Whitcomb House.

At the bottom of a carton of picture books was the

leather cover of an old scrapbook. She pulled it out carefully. Scrapbooks could hold nineteenth-century Christmas cards or valentines or advertising cards, and if the contents were beautifully lithographed and not glued in, they might have value. Of course, she didn't hope too hard. Scrapbooks could also hold junk or recent memorabilia or pictures of interest only to the owner, not to an antique dealer. Maggie balanced the album on the pile of picture books she'd selected and opened it.

The album was filled with page after page of carefully dried and pressed seaweeds—or sea mosses, as they were called in the nineteenth century. Drying sea mosses and wildflowers was a Victorian lady's craft and amusement. But dried plants were fragile; rarely had an album like this survived. Maggie handled it carefully. On the inside cover was handwritten, "Sea mosses I collected on Long Island, summer, 1883. Eloise Hammond." Provenance!

They would have to be handled with care, but they could be spray-glued, placed in deep mats, and then framed. They would look spectacular on someone's wall. And the price was?

Maggie casually took the album and the picture books to the women behind the cash box. "I have six children's picture books, and this old album," she said. "How much will that come to?"

"Oh, why not a dollar each for the children's books, and you can have that old album for five. It's been in my grandmother's attic for years."

Maggie smiled and pulled out $11.

She'd have to handle these pages carefully, and pay Brad and Steve to do the framing, but there were at least twenty pages of dried sea mosses. She could hang them on one wall at a show and ask $200 each.

Some dealers didn't take the time to go to suburban garage sales. Maggie couldn't help grinning as she carefully put the album on the front seat of her van. Some dealers really missed out.

Chapter 27

Gold Fish (Carassius auratus [Linnaeus]). *Lithograph of a goldfish, in the style and period of Denton's fish, c. 1890, but not attributed to a specific painter or engraver. Goldfish originated in China, like their cousins the carp, or koi. Compared with other fish species, goldfish have a long life span. Their hardiness makes them popular in the United States for both aquariums and outdoor ponds. 8 x 11 inches. Price: $60.*

Maggie ate the bread and cheese on her way back to campus. She loved the richness and texture of a soft blue cheese, but it was messy. Before she left the car, she wiped her fingers, and then the steering wheel, with a tissue and dusted the bread crumbs from the driver's seat. "You'd think I was old enough to eat without making such a mess," she said to herself. But the bread and cheese had been good, the garage sale had been terrific, and she felt more in control of life than she had an hour before. There was food in her house; she had no classes scheduled for the afternoon. And she'd made a major purchase for Shadows.

Maggie felt a pang at the wave of self-satisfaction. How could she feel good about life when Sarah was still in the hospital and Tiffany was dead? Life could change so quickly. And for those two young mothers . . . She hoped Tyler's grandparents had arrived to smother him with hugs and take care of him. She'd never heard Tiffany say anything negative about her parents, other than that she was too old to have to depend on them. But there was no statute of limitations on parenthood. Today Tiffany's parents had most likely become de facto parents to their two-year-old grandson.

After a stop in the ladies' room to wash up and check her sweater for lingering crumbs of blue cheese, Maggie headed for Max's office.

She walked quickly around the corner and almost ran into the large tank of tropical fish Max had installed in his reception area. Above the tank was the late-nineteenth-century print of a goldfish that she and Michael had given Max for his birthday two or three years ago. They'd meant it as a bit of a joke, but Max had triple-matted it and hung it in a place of honor.

Jennifer waved Maggie in.

"Maggie. It's about time. I've been trying to contact you all morning." Max's usually complacent round face was lined by wrinkles, and the dark shadows under his slightly pink eyes implied he'd had a rough night.

She looked past him at the medium-folio Currier & Ives *Windsor Castle and the Park* on the wall behind his desk. Max was proud of that lithograph. Every time

Maggie saw it, she remembered reading that the reclusive nineteenth-century poet Emily Dickinson had an identical one hanging in her home. She'd always felt there was a strange connection between those two very different people. Emily Dickinson's home and Max's office were each private castles. Few people were allowed to climb the battlements of either.

"I was teaching one of Linc James's courses; we trade off once or twice a semester. Seeing a different face keeps the students interested. I called as soon as I got your message." Maggie didn't mention that by then Max had been out having lunch. Or that she'd gotten in some grocery shopping while he'd been having what his slightly rosy nose hinted had been a drink or two *with* his lunch.

"Jennifer told me. I know." Max sighed and held out his arms in a gesture of helplessness. "Have you seen the headlines in today's paper?"

"Yes."

"Then you know it's all over the media. Every newspaper and television station and wire service out there is carrying a story about Tiffany Douglass. And most of them mention Sarah Anderson, too." Max sighed again. "Have you any idea what this is doing to the reputation of Somerset College?"

Maggie almost mentioned what it might be doing to Tiffany's family, and to Sarah, who had hoped the foster father from her past would stay in her past, but for the moment she held her tongue. Clearly Max had other issues on his mind.

"I've had calls from several members of our Board of

Trustees questioning how we could allow this to happen, and asking about their own liability for it, should either of the girls' families sue. The mayor is talking about the possibility of new zoning regulations to prevent our locating dormitories off-campus . . . even if they're just across the street and had already been approved last year. Two of our biggest donors are threatening to cut off funding if we can't pull this together. Not to mention the students who are talking about dropping out of school. Or the high school guidance counselors who've called to tell me they can't recommend our campus until we can assure them Somerset College provides a safe and healthy environment."

Maggie paused. What was there to say? "You're right. We need to provide a safe environment for the students. And for the professors and administrative staff," she added, thinking of what Jennifer had said earlier. "I was at Whitcomb House this morning. The police were there, and the students were shocked and scared. Angry that this has happened. We need to promise all our students, especially those at Whitcomb House, that this was an aberration. It won't happen again. We need to take an active role in working with the police to make sure Tiffany's killer, and the person who poisoned Sarah, are caught and punished. Soon."

"We're doing all that, of course, Maggie. Don't you think we are? We talked about that early this morning. I've hired extra security guards for the campus buildings, especially the dormitories, and the police have agreed to patrol the campus more often. But until they find the killer, or killers, or until this incident dies down, the entire campus is going to be affected." Max banged his fist hard against his desk and several pencils rolled off the other side. "After what I've done, what we've all done, over these years to make Somerset College the respected institution it is, we give an opportunity to six unwed parents and they ruin a reputation that's taken decades to build."

"Max." Maggie was shocked and couldn't control the anger in her voice. "It's hardly Sarah's or Tiffany's fault that they were victims. We've been giving them a chance most colleges wouldn't have even considered— a chance to pull their lives together and give them, and their children, a better future. That's what you've been telling the media all fall. We can't turn around and blame these horrors on the victims!"

"Don't be so simplistic and sentimental, Maggie. This isn't a romantic little drama where everyone walks off into the sunset hand in hand. We've never had this sort of problem before. If we hadn't opened our doors to those sorts of people, this wouldn't have happened. Right now, because of two irresponsible young women, the name Somerset College is synonymous with fear and violence and distrust and is known for promoting the advancement of unwed parents."

"Max!" Maggie was incredulous. "Stop talking about them as if they're criminals! As if one mistake has colored their entire futures! You're being totally insensitive and unfeeling." She steadied her voice a bit. "And besides, it's temporary. As soon as the police have this tied up, people will forget."

"They're going to forget now, so far as I can make

them." Max stood up and pointed at her. "Maggie, you're in charge of Whitcomb House. I want you to tell everyone still living there to leave. I want the house closed."

Maggie stood up, too. She was slightly taller than Max, but he had the power advantage of his position, and of the wide mahogany desk between them. "You can't do that! Some of them have no other place to go!"

"That's their problem! I don't care what you tell them. I want the students out of there this week." Max sat back in his chair. "They have tuition scholarships. They're welcome to continue as students. But I don't want them living on campus. I don't want any children in our dormitories! Dorms should be for adult students, not for preschoolers. We have a day-care center. That's already going a bit too far. If someone has children, then they're responsible for caring for them. Not us. Not me. Not Somerset College."

Maggie was silent for a moment. "Have you talked with Dorothy and Oliver Whitcomb about this?"

"Right now I've had enough of Dorothy Whitcomb's plans for the morally deficient of the universe. The last I heard, their home was considered a crime scene. Right now the Whitcombs are not exactly an asset to Somerset Community College either."

"Are you sure this is what you want to do, Max? Throw these poor students, who are already scared and nervous, out on the street? With their children?"

"That's exactly what I want to do. Dorothy Whitcomb talked me into this crazy program. She said it was the right thing to do. That Somerset College would be respected for it. Well, those students have been here a little over two months, and we have reporters and photographers swarming all over our campus asking, 'How could it happen here?' I want to make sure it never happens again." Max stood up again. "Maggie, I want Whitcomb House empty by Friday afternoon. I don't care how you do it."

"Max . . ."

"And I don't want to hear any sentimental reasons why it shouldn't be done. Whitcomb House was a mistake. As intelligent, educated human beings, we know mistakes can't be erased. But they can be corrected. And I want this situation corrected. Now."

Maggie turned and started for the door, her mind spinning. At the door she turned around. "But, Max—"

"That's it! No discussion. My decision is made! And if you can't take care of this, then you can look for another job at some college where insubordination isn't taken seriously." Max's round face was red and his eyes bulging.

"Max, I can't—"

"And what do *you* want?" Max yelled at someone behind Maggie. She turned. It was Claudia.

"President Hagfield, Professor Summer, please don't be upset, but I wanted you to know as soon as possible. I must have been in the cafeteria, and no one was in any of the offices. Mr. Turk found it. But I called the police. It's just awful. On top of everything else that has happened. I'm so sorry. But I thought you both should know as soon as possible."

"Claudia, what happened?" Maggie put her hand on

the woman's arm to try to calm her.

"Who's been hurt—or killed—this time?" Max asked, coming toward them.

"No one's been hurt, President Hagfield. Not that I know of. It's Maggie's office. It's been trashed."

Chapter 28

Human Head. *Lithographed cutaway of a man's head, painted by Holmes W. Merton, 1912. The top layer of the lithograph shows the skull, nerves, veins, and arteries. That layer lifts to reveal the interior nerves, sinuses, upper spinal cord; and finally, the third layer illustrates the sections of the brain and bones of the skull. From a medical textbook published in 1913 by I. W. Wagner. 6.25 x 7.75 inches. Price: $100.*

Max stayed in his office, no doubt stewing, but Maggie and Claudia ran to the American Studies department. Paul was standing off to one side. He'd run his hand back through his hair, leaving it standing up in a manner far from its usual careful arrangement.

Two policemen were standing in the door of Maggie's office. Not Luciani and Newton this time, she noted. Thank goodness. At least her office didn't merit the attention of homicide detectives.

"What happened?" she asked, trying to look between the two of them. Their bulk filled most of the doorway, but not enough for her to miss the condition of her office. She gasped. "When? Who?"

In the little over an hour since Maggie had left her office, it appeared to have been hit by a tornado. Her file cabinet drawers, which she had neglected to lock, had been opened, and the files randomly tossed on the floor. Student papers that had been on her desk were now on the floor, along with the contents of her wastebasket, which had been overturned. Most of the books in her ceiling-high bookcases had been dumped. Her snake plant was upside down, the dirt creating a small hill on top of student papers. Uncle Sam was happily scratching in the dirt, scattering small stones and pieces of leaves and roots in various directions. The center drawer of Maggie's desk was open, and the half-empty can of diet cola she'd left on the desk had been poured into the drawer and on top of the papers on the floor.

Thank goodness none of my portfolios were here, Maggie thought. "Oh . . . hell." Maggie squeezed her way between the two officers. Her Currier & Ives *Maggie* had been taken off the wall and hit or kicked so that the glass was broken. She picked it up and looked at it carefully. Luckily, the streams of cola had not gotten this far. The frame was damaged, and the glass was broken, but the print was intact. Maggie hugged it to her chest, as though that would make a difference. Then she turned to the policemen.

"Assuming you're Professor Summer," the taller of the officers asked, "can you tell if anything is missing? Were there any valuables in here?"

"Nothing of value to anyone but me," answered Maggie quietly. She looked around again. Had someone been looking for something? Tiffany's briefcase! She made her way through the mess to the back of her desk and saw marks, maybe from a knife, around the lock to the drawer she'd hidden the briefcase in. But the drawer remained locked. "My drawer holding student records," she explained. "Someone tried to get into it, but it's okay." She looked at the police, and at Paul and Claudia, who were standing helplessly outside her office door. "Didn't anyone see anything? How did this happen in the middle of the day?"

"Everyone was out. Mr. Turk found it when he got back from lunch. Your secretary arrived just after him. She called campus security and us."

"Maggie, I'm so sorry. I can't imagine who would have done this to you! And with Tiffany and Sarah, and everyone being so cautious just now, I thought we had to call someone!" Claudia looked at her. "I should have been here. Usually I eat my lunch at my desk, but today I needed to get away from the phones. I went to the cafeteria. And look what happened!"

"Maybe it's just as well you weren't here. Whoever tossed the office must have been pretty angry," said the policeman closest to Claudia. "Professor Summer, can you guess who might have done this? Anyone you've had trouble with recently? A student you gave a low grade to?"

"I wish I could think of someone." Maggie looked around her devastated office, still holding her print. "If it was one of my students, that student had better drop my class. Now!" She attempted a smile. "I suppose a student might be looking for papers, or records. Something might be missing. But it will take days to sift through everything."

"A student might be looking for your grade book."

"That's the drawer I checked first. It's still locked." And still holding Tiffany's briefcase.

"You're sure you can't think of anyone?"

"I have no idea. I've been so busy with Whitcomb House, and with my business, and my classes . . . but there haven't been any personal problems recently."

"No threatening notes or e-mails or phone calls?"

Maggie shook her head.

"Wait—you said you've been busy with Whitcomb House?" The taller policeman was paying attention. "What do you have to do with that situation?"

Maggie sighed and kept looking at her office. It would take hours, maybe days, before she could get this straightened out. Hours and days she didn't have. Someone had violated her space. The shock began to wear off, and she felt her anger growing. "Don't you people compare notes? I've already talked to Detectives Newton and Luciani about Whitcomb House. Twice in the past two days!"

"It might be important," said the cop nearest to her, gently, trying to keep her calm. He was holding one of those black notebooks they must issue along with badges.

"I'm the adviser to the students at Whitcomb House." Or at least to the students who *thought* they lived at Whitcomb House, Maggie reminded herself. She still had to deal with Max Hagfield's latest inspiration. How had she ended up in the middle of this whole mess? Why did everyone count on her to make things right? Students; Dorothy; Max; and now she had this disaster to cope with. Even if someone was looking for something . . . even if they were looking for the briefcase . . . why would they go to the trouble and take the time to trash her office?

The two policemen took a few notes and then conferred in the hallway. Claudia took advantage of their leaving Maggie's doorway to remove Uncle Sam, who meowed plaintively as she took him away from the lovely pile of dirt and snake plant leaves on Maggie's floor.

"I'm sorry, Maggie. I went for lunch and I didn't see anything, and then when I came back . . ." Paul shook his head. "Who would do this to you?" He moved closer to her, as though to touch her arm.

"I don't need your sympathy, Paul!" He was trying to be understanding, but what she needed was for everyone to leave her alone. Life had turned into a kaleidoscope; events were happening too fast for her to think them through logically. She depended on logic to keep her life in focus.

Nothing was in focus right now.

The shorter policeman returned. "Professor Summer, when something like this happens, we usually assume it's some sort of prank, or a student who's upset because you didn't give them the grade they felt they deserved. But in light of your connection with Whitcomb House, we'd better dust for fingerprints. We'll share our notes with Detectives Luciani and Newton, just in case there's some connection between the two situations."

Maggie nodded, concentrating on not falling apart in front of the police and her colleagues. She felt light-headed and confused. She'd always been so capable, so organized. She'd been able to cope with Sarah's illness, and even with Tiffany's death. But right now she felt like screaming. This time the attack was personal.

"I'm afraid you'll have to leave your office for now. We'll close it off. There is a key, right?"

Maggie sighed. If only she'd used that key before she left to do her errands! But faculty office doors were often left unlocked, and even open, during the day. She tried to remember to lock hers at night, and sometimes didn't even do that. She wouldn't forget again.

"You can use my office if you need to make any calls," Paul said. "Until you can get back into yours." He turned to the police. "How long will you need?"

"By tomorrow morning she should be able to get back in and clean up."

"Tomorrow morning I'll help you, Maggie. If you'll let me," Paul said, raising his eyebrows questioningly.

Maggie looked at him numbly. "I'll take you up on the offer to use your telephone." She couldn't do anything here now. But maybe she could still help Kendall, Maria, Kayla, and Heather. She'd call Dorothy. If anyone could convince Max to reconsider the fate of Whitcomb House, it would be Dorothy. Or Oliver.

Chapter 29

Carnivora: Gray Wolf, Coyote, Jackal, Red Wolf, Prairie Wolf, White Wolf, Black Wolf. *Chromolithograph, 1880, by Henry I. Johnson for natural-history book on classifications of animals. Seven animals in generic grassy location, showing differences between species. 7 x 9.5 inches. Price: $55.*

"In addition to this mess, now there's another problem related to Whitcomb House," Maggie said as she joined Paul in his office while the policemen called for a unit to dust for fingerprints in hers. "I just came from Max's office. He's overreacting; he wants to close Whitcomb House. This week. He told me to get the four remaining students and their children out."

If they left, Maggie thought, then where would Aura go? In a moment she knew the answer. Aura would go home with her. That's what Sarah would want. And Sarah could come to stay with her, too, when—if—she got out of the hospital. She had extra bedrooms. "Max thinks closing Whitcomb House will end the negative publicity."

Paul snorted. "That's ridiculous. He really thinks throwing four students and their kids out on the street will *solve* the problem?"

"That's exactly what he thinks. He ordered me to tell them to be out by Friday afternoon. Although he did agree they could continue attending classes here."

"And live where? From what you said the other night,

those aren't young people who can just move home and live with mommy and daddy and commute to college. They're adults, and Whitcomb House is their only home."

Maggie nodded. "For the most part. Tiffany had parents in South Jersey. I assume they'll take Tyler, thank goodness. And Maria's family isn't too far away, so she might be able to move in with someone. But I don't think the others have any place they could go on a couple of days' notice."

"What are you going to do?"

"Talk to Dorothy and have Dorothy talk to Oliver. They're the only people who might be able to convince Max to change his mind. Even if he feels strongly, their donations to the college—or lack thereof—might make the difference. And Whitcomb House is a project Dorothy strongly supports."

Paul nodded. "You're right. But they're not at their home right now. It's been closed as a crime scene."

And Oliver might have been having an affair with Tiffany, whose briefcase was locked in the file drawer of her desk. Who could have known Maggie had it? She wished she could get it now, but too many people were watching. She was the only one who knew for sure that she had it, and she couldn't trust anyone. Certainly Dorothy or Oliver wouldn't have come to her office and created that mess. Although Oliver could have hired someone to do it. . . . "Do you know where they're staying?"

"At the Somerset Hotel. They took a room for a couple of days until all this can be sorted out. Oliver called this morning to tell me. They're very upset, of course."

"Of course." Maggie picked up the phone.

The call was put through to their room's voice mail. "Hello, Dorothy and Oliver? Maggie Summer. I need your help for the students at Whitcomb House. It's urgent. Call me. This afternoon if you can." Maggie realized she wouldn't be in her office. "Call me at my home. I'll be working there." And making lasagna, Maggie thought. She had to do something constructive, or she would scream.

"They're not in?" Paul asked.

Maggie shook her head. "Maybe out for lunch. Paul, last night at dinner you implied Oliver had a relationship with one or more of the women at Whitcomb House. Do you know that for sure?"

"I didn't say that, Maggie." He didn't look at her directly and started sorting through piles of papers on his desk. "Oliver cares about the students there, of course, because they're of special interest to Dorothy. I didn't mean to imply there was anything improper about Oliver's relationship to any of them. Oliver is a fine man. He wouldn't do anything like that. Certainly not at Somerset College."

Could she have misunderstood? Maggie didn't think so. Paul was drinking last night, but she couldn't imagine him inventing such an allegation. And it had been an allegation. She was sure. Tiffany's housemates had seemed pretty convinced she was having an affair with someone. If not Oliver, then who?

Why wasn't Paul telling her the whole truth? Whatever the reason, she wasn't going to get it out of him now.

"I'm exhausted. It's been a difficult day, and I have a heavy week ahead of me. I'm going to go home and work there this afternoon. If anything happens that I should know about, please let me know, Paul."

"Aren't you going to talk to the Whitcomb House students first?"

"I'm not giving up yet. I'm not giving up until I hear Dorothy Whitcomb say there's nothing she can do. In the meantime I don't want to give those students anything else to be worried about. They've had an incredibly difficult past two days."

At home, Maggie put away the rest of the groceries, resisting the urge to slam the kitchen cabinet doors in frustration. She needed answers to too many questions. Winslow watched as she moved around the kitchen, clearly hoping her activity meant the possibility of extra treats for him. She found a small piece of leftover roast chicken in the refrigerator and he jumped to get it.

No wonder people loved animals; they were so easy to please, and they loved back so simply. She reached down and scratched between Winslow's ears. Clearly he would have preferred more chicken. Today it appeared she couldn't even please him.

Then she thought of her e-mail. Had Will sent her a message? She could use a hug, even if it was a cyber-hug.

At least her home office was still in order. She tried not to think of the mess she had left at the college. As the computer booted up, Maggie picked out a CD to play. Baroque music could be depended on.

Dear friend,
You're probably busy grading midterms and coun-
seling students and baking apple pies and matting
Jessie Willcox Smith prints, but, when you have a
moment, give a thought to your friend on the road.
Weather in Ohio is still wet and cold. I slept in the
RV last night. Saved motel expenses, but missed a
hot shower this morning. I have a list of antique
barns and shops to check out today. Remember the
ones we searched in Maine last summer? I did find
a nice set of devil andirons yesterday . . . the devils'
mouths are open and designed so flames will show
through. Very ferocious, and I'm tempted to keep
them myself. The perpetual lure of the perfect
antique. Fortunately for my budget I suspect I can
get a good price for these and can't afford not to sell
them. Unless you have any prints of devils, and we
could plan a room around them. Take pity on a cold
and lonely traveler, and write soon. I miss you. And
I hope that student of yours is feeling much better.
She's lucky to have you to care about her.
                                                    Will

Maggie smiled and clicked REPLY.

Dear Will,
So glad you have company, even if the friend is a
devil of a guy. He should be able to add some warmth
to your days. And nights. Unfortunately I have no
prints of devils. No apple pies either, but right now
I'm heading into the kitchen to make an enormous

pan of lasagna. Gussie and Jim are arriving tomorrow night, late, and will be here through the weekend. Wish you were here, too. My student is still in the hospital. No changes there. Although there are a lot of things happening on campus, so I'm running a bit. Smiling west, in the general direction of Ohio—

Maggie

She clicked on SEND. Sweet and breezy. That was her. She frowned. Should she have told him what was really happening? But at least she wasn't ignoring him. If she told him about Tiffany's death, and Sarah's poisoning, and her office being trashed, he'd worry, and there was nothing he could do, even if he were here. Although she could sure use a hug. Or three.

She thought of Paul's hug last night. Despite everything, for a moment she had felt warm, and safe. And maybe more . . .

She shook off that feeling, headed for the kitchen, and started pulling out the ingredients for lasagna. She must be crazy. Feeling safe when she was with someone who was obviously hiding information that might lead the police to a killer. Why should she feel comforted just because a man hugged her? It certainly wasn't logical. She had just begun layering sausage, sautéed mushrooms, and tomato sauce with the spinach and cheeses and noodles when the telephone rang. She wiped her hands on a nearby dishtowel and picked up the phone.

"Dorothy!" Maggie glanced at the clock. "Yes, it's important. I could get to the Somerset Hotel in half an hour. Could you meet me in the bar?"

Chapter 30

Sparrow Hawk. Pair of hawks; one on branch and one looking out from hole in tree. Sparrow hawk egg and maple leaves in foreground. Lithograph, 1882, from Nests and Eggs: Birds of the United States, *by Thomas G. Gentry, published by J. A. Wagenseller, Philadelphia. 8.5 x 11.5 inches. Price: $75.*

Dorothy was waiting for her at a small, round table in the oak-paneled hotel bar, hair immaculate as usual, dressed in an elegant pale pink pants suit. Maggie smoothed her wrinkled navy slacks and wished she'd checked to make sure there were no tomato stains on her navy-and-white sweater.

"Sherry?" Dorothy offered, gesturing at her own glass.

Maggie gave in to temptation. "Dry Sack, please. On the rocks with a twist." Thoughts of Diet Pepsi disappeared when a bottle of Dry Sack was near. At least when the day had been as long and dreadful as this one. "Paul told me your house is now a crime scene and you're living here temporarily."

"Yes. I just hope they find some answers soon, so we can go home. It's horrible to think that someone may have poisoned Sarah. Did you see her today?"

"I was at the hospital this morning. And you?" Maggie wondered if Sarah's foster father was still there.

"I stopped in just after lunch. That's where I was when you left your message. She's about the same."

"At least she's no worse." Maggie held her glass, swirled the liquid slightly, and savored the scent. Deeply rich and slightly sweet. A perfect sherry. She sipped. Good sherry should never be gulped.

"I still can't believe the news about Tiffany. Two of my girls, in two days. They all seemed so young and lighthearted just Sunday night."

At the Whitcombs' home. "Dorothy, we have another problem."

"Beyond Sarah and Tiffany?" Dorothy put her glass down on the small table between them and looked stricken. "Has someone else been hurt?"

"Oh, no!" Maggie realized her manner had suggested something even worse than what Max was suggesting. "But it is a major problem for the students still living in Whitcomb House."

"Have they sealed it off as a crime scene, too?"

"No. Worse than that." Maggie took another sip of the sherry. "I just met with Max. He's convinced Whitcomb House and its occupants are dragging Somerset College's reputation down. He wants to make Whitcomb House disappear. He told me to have the students moved out by Friday afternoon."

"No!" Dorothy stamped one of her pink-shoed feet under the table. "He can't do it! Not after all we've been through—and they've been through."

"He gave me direct instructions to get them out. Said they could continue attending school on their tuition scholarships, but that they couldn't room on campus."

"That's ridiculous. We have agreements with those students. We can't go back on our word." Dorothy hesitated a moment. "We need to get Oliver involved. He knows more about legalities than I do." Maggie nodded. Dorothy walked to the bar, telephoned, then returned. "He'll be right down. He's upstairs, listening to CNN. Sometimes I wonder what he'd do in retirement without television news."

"It must be very different for you, having him home all of the time."

"So far it's worked out. I have my projects; he has his. And we have our own regular evenings out with friends, so we're not together all of the time. Some couples are overwhelmed by togetherness when one of them retires. We haven't had that problem."

"So you've each kept your own friends?"

"We always have. He had his friends in New York, and I have friends here. I come to your seminars at Whitcomb House some Monday evenings. There are meetings about the hospital. And Oliver has always gone to his gym—now the gym at Somerset College. Monday nights he and Paul play poker with some other corporate survivors, and Thursdays he plays squash. We both keep busy. Even without the disruption of police investigations." Dorothy looked beyond Maggie's shoulder. "Here he is now."

Her husband stopped at the bar and picked up a draft of Guinness on his way to join them. "Well, now, what seems to be the problem? Max is upset about what?"

Maggie explained. "He wants the Whitcomb students out by Friday afternoon," she finished.

"I don't think he can throw them out. Don't say anything yet, Maggie. I'll check with my lawyer to be sure, but by offering them scholarships and room and board for a year, on the condition they keep up their grades, I think they have an implied contract with the college. If we throw them out of Whitcomb House and don't offer them an alternative dormitory, we'll be in breach of that contract."

"Plus," added Dorothy sweetly, "someone might call the media who are so interested in Sarah and Tiffany and tell them Somerset College is throwing four or five destitute single parents and their poor children out on the streets, just because one of their friends was murdered. I would think that publicity for Somerset College would be considerably worse than it is now."

Oliver reached over and touched Dorothy's hand. "My dear, what a thought! And who do you think would call the media?" Oliver and Dorothy smiled at each other in understanding. Oliver was the one who broke the connection. "Maggie, leave it up to Dorothy and me. I promise that by noon tomorrow, if not earlier, Max will be begging those students to stay . . . perhaps he'll even offer them a guaranteed extra semester to help make up for all the stress they've endured."

Maggie raised her glass. "I truly thank you. You've made my job much, much simpler."

"Oh! There's Susie Wylie. She said she might stop in. Do you mind if I just say hello to her for a moment?" Dorothy waved to a portly woman in blue silk who'd walked in the door, then got up and went to join her.

"A rough week, Maggie," said Oliver, taking a deep drink of his beer. "Very rough indeed for Sarah and Tiffany, and for those of us who were close to them."

Maggie saw her opportunity. She and Oliver were alone. "Oliver, I hope you won't consider this interfering, but there are a lot of rumors going around."

"I'm sure there are. With a campus full of young people? No doubt."

"Would you mind if I asked you about a couple of them? Just so I feel more confident when I talk to the Whitcomb House students. They're already so nervous."

Maggie took a deep breath, checking to see that Dorothy was still with Ms. Blue Silk Dress. "I've heard you've been involved in nonacademic activities with one or more of the Whitcomb House students."

Oliver's smile hardened. "Is that an accusation?"

"No, it's a question. Specifically—were you having an affair with Tiffany Douglass?"

Oliver put down his drink. "Who told you that?"

"Tiffany implied to several people that she was seeing an older, married man. She was away from Whitcomb House in the evenings fairly frequently. Often on Monday nights, when I held my seminars there." Maggie took another sip of sherry. Would Oliver really confess to having an affair with a Somerset College student? What if Tiffany had blackmailed him? What if he had killed her? Would Maggie's questions put her in danger, too? "Dorothy told me you play poker on Monday nights. That means you're not home on Monday evenings."

"Maggie, I'm hurt that you would even consider me capable of betraying my wife by involving myself with one of the Somerset students. Even such a lovely young lady as Tiffany. I don't know what Tiffany said, or who she said it to, but if she was having an affair, it was with someone else, I assure you."

"It was just a rumor."

"Well, you can put that rumor back wherever you found it. And, for the record, I was not having an affair with Sarah Anderson either. Just in case anyone asks. Dorothy and I were trying to help these young people make futures for themselves. Someone chose to cut those futures short. It was not Dorothy or me."

"Was Tiffany blackmailing you, Oliver?"

Oliver flushed red, then white, and then stood. "I think you've said just about enough, Maggie. You will excuse yourself and leave this hotel and you will cease and desist from asking any more insolent questions."

Maggie stood up. "I didn't mean to be insulting. But today my campus office was trashed. I think whoever did it is looking for pictures Tiffany Douglass may have had. Pictures she may have been using to blackmail the man she was having an affair with. If it was you, Oliver, then I thought I'd warn you that the police know about the blackmail. And if it wasn't you, perhaps you'd have some idea of who it was."

"I was not being blackmailed by Tiffany, nor by anyone else. I have no idea who might be. And if your office was trashed today, I'm sure it looks no worse than my home, which is being searched as a crime scene." Oliver didn't smile as he looked at Maggie. "I'd suggest you think very hard before you ask any more insulting questions of anyone. Especially questions that fall into the category of defamation of character."

"Tiffany Douglass is dead, Oliver. Someone might consider that insulting, too. If you have nothing to hide, you have no reason to mind being asked questions. And that's good, because my questions were easy. I suspect the police will be asking them in a different way."

Oliver was right. It was time for her to go.

She needed to think. For her own peace of mind she needed to do something, anything, to help find Tiffany's killer.

Chapter 31

A Child's Garden of Verses. *Romantic, sentimental lithograph from painting by Jessie Willcox Smith (1863–1935) of mother in long pink gown, surrounded by eight happy, laughing toddlers. 6.75 x 9 inches. Price: $60.*

Police cars were still parked outside the college office building when Maggie drove through the gates and around the circular drive. She knew she should go in and open her desk drawer and give Tiffany's briefcase to the police. And then answer questions about it. But she couldn't cope with any other issues or police or victims or possible suspects, today. She idled her van for a moment. She should go home; she still had to straighten up before Gussie and Jim arrived tomorrow night. She had a sink full of dirty dishes. And she could try to get a good night's sleep.

Or she could go back to the hospital. Had the police convinced Sarah's foster father to return to Princeton? If

Sarah came out of the coma, would he still want to reestablish contact? Was he Aura's father?

Or she should visit the day-care center to see Aura. No—the Whitcomb House students hadn't planned to leave their house today; they were at home, with the children. Aura was fine.

Maggie felt her heart beating hard. Aura had people with her. Sarah was being cared for. Tiffany's parents had no doubt come for Tyler. She hoped the joys of raising Tyler would ease their mourning for their daughter.

The Dry Sack had tasted good and relaxed her just enough that she didn't want to go home and deal with telephone messages and dirty dishes.

She headed instead for her favorite Greek restaurant. She would treat herself to a quiet dinner. A peaceful dinner.

It was still early, and Gorka's was almost empty.

The waitress showed Maggie to a small table near a blue-curtained window and a watercolor of the Acropolis and handed her a menu. Maggie ordered a glass of ice water and another Dry Sack. Just one more drink. She would be driving home. She started by sipping the ice water. She needed time, more than anything else.

So much had happened. So little made sense.

Maggie had not told anyone of her tentative decision to adopt, but she had signed up to attend an agency orientation meeting in early December. There was a day-care center at Somerset College; good public schools were nearby. One of her guest rooms could be for her daughter. Or son. That was a decision she hadn't made yet. There were so many children who had no one. Was she considering adopting a child because she wanted to help a child? Yes. But she had selfish motives, too. She wanted to be a mother, to take care of someone, to teach them about the world. To hug them. She wanted to get hugs, too. To be loved.

Was she substituting her vision of a mother's relationship with a child for her lack of a permanent relationship with a man? A therapist might ask. Or an adoption caseworker doing a home study. But the relationships between a mother and child and between a woman and a man were so different. Although no relationship was permanent. That was for sure.

The timing of her assignment advising the students at Whitcomb House had been perfect; she'd been able to see, firsthand, what it was like to be a single parent.

Maggie sipped her Dry Sack and remembered Sarah, young and enthusiastic, when she had asked Maggie to be Aura's guardian, "in case anything should happen to me." Maggie had agreed; neither of them had dreamed the agreement would be anything but a temporary contingency plan.

Maggie looked at the poster of the Aegean Sea on the opposite wall. The water was crayon-blue, and the clouds cottonlike. All very far away from Somerset County, New Jersey. She'd never been to Greece. It was on her "someday" list. A lot of possibilities were on that list.

She ordered the shish kebab with broiled vegetables and pilaf with pignoli and alternated sipping water and sherry.

Dorothy had made it clear that she wanted custody of Aura.

The battle wouldn't be worth fighting.

Maggie wanted to love a child whom no one wanted; a child without a family. Aura had a mother who was still alive, a grandmother who wanted her—and possibly even a biological father.

Could the father have found out that Aura was Dorothy's granddaughter; that his biological daughter had a wealthy relative?

No. There was no way that man at the hospital could have known.

But if he was Aura's father, his presence could further complicate any custody case. Could the name of Aura's father be on her birth certificate? According to the adoption books, a single mother could either name a father on the birth certificate or indicate "unknown." Perhaps Sarah hadn't wanted to imply she hadn't known who Aura's father was; perhaps she'd put someone's name on the certificate. That would give that man parental rights—and obligations. Would Sarah have contacted a lawyer to see if those rights could be voided? It was possible. The lawyer speaking at Whitcomb House had clearly told the single parents to ensure that their children's legal status could not be questioned.

Sarah has to live, Maggie thought. Somehow she has to survive, and she has to sort this out. Aura needs her.

Maggie's mind swirled with the contradictions of the situation. Emotionally, she knew what she wanted. Rationally, she knew what she would have to do.

Most of all, she wanted Sarah to live.

Tiffany had died—also from poison.

But in Tiffany's case there were possible motives.

Her older, married lover? And what about Maria's guess that Tiffany had been planning to blackmail someone or was doing so? Blackmail was certainly a motive for murder. But, again—who? Maggie was trying to think logically. But was any murder logical?

Tiffany had been with someone until two early Tuesday morning. Dorothy said Oliver played poker Monday evenings with Paul. But last night, Monday night, Paul had dinner with me, thought Maggie. And although we finished early, he was in no condition to go and play poker.

Paul had said he and Oliver had covered for each other in the past. Could one be covering for the other now? And, if so, who was covering for whom?

Could Tiffany have been having an affair with Paul?

Paul wasn't married. Had been, but wasn't now. Tiffany had told her housemates that her lover was married, hadn't she? No; the phrase was "had other commitments." The commitments could have been to a marriage . . . but they could have been to something else . . . perhaps commitments to Somerset College? Public allegations of sexual harassment at colleges and universities had made faculty very conscious of the dangers of student-teacher relationships.

Paul was the only one she'd talked to who'd hinted he knew something and hadn't seemed totally honest with her.

She finished dinner and resisted the idea of baklava for dessert.

She would go home, cope with the dishes, make the guest bed, and then call Paul and talk to him again about

Oliver and Tiffany. He hadn't wanted to talk at school this afternoon, but maybe from the privacy of his home he could make the pieces of this puzzle fit. She had to speak with him again.

Chapter 32

A Friendly Game. *A 1908 lithograph from a drawing by Jessie Willcox Smith (1863–1935) of a boy and a girl sitting on parallel chairs, balancing a checkerboard on their knees. The children have similar haircuts and are wearing round, white collars with black, floppy bows and loose orange outfits, in a style reminiscent of Maxfield Parrish's. Both Parrish and Smith were members of Howard Pyle's Brandywine Group. 10.5 x 14 inches. Price: $75.*

Usually Maggie just parked in her driveway, but tonight, with the van full of prints and the sight of her trashed office fresh in her mind, she parked in her garage and locked both the van and the outside garage door. Paranoia is not necessary, she told herself as she double-checked the locks on all the doors of the house. But tonight she wasn't comfortable being alone. She was glad Gussie and Jim would arrive tomorrow. She could use some conversation with people who were not living in or near a crime scene.

Winslow meowed and followed her as she checked the doors and windows. "I know you're here, Winslow. I know I'm not alone. But much as I love you, I don't think you're much of an attack cat." He followed her into the kitchen and demanded dinner, which she provided. Herring tonight.

While Winslow was licking every corner of his dish, Maggie made the bed in the first-floor guest room, which Gussie could negotiate in the electric wheelchair she now used because of her post-polio syndrome.

Maggie chose the soft yellow sheets she'd found on sale last spring. The bed was carved oak, and the yellow went well with the beige blankets and the tone of the wood. She covered the bed with a double crazy quilt with a square-cut New England foot that fell straight around the sides of the four-poster bed, then made sure there were fresh yellow towels in the guest bathroom, a new cake of soap and tube of toothpaste, and a box of tissues on the table next to the bed.

A hand-colored engraving of a duck and a fish by Mark Catesby hung over the bed. Catesby (1682–1749) was the first person to picture the animals and plants of what is now the eastern United States. He did his own engraving and coloring, and his *Natural History* preceded Audubon's volumes by about a hundred years. His unique way of combining animals, insects, fish, and plants in single prints made for striking compositions.

Maggie had been lucky and gotten the Catesby at an auction where the auctioneer had not recognized its value. Catesby was not as well-known as Audubon, and his signature was an *M* and a *C* intertwined, which might be missed or misread. She had gotten this one for $1,000 and decided to keep it for herself. She thought of it as a savings account. If she decided to sell, it could be the centerpiece of her exhibit in any show, and she'd price it at $3,500. Or more. There weren't many Catesbys in circulation.

For now, though, it was staying right where it was.

Paul had said he didn't know what a single person would do with a house, but she had no trouble filling hers. Especially when the space meant she was able to enjoy beautiful furnishings and the company of friends.

Maggie set up a brass luggage rack and checked the clock in the bedroom to make sure the time was correct. Almost nine. She'd better call Paul before it was unreasonably late.

Her Somerset College staff directory was in her study. She dialed Paul's home number. No answer. Should she leave a message? No. She'd already asked Paul about Oliver, and leaving a message might only make him more cautious. He'd volunteered to help her clean and straighten her office in the morning. She'd save her questions until then; that way they'd seem more casual. Less threatening.

Maggie mechanically washed the cutting board, colander, and cutlery she'd used to make the lasagna. Usually Gussie liked to eat at the local Chinese restaurant when she was here; there weren't any good Chinese places near her home on the Cape. But in case she was tired and wanted to eat in, Maggie'd made enough lasagna for both Thursday and Friday nights. She had salad ingredients, and she made a note to stop at the bakery Thursday for some éclairs or cream puffs to have for dessert. And bagels, she added. Jim liked bagels. With cream cheese and lox.

Clearly she'd have to make another grocery run. But

some cranberry muffins she'd made a couple of weeks before were in her freezer, and she had eggs and ham. If tomorrow turned out to be as crazy as today, she could wait until Thursday to get to the store.

Maggie stretched out in her most comfortable living-room chair. The effects of the sherry had worn off, and she went over the day's events once again. Maybe she'd forgotten something that would make a difference. That would answer some of the questions. Tiffany dead. Sarah still in a coma, she assumed; she'd had no calls from Dr. Stevens.

And Maria suspecting Tiffany of blackmail.

She wished she had Tiffany's briefcase. Maybe if she'd played with the lock . . . but there'd been no time at school today. Tomorrow, after the police had finished with her office, she could easily get the briefcase.

She was too restless not to do something. The number for Whitcomb House was on her speed dial. Maria was the one who answered.

"Professor Summer? Have you heard anything new about Sarah?"

"No, I haven't. How are you all doing?"

"We're okay. The detectives left about noon, after taking pictures and fingerprints. They did look at Tiffany's room, but they didn't go through the whole house again, thank goodness. Kendall went out and got some groceries for us and we just made a big pot of spaghetti and meatballs tonight. It was easy, and the kids love pasta."

"Did Tiffany's parents come for Tyler?"

"They got here late this afternoon. Tyler was really

glad to see them. He's too little to understand his mother's dead. All he wanted to do was help them pack his toys and go for a visit. They took some of Tiffany's things, but left most of her clothes and books and said any of us could have them." Maria's voice dropped off.

"That must have been hard."

"Yeah. They said they'd call when final arrangements are made, but the funeral will be in South Jersey, so I don't know if all of us will be able to go. If it's on Saturday, I think we'll try, though."

"Let me know about the arrangements when you hear," said Maggie. "I have a show to do this weekend, but maybe I could get someone to booth-sit for me . . ." That wouldn't be a good idea, and she knew it. No one could answer questions and make consistent sales in someone else's booth. And a funeral in South Jersey would mean being away for the whole day. But at least she could send flowers.

"I'll let you know. I promise." Maria was silent. "It's awfully quiet here, you know? The kids are in bed, and with just the four of us here the house seems empty."

"Maria, can you help me with one more thing? This morning you said you thought Tiffany was going to blackmail someone."

"I thought that's why she needed pictures."

"You said your old boyfriend, Eric, was a photographer and Tiffany wanted his number. But you didn't give it to her, right?"

Maria hesitated a moment. "I told you I didn't want Tiffany contacting him, and so I didn't give her his number. And that's what I told the police. But Eric called this afternoon. He'd read about Tiffany in the paper and wanted to make sure Tony and I were all right. He *had* talked to Tiffany. She got his number from my address book."

"Did he take pictures for her?"

"He said no, that he didn't do the sort of thing she wanted. But he did loan her a camera."

"When did he do that?"

"A couple of weeks ago. It was the kind of camera you can set to go off automatically, or activate from a distance. He said she had it for a few days, and then she returned it."

"Did he say what she was taking pictures of?"

"That she wanted pictures of herself and a friend. A memento of their relationship. But she asked him how to muffle the sound of the shutter, and how to put the camera somewhere it wouldn't be noticed."

Maggie thought a moment. "Was it a digital camera? Or did he develop the film for her?"

"That's the really weird part. He wouldn't tell me anything about it. He just said he wasn't into that sort of thing, and it was against the law to take pictures like that."

"How would he know if he didn't develop them?"

"I think he did, Professor Summer. He just wouldn't tell me."

"Do you think he has a copy of them?"

"He said Tiffany had everything she wanted, and he didn't want to get involved; he didn't have anything the police would be interested in. So if he had photos or negatives, I don't think he has them now. He was worried I'd tell the police he was helping Tiffany."

"But you haven't."

"No. When I told them about Tiffany possibly black-mailing someone, I told them I wouldn't give her Eric's number. I didn't even tell them Eric's name; I just said he was an old friend of mine. And that was the truth." Maria paused again. "Eric's had some problems in the past, Professor Summer. If the police knew he'd gotten involved with something like blackmail, he could end up in jail again. He's pretty upset right now that Tiffany got herself killed. He kept saying she was a stupid bitch—sorry, Professor Summer—and that at least he had his camera back. I don't think he has anything that would help the police."

"Except that he knows she took some pictures. Her fingerprints might be on the camera. And maybe he saw the pictures and could describe them."

"Maybe he could, but I don't think he will. Eric doesn't want to help the police in any way. He's not exactly a supporter of the Police Benevolent Fund."

"I understand, Maria."

"And if he gets in any kind of trouble, that could be trouble for Tony and me, too," added Maria. "Eric gets awfully mad sometimes. Especially when someone gets him in trouble."

"Is that why you had a gun in your room?"

"I'm sorry, but, yes. I know how to use it, too. But I think Eric will be okay. As long as no one tells the police he had anything to do with Tiffany."

"You know if the police don't find those pictures, then an important piece of evidence is missing."

"I want them to find whoever killed Tiffany."

"Then give me a little time," said Maggie. "I'll do everything I can to keep Eric from getting involved."

"Thank you. I need you to do that if it's at all possible."

Maggie sat with the telephone. Tiffany had taken pictures. That seemed certain now. And if she had already given the pictures to the man she was blackmailing, then there would have been no need to kill her. Unless he was afraid she would talk to someone. And tell them what? Maybe he thought she had the pictures or negatives with her when she was killed. But she didn't. And someone knew she'd visited Maggie that afternoon and figured out the photographs might be in her office. They had to be in the briefcase.

Maggie brushed Winslow off her lap and paced. Photographs. Photographs sometimes were reminders of things you'd rather forget. She walked over to a small group of photos hung near the window seat. Michael had put them there. Several times since his death she'd thought of taking them down, but hadn't done it. There was a picture of Michael and Maggie on their wedding day. So full of hope for their future. A picture of Michael's parents and two sisters. And a picture of Maggie as a little girl, her long hair in braids, with her parents and her big brother, Joe. She'd been six when Joe left home, so the picture must have been taken sometime in that last year. Now her parents were dead, and Joe . . . Joe might be anywhere.

She'd had a postcard from him a couple of years ago, postmarked Arizona. But not a word since then, and no way to reach him. He didn't even know Michael was dead. Although he probably wouldn't have cared; they'd only met once, at Maggie's parents' funeral. Joe had always lived life in a lane separate from everyone else's. He'd seen life from a little different perspective.

Maggie wondered where Joe was now, and whether he was all right. She hoped so. She didn't think about him often, but when she did, it was always with the regret that she knew almost nothing about her closest living relative.

And that his leaving had changed her relationship with her parents forever. Scared that she, too, would leave, they had been controlling and insistent that she could trust no one in life but herself.

That was one lesson she'd learned all too well.

Maybe that was one reason she wanted to have a family. A family that stayed close. Although maybe her parents had wanted that, too. They just hadn't known how to do it. Why did she think she could do any better?

Chapter 33

Night of the Raven. *Signed proof of black-and-white wood engraving by Margaret K. Thomas, listed mid-twentieth-century American artist. Bare tree on hill whose scraggly branches reach menacingly toward the sky as a raven flies by. An enormous moon, its light dimmed only slightly by clouds, illuminates the scene. 12 x 19 inches. Price: $275.*

Maggie swallowed a Tylenol, turned off the brass lamp

on her bedside table, and snuggled down under the comforter. There was nothing else she could do tonight.

Morning would come quickly enough. She'd tackle her office, talk with Paul, and find a way to open Tiffany's briefcase. In the meantime, both her body and her mind craved sleep.

She lay still, drifting into sleep, lulled by the usual creaks and moans of an old house on a chilly night in early November. The wind must have picked up, she thought drowsily. She trimmed her trees and bushes every summer so they wouldn't hit the side of the house in winter snow and ice storms. But tonight the noises of the branches were different. She heard a scraping, or scratching, as though the wind were trying to get in through one of the windows.

It wasn't the wind.

Maggie froze. Every nerve in her body was on alert. She listened intently. One after another she heard the windows on the first floor of the house shake. No wind would shake windows sequentially. Someone was trying to get into the house. A burglar? Someone looking for those photographs? Someone looking for her?

Maggie's first instinct was to scream. But no one would have heard. Instead, she lay still in the bed, her body stiff with fear. She could hardly hear the windows shaking. All she could hear was her own heartbeat, which was suddenly the loudest noise in her universe.

She kept most of the windows locked at this time of year; she had put down the storm panes only a week ago. But she had left screens on several, in case warm late-fall days encouraged her to air the house out again before winter arrived to stay. Those windows she might have left unlocked.

She couldn't hear anything now. Had she imagined it? Had she let her imagination and the events of the past two days convince her that someone was actually trying to break into her house? For a few instants she wondered. Then she heard the noise again. Whoever it was had passed the kitchen door and was now near the ramp she'd built as an alternative entrance to the French doors in her study. Convenient when Gussie visited in her chair; convenient for wheeling a dolly loaded with prints directly from her study to her van. Convenient for someone else tonight?

She'd double-checked all of her doors tonight. They were locked.

But—yes—someone was shaking the door at the top of the ramp, making sure it was secure.

Maggie felt cold and rigid. She could hardly breathe as she reached out to the telephone next to her bed. This was no time for bravery. She dialed 911.

The three rings felt like thirty. "Please?" Maggie whispered. "Someone is trying to break into my house. . . . Yes. Now!" They got her address from their caller ID system. How long would it take for someone to arrive?

Park Glen was a small town; after midnight few police were on duty. Suburban police departments often took turns covering for each other to save costs. There might be a patrol within a block of her house. Or, more likely, no one within fifteen minutes. Or the only policeman could be on another call somewhere. Somewhere far from her house.

Was the intruder looking for her? Or for something he thought she had?

She'd have to gamble that he didn't want her. She'd parked her packed van in the garage tonight. Most nights she left it in the driveway. Whoever was in her yard might have assumed she wasn't home.

Television commercials for burglar alarm systems—why had she never installed one?—said burglars didn't want to confront people. She could hear the windows shaking in the study now. If the person still circling her house knew she was at home, would that scare them away?

Or would that give them an added incentive to break in?

She had to do something. Maggie reached over and turned the light on next to her bed. Then she got up, automatically put on the bathrobe she'd left at the foot of the bed, crossed to the door, and turned on the light in the hallway that ran the length of the second floor. She could still hear rustling and shaking. Emboldened by the light, she walked into the small bedroom next to hers, at the front of the house. The room that would perhaps someday be for her son or daughter. Tonight she was glad she was alone. How would a single parent deal with this situation?

She knew immediately. They'd be even more afraid than she was now, because they'd be afraid for their child as well as for themselves. And they'd have to be braver. They'd have to show their child that there was nothing to fear.

Inspired by that thought, Maggie walked to the front window and looked down at the street. Her feet were frozen, with cold and with fear. The night was dark; clouds covered the moon. But a car was parked two houses down, just visible beyond the glow of the imitation gas streetlight in front of Maggie's home. It was unusual to have a car parked on this quiet street so late on a Tuesday night. In this neighborhood most people, and their guests, parked in driveways. She couldn't see the color of the car or the license plate number; all she could tell was that it was a dark sedan. Not a sports car or compact. She wished she paid more attention to automotive ads.

Emboldened, she left the window, where she might be seen, and turned on the light in that room, in the other front bedroom, and then in the second-floor bathroom. There was a switch for the light over the staircase to the first floor. Should she turn it on, too?

She listened again. Her feet felt like weights. Frozen weights. Did she dare go down the stairs where she might be seen? She needed to know who it was.

Footsteps crackled in the dry leaves below her as she stood next to the window in the hallway. Maggie lifted the lid of the pine captain's chest she kept in the hall for storage of extra blankets and towels and . . . flashlights. The large torch she used during electrical outages was right where it should be. Next to it was the box cutter she used to remove prints from books with broken bindings. She must have left it here after taking that volume of Volland nursery rhymes apart in her room a couple of weeks ago. She slipped the box cutter into the pocket of her bathrobe and picked up the flashlight.

Pointing the light toward the floor, she clicked the button to turn it on. Nothing. Damn. Could she have forgotten to replace the batteries? Her heart sounded louder with every beat. She shook the torch and pushed the button again. It lit. She started to raise the hall window. Would the light shine down far enough so she could see who was there? She listened. She could still hear footsteps in the leaves. Whoever was there hadn't been discouraged by the lights on the second floor.

She hesitated. What if he—or she—had a gun?

She couldn't think about that. Gently she opened the window. Thank goodness she'd oiled the inside of that frame last summer. It didn't stick. But she'd have to raise the screen, too, to be able to see out. The screen squeaked no matter how carefully she moved it.

She pushed it up, holding her breath as though that would silence it. It didn't. But there was no sound from below. Maggie leaned out, directing the torch so it would point into her yard. The beam only covered a small area. She couldn't see anyone. Slowly she turned it so she could see more of the yard.

As she looked the sound of a siren and the flash of a revolving light broke the stillness. Police!

The cruiser pulled up and parked in front of her house. Maggie began to breathe again. She rotated the beam of the large flashlight around the yard once more. All was quiet.

She backed her upper body in through the window, bumping her head on the frame. Hard. The flashlight slipped from her hands and fell into the yard.

"Hey, lady! You the one who called 911?"

Maggie looked down. A uniformed officer was standing there, rubbing his head.

"There was someone here. He tried all of the windows. I could hear them shaking."

As she spoke, a nearby car started up and accelerated. The patrolman ran toward the noise as Maggie went downstairs. She met him on the small porch in front of her house.

"Did you see the car?"

"It drove off too fast. Are you sure no one got into your house?"

Maggie felt like a quivering, helpless female, but under the circumstances she didn't care. "I don't think so. But I don't know for sure." She realized she was standing in bare feet, wearing her blue flannel nightgown and old robe, shaking with cold and fear. But she did have a box cutter in her pocket.

"I'd like to check the house to make sure," said the patrolman, and Maggie nodded, filled with relief. "My partner can check your yard."

"Yes, please," she said quietly. "Can I make you some tea or coffee?"

"No thanks, ma'am. You just sit right here by the door, and if you hear or see anything unusual, you scream. Promise?"

Maggie nodded. Right now she didn't care if she was being treated like a ten-year-old. The relief of having someone else in charge for a few moments was too much. She started to cry.

Sniveling idiot, she told herself with embarrassment.

She ignored the patrolman's instructions and went into the kitchen, got some tissues, and blew her nose. Everything was as she'd left it. Winslow meowed at her from the top of the kitchen table. She moved him to the floor. "Big help you were," she scolded. She sat down and waited for her pulse to return to normal.

After a few minutes the policeman returned, and his partner handed Maggie the torch. "Wicked weapon you've got here," he said, grinning, and rubbing the back of his head. "Unfortunately it got one of the good guys."

"Sorry." Maggie could see the torch had major problems; the plastic lens had split and the side was dented. She hoped the patrolman's scalp was in better shape.

"There was someone here, ma'am; the ground next to the house is just damp enough to show some footprints outside the windows in the back, and by the ramp. But whoever it was has left. Make sure you lock up tight. We'll take a drive through every hour or so to check, but I don't think you'll have any more company tonight."

Maggie felt numb. "There's nothing else you can do?"

"Probably it was someone trying to pick up computers or jewelry to sell for drug money. I'm surprised he didn't disappear when you turned on the upstairs lights. That's what they usually do." He looked at Maggie. "You'll be fine. We'll file a report. If you should hear anything, call 911 right away, all right?"

Maggie nodded.

The police left. She checked all of the doors and windows again, this time locking the couple of windows she'd left open before. She locked the ones on the second floor, too, just in case.

By the time she got back into bed it was almost three. She lay stiffly under the comforter, no longer lulled by the night.

The world had become too frightening, too close.

Her office . . . and now her home. Her sense of security was gone. Who would do this to her?

Who would poison Sarah and Tiffany?

The world of Somerset, New Jersey, where she had always felt comfortable and at home, no longer felt safe.

She finally fell asleep, but only into dreams of falling and footsteps and fear.

Chapter 34

Tell Tale Tit, Your tongue shall be slit; And all the dogs in the town Shall have a little bit. *Colored engraving of old nursery rhyme, with verse, from* Mother Goose, *1881, London, illustrated by Kate Greenaway (1846–1901). Greenaway's quaintly dressed children were extremely popular during the 1880s and 1890s, and reproductions of her work are being printed today. 4 x 6.5 inches. Price: $60.*

Maggie's night was too restless and too short. At seven she forced herself to get out of bed, poured a soda, and logged on to her computer.

Good morning, Dear Lady. Weather in Ohio is improving, and so, I'm hoping, is yours. Found some small treasures in a shop yesterday—an early brass trammel in perfect condition, and a wonder-fully quirky Victorian, homemade wire flyswatter. No prints, though, so you didn't miss any bargains. But I miss your smile. As I remember, Gussie and Jim are arriving tonight, so give them my best. Hope you're taking some time for long baths and relaxing music, but suspect you're not. If you're up to a plane ride or a long drive, think about spending Thanks-giving in Buffalo. . . . I should get there a week in advance, so the house might even be vacuumed. And you once said you'd never seen Niagara Falls. So— consider the possibilities. And me.

Will

Maggie sighed and read over the message. She had planned to clean her own house and reorganize portfo-lios during Thanksgiving break. But after the events of the last few days, spending her first Thanksgiving without Michael alone didn't sound like fun. Being alone at all didn't sound like fun. Although it was a lot easier when the sun was shining.

If only she could tell Will what was happening . . . but there was too much, and it was too complicated. Soon, Maggie thought. Soon it will be a "you'll never guess what happened" story, and I'll be able to share it. Long-distance relationships had their challenges.

And even when Michael had been there, Maggie had managed most of life on her own.

Dear Will,
And a wonderful Wednesday to you! Your finds of

yesterday sound great—would love to see the folk-art flyswatter! When do you think we'll get techno-logically hip and have digital cameras? Or those little telephones that send pictures? For now, e-mail is about as challenging as I want technology to be. I'll think seriously about Thanksgiving. Right now I'm in the middle of a busy week, and not ready to focus on something three weeks away. But I will be. Soon. I promise. Sending you a cyber-hug . . .

Maggie

She deleted the four junk e-mails that had arrived overnight and skimmed a notice from an international adoption agency headquartered in Pennsylvania that was hosting an orientation meeting on Saturday. She would have liked to attend. But the Morristown Antique Show would keep her occupied this weekend. She wrote back to the agency asking when the next Saturday orientation meeting would be. Not Thanksgiving weekend, she hoped, turning the regard ring on her finger. It would be hard to choose between Will and the adoption meeting; between Will and children; and this morning she didn't feel up to making difficult decisions.

Before today gets any more complicated, Maggie told herself, you are going to school and getting that brief-case. She put on a long, red-plaid flannel skirt and a red turtleneck and picked up the large navy canvas tote bag she sometimes used for shopping. It would be big enough to cover the briefcase from prying eyes.

As she'd hoped, she was the first this morning to get to the American Studies office area. She unlocked her office and tried not to look at the mess left after the trashing and then the fingerprinting. Her hand shook a little as she isolated the correct key on her key ring and unlocked the desk drawer. Tiffany's briefcase was right where she'd left it. She hastily slipped it in the canvas bag, relocked the desk and office, and walked back to her van, trying not to look behind every tree to see if anyone was watching. But if she didn't count the one student who had arrived early and was sipping his coffee on the steps of the administration building, no one was nearby.

At home, Maggie pulled her bag of tools from the van and took the briefcase inside. It had a combination lock. Maggie looked at the other side of the case. She hated to ruin the soft leather. But there was no other way. She found her narrowest screwdriver, a small brass hammer, and two clamps she used to fasten Peg-Boards to the back of tables at antique shows. She clamped the brief-case to the wide, heavy table she used for matting to hold it steady as she carefully inserted the screwdriver between the top and bottom of the hinges. It wasn't easy. It took more than a few minutes. And the briefcase would never be the same again. But Maggie was finally able to pry it open far enough to start sliding papers out.

A small address book. Maggie was tempted to stop there, but she wanted to see everything that was in the case. Were there photographs? She felt her pulse racing as she pulled out the next item. An appointment cal-endar. No appointments were listed for the night Tiffany was killed. But the initials O.W. did fill at least one night a week for the past month.

So Tiffany had been seeing Oliver Whitcomb!

Several pages of notes from a mathematics class.

A picture of Tyler with a clown at what looked like an amusement park. Maggie hesitated. Did she really want to see what Tyler's mother had in this case? The police should be doing this. Probably everything she was looking at should be fingerprinted. But, then, everything here was Tiffany's. It shouldn't have any prints other than hers.

And now Maggie's.

A paper from an English class. An overdue credit card bill. A tiny, free sample lipstick from a department store cosmetics counter.

A large brown paper envelope.

As soon as Maggie pulled it out, she knew. These were the pictures someone was so anxious to get. These were the pictures someone had killed Tiffany for. The pictures someone had trashed Maggie's office and tried to break into her home to find.

She slid the photos out. There were only half a dozen, but they were enough. Enough to know that Oliver Whitcomb was going to be in a lot of trouble. And that he had a motive for murder.

Chapter 35

Major General Benedict Arnold. *Steel engraving by H. R. Hall, printed by W. Pate and published by G. P. Putnam & Co., 1852. With steel-engraved reproduction of Arnold's signature. Benedict Arnold (1741–1801) was a general in the U.S. Army during* *the American Revolution. In 1780 he was given command of West Point; his correspondence with the British revealed his plan to betray West Point for a British commission and money. The plot was discovered, but Arnold escaped and went into exile in England and Canada. 6.5 x 10 inches. Price: $45.*

It had been two days since she had visited Aura, Maggie thought guiltily as she headed toward campus and the Wee Care Center. Here she was thinking about adopting a child, and Aura was a little girl who needed her now and she hadn't even found time to visit her every day.

The day-care worker held Aura's hand as she led her toward Maggie. Aura was much quieter than she'd been Monday. Now she'd had the double shock of her mother being gone and of finding Tiffany's body. Maggie wondered how much Aura understood, and how much she'd remember. Maggie needed to read a lot more books on child psychology before becoming a parent.

"Good morning, Aura," said Maggie. "I took the picture you drew to your mommy."

Aura brightened immediately. "Did Mommy like it?"

Maggie thought of Sarah, lying in the hospital bed, unconscious. "I'm sure she did, Aura. But she's still sleeping a lot. I put the picture up where she would see it when she wakes up, though."

"Tiffany is sick, too," Aura said. "The policemen took her away. And then Tyler went away."

Did Aura think someone was going to take her away? The events at Whitcomb House in the past few days had to be incomprehensible to a four-year-old.

"Tyler went to stay with his grandma and grandpa," said Maggie.

"Will I go to stay with a grandma and grandpa?" asked Aura.

Aura had never met anyone she could call grandma or grandpa. But Dorothy was her grandmother. This morning Maggie didn't want to think about what Oliver was.

"You're not going anywhere, Aura. At least not now. You're going to stay where you live, and Kayla is going to take care of you, and Heather, and Maria, and Kendall are going to be there."

"That's what Kayla said, too. She said Mommy would be home soon."

"I hope she will be, Aura."

"I'll make her another picture today," said Aura. "Will you come and see me tonight and get the picture and take it to Mommy?"

Maggie nodded. "I'll do that."

"I'll make a special picture for her." Aura turned to go back into her classroom, then turned back. "Would you like me to make a picture for you, too?"

"I'd like that very much, Aura." Maggie's eyes filled with tears.

"Bye-bye." Aura disappeared behind the classroom door.

Maggie stood silently for a moment. Sarah had to get better. She had to.

For the second time that morning Maggie headed for her office. This time she was carrying photographs, safely tucked in a brown portfolio like those she used for prints, and notes for her nine-o'clock class. Thank goodness she'd kept the outline for today's lecture at home; she wouldn't have to hunt for it in the mess that was her office.

Claudia raised her head from the pages of a magazine and frowned as Maggie passed her desk. "I thought something must have happened to you, too. Your class is in five minutes." She handed Maggie a pile of pink message slips and a chocolate Kiss.

"I know," said Maggie.

"If you could be a flower, what would you be?"

"What?" Maggie looked at Claudia.

"It says in this article that most men want to be roses. With thorns. But women want to be all sorts of flowers. I can't make up my mind whether I'd rather be a daffodil or a Johnny-jump-up. What would you like to be?"

"This morning—poison ivy! Maybe then everyone would leave me alone!" Maggie stuffed the messages into her pocketbook.

Claudia shook her head and handed Maggie three more chocolate Kisses. "The janitor wanted to clean your office last night, after the police were finished, but I was sure you'd want to go through all those papers yourself. I did convince him to leave you some cleaning supplies, though." She moved aside and pointed under her desk to a pail filled with cloths, paper towels, and glass cleaner.

"Thank you, Claudia. I'm sorry I snapped at you. I didn't even think of things like that, and I'll need them. But not until after this class. I just stopped to get my messages."

Maggie held tightly to the portfolio as she walked through the halls. She didn't dare leave it in her office or her van.

Her van. If someone thought she had the photographs, would they search her van? The van that was full of prints! Maggie blanched, but kept walking. The faculty parking area was in a well-traveled area near the library, and it was morning. Too many people would be around for anyone to try to break into it now. And she had locked all the doors and windows.

Her "Myths in American Culture" class was waiting. Maggie put the portfolio down on the desk she was using and began. It was 9 A.M. Wednesday. Life, and classes, had to continue.

"This morning we're going to talk about the myth of the self-made man. It's a myth closely related to the myth of America as Eden; as a place to begin. It grew out of the reality that, if there was not land for everyone here, then at least there was land for more people than there had been in Europe. And whereas in European societies position, power, and money were all primarily hereditary, in America inheritances were not as important.

"Of course, even some of those who sailed on the *Mayflower* had more money and position than others. But the illusion was that once you were on American soil, hard work could make up for any differences in birth.

"This myth was encouraged by politicians, who advertised the successes of Andrew Jackson, whose wife taught him to read, and then of Abraham Lincoln, who may have been born in a log cabin. And if anyone doubted the myth, then Horatio Alger's stories proved it.

"Today the name Horatio Alger is used to describe someone who has risen from the bottom of society to a position of wealth and power. The real Horatio Alger was a writer and minister. During the Civil War he was the chaplain of the Newsboys' Lodging House in New York City, a refuge for homeless boys who lived in Five Points and other slums in lower Manhattan. Many of these boys, some orphaned by the Civil War, some deserted by their families, tried to make their living selling newspapers. Alger wanted them to believe they had a future. That their destinies depended on their own actions, not on their current situations.

"Beginning in 1867, with the publication of *Ragged Dick*, Alger wrote action-filled books about boys who were on the lowest rungs of society with titles like *Tony the Tramp* and *Phil the Fiddler* and *Only an Irish Boy*. All his heroes are boys who are poor but honest and hardworking; they struggle against poverty and against temptation. And, inevitably, their efforts are recognized by older men who reward them by offering them economic and social opportunities. All of Alger's young heroes achieve wealth and position and power. His one hundred and thirty books were bestsellers from 1867 until the early twentieth century, and one or two are still in print today. Over the years, more than twenty million copies of Horatio Alger's books have been printed.

"A generation after he wrote *Ragged Dick*, Alger's books were often used by the Social Darwinists of the

Gilded Age—those who believed that the wealthiest Americans were examples of the 'survival of the fittest' doctrine—to justify that wealth. After all, Americans were self-made men, and only the most honest and hardworking could have made it to the top.

"At least, that was true in Horatio Alger's books."

Maggie paused. "Today we smile at some of those beliefs. We know, for example, that honesty is not always rewarded and dishonesty sometimes is. The robber barons of the Gilded Age proved that, and certainly we could all think of many more recent examples. And yet many of you or your parents or grandparents came to the United States with the same beliefs Horatio Alger had. That's why you're sitting here, in this classroom. You believe that if you work hard and prove yourselves, then you, too, can have a better job, and a bigger house, and, ultimately, a happier life. Am I right?" Maggie saw some smiles and nods around the classroom.

Certainly young mothers like Sarah Anderson and Tiffany Douglass would have fallen within Horatio Alger's definition of "starting from the bottom." Although, since they were single mothers, Alger would no doubt have dismissed any possibilities of success for them. Not only were they women (none of his books were about girls) but they were "immoral."

"Let's take the rest of this class time to discuss the idea of the self-made man—or woman," Maggie continued. "Is it a myth? Or can a man or woman who starts with nothing, but who works hard, still find that America is a land of opportunity?"

Chapter 36

Lithograph of four folk-toy weapons: a slingshot, a pistol, a rifle, and a crossbow. From Folk-Toys: Les Jouets Populaires, *a book of designs of Czechoslovakian folk toys by Emanuel Hercik, printed in Prague, 1941. 8.5 x 11.5 inches. Price: $50.*

Maggie's office didn't look any better than it had earlier.

She put down the papers she was carrying, dusted most of the fingerprint powder off her chair, and retrieved the plastic pail of cleaning aids from Claudia. She'd start by the door and work her way around the office. "Fall cleaning," she muttered to herself as she wiped the top shelf of the bookcase nearest to the door and began dusting and replacing books. There was one good side to all of this: by the time she'd finished, her office would no doubt be cleaner than it had been before the damage. She hadn't dusted these bookcases thoroughly for over a year.

After most of the books were off the floor and back in the first bookcase (and several volumes were rediscovered and piled in the corner to take home to read), she scrubbed spilled soda off the desk and floor, and out of the top drawer in her desk. The loose papers would take hours more to organize and file. She piled all of them, some stained with Pepsi and some not, on the guest chair where Tiffany had sat less than forty-eight hours before. It seemed so long ago. She hesitated, then plunged back into the cleaning. It had to be done. Her sanity, if not her job, depended on her putting at least part of her life back in order.

She put the Currier & Ives *Maggie* in a portfolio to take home so she could replace the glass and try to repair the frame.

The telephone didn't ring, and no one bothered her. It was heavenly.

Over an hour later, when Maggie had finished about half the cleaning, Paul stuck his head in. "Hey! I told you I'd help with this! You started without me." He took off his jacket and rolled up his sleeves. "So—what can I do?"

"You can clean the shelves in the bookcase on that side of the room," Maggie said. "Claudia scrounged some Windex and paper towels. If you find any stray papers, put them on the chair over there. I'll go through them later."

"Aye, aye, captain!" Paul said as he tore some paper towels off the roll and headed for the designated book-case.

They worked in silence for a few minutes. Paul spoke first. "I hope you had a peaceful evening last night. After everything that happened yesterday, you deserved one."

Could he already know what had happened last night? Or, if he didn't, then should she tell him? "I went out for a quiet dinner, but then later had a little excitement. A prowler tried to break into my house."

"No!" Paul stopped dusting and looked genuinely concerned. "After what happened to your office yes-terday? That can't be chance."

"The timing doesn't sound coincidental, does it?"

"Did you call the police?"

"Whoever it was drove away before they could catch him—or her."

"What are you going to do now?"

"Clean up my office, teach my class this afternoon, and keep my eyes and ears open. I don't want to fall into the same category as Sarah or Tiffany."

Paul was silent. "This is tough for me. I'm new here, and I want to help. But . . ."

"But you don't want to get your friend Oliver in trouble, right?" Maggie walked around the desk and stood next to Paul so their conversation wouldn't be overheard. "Paul, if Oliver is poisoning students and burglarizing my office and home, then he's not worth protecting."

"Professor Summer? And Mr. Turk." Detective Newton was in the door of Maggie's small office, Detective Luciani behind her. "I'm glad you're here. We need to speak with both of you."

"Yes?" Maggie moved over, shifted some papers, and sat down on her chair. The cola she hadn't yet cleaned off stuck to her skirt. Paul stood near the bookcase, still holding paper towels. Had the detectives figured out she had the photographs? Should she tell them?

"Professor Summer, your office was clearly the object of someone's search yesterday, and we just found out you called 911 last night reporting that someone attempted to enter your home."

"Yes."

"We're trying to make sense of the poisoning of Sarah

Anderson, and then Tiffany Douglass, but we keep coming up with dead ends." Detective Newton, as usual, was taking the lead questioning Maggie. Perhaps because she was a woman. Maybe Luciani questioned men. "Professor Summer, you knew both of the victims. And Mr. Turk, you're a friend of the Whitcombs. Somehow the two young women and the Whitcombs seem to be linked in this investigation. We need to talk with both of you again." She looked at Paul. "But separately. Mr. Turk, would you mind waiting for us in your office?"

Luciani closed the door after Paul. It was a bit too cozy with Maggie and the two detectives there amid the mess, but it was more private.

"Professor Summer, what do you have that someone is looking for?" Detective Newton looked directly at her with an intensity Maggie had not seen before.

Maggie hesitated only briefly. The police needed to know. Someone needed to find whoever had poisoned Sarah and Tiffany. "Yesterday I didn't know for sure. But I do now. Tiffany visited me Monday afternoon, to talk about Sarah, as I told you earlier. I didn't consider it anything out of the ordinary."

"Did she know anything that might pinpoint who had poisoned Sarah?" asked Detective Luciani.

"No. Quite the opposite. She had no idea. We talked for a while, and then she left, and I did, too. I didn't notice until yesterday that she'd left her briefcase here."

"In your office?"

"Yes."

"Where is it? Did whoever disturbed your office take it?"

256

"No. When I found the briefcase, I locked it in the desk drawer with my grade books. I came in early this morning, got it, and took it to my home."

"You realize you should have turned it over to us," said Detective Newton. "You knew that anything belonging to the deceased might be critical to our investigation."

"But I didn't know for sure, and . . . in any case, that's what I did."

"So the briefcase is now in your home."

Maggie nodded. "But I opened it." She didn't feel ready to tell them she had broken into the briefcase. They would find that out soon enough. "I have the contents here." Maggie handed the portfolio to Detective Luciani, who had come around to her side of the desk. Tiffany's address book and appointment book were there. So were the photographs.

Luciani handed the rest of the papers to Newton, and they spread the photos out on a relatively clear area of Maggie's desk.

One of the pictures showed Oliver Whitcomb, naked, holding a whip. Others showed Oliver and Tiffany, both nude, or close to it. In two of them Tiffany was tied to a bed with what looked like a red rope. In one she was handcuffed. The pictures showed two apparently consenting adults having bondage sex.

"Not pretty stuff," said Luciani.

"That explains the bruises Kayla said she saw on Tiffany," said Newton.

"And it would explain, graphically, why Tiffany might have been able to blackmail Oliver Whitcomb," said Luciani, gathering up the photos. He put them back in the portfolio. "Professor Summer, you might be interested to know that the toxicology tests came back on Tiffany Douglass. She was poisoned by potassium permanganate, most likely mixed with red wine. Not the same poison Sarah Anderson ingested."

"Potassium permanganate?" Maggie went white with shock. "Are you sure?"

Chapter 37

Hand-colored steel engraving of a whale beached on a glacier; two clipper ships are in the background, and two dories are on their way toward the stranded mammal. Printed by Frillarton and Company, London and Edinburgh, in 1853 for Oliver Goldsmith's History of the Earth and Animated Nature. *As with many engravings of the period, the central figure, the whale, is hand-colored; the rest of the engraving is left in black and white. 5.5 x 9 inches. Price: $60.*

Maggie spoke with the detectives for a few more minutes, then Luciani and Newton went next door, to Paul's office.

Maggie sat quietly, pulling her thoughts together. She looked around her office. She still didn't know who'd trashed it, but now she thought she knew who'd killed Tiffany. Who had to have killed Tiffany. And if that person had killed Tiffany, then perhaps that person was also responsible for Sarah's poisoning. Responsible for searching Maggie's office, and for trying to break into her home last night. She had the major pieces. All she had to do now was make them fit. And get some proof. Then she could share her theory.

Detective Newton came to her door. "Professor Summer? Would you join us for a few minutes in Mr. Turk's office?"

She nodded and followed the detective. As she got there, Paul, his face ashen, was being read his rights.

"You think I killed Tiffany? Or poisoned Sarah?" His voice was barely audible.

"You helped set up the bar where Sarah was poisoned, your fingerprints were all over Professor Summer's office, and you haven't told us everything you know."

Detective Luciani then spread the photographs of Tiffany and Oliver out on Paul's desk. Luciani leaned over the photos, shouting at Paul, "For example—do you know anything about this?"

Paul's shoulders sagged. "All right! Yes. I knew Oliver Whitcomb had . . . different sexual tastes. But I didn't have anything to do with Tiffany's death! Oliver used to tell me about his . . . friends . . . when we were in New York. And I knew he was seeing Tiffany Douglass. I didn't know for sure he and Tiffany were into that kind of stuff together. And I didn't know until yesterday that there were pictures. He called after he heard about her death. He said it would be very embarrassing if anyone found them, and he'd do anything to get those pictures and negatives and ensure they were destroyed."

"Embarrassing?" said Luciani.

"I assumed to him. And to his wife. Maybe even to the school."

"And . . . ?" said Detective Newton.

"I told him I'd seen Tiffany in Maggie's office Monday afternoon. He asked me if she'd had the briefcase he'd given her. I said I thought so. He asked me to see if she'd left it there."

"You were the one?" Maggie said, her voice rising. "You totally dumped my office looking for dirty pictures of Tiffany and Oliver?" Paul had lied to her and had pulled part of her life apart.

Paul nodded. "Oliver said to make it look as though a student had done it. I tried not to ruin any papers that looked critical. And, after all, I couldn't find the briefcase. I'm sorry. I didn't know what else to do. I owe so much to Oliver."

"Did you owe so much to Oliver that you killed Tiffany to get those pictures? And then panicked when she didn't have them and trashed Professor Summer's office?" asked Detective Luciani.

"No! I don't know anything about Tiffany's death! I searched Maggie's office. That's all!"

"You didn't find the briefcase because Professor Summer had already locked it away," said Detective Luciani.

"I didn't know. I told Oliver Tiffany must not have left her briefcase there after all."

"And you were the one who came to my house in the middle of the night and almost scared me to death?" Maggie was getting angrier by the minute.

"That wasn't me! I swear it! I was at home last night.

By myself. Feeling guilty about messing up your office." Paul's head dropped. "Oliver did me a big favor in recommending me for this job. He knew I didn't have any teaching experience. It wasn't just my choice to change careers. I was about to be laid off. Oliver came to my rescue."

"Did Oliver Whitcomb poison Tiffany Douglass?" Detective Newton asked.

"No! I can't believe he would do that," said Paul. "He's not like that. He's got some kinky tastes in sex, but I can't believe he'd intentionally hurt anyone!"

Detectives Luciani and Newton looked at each other. Newton spoke. "Mr. Turk, we'd like you to come down to headquarters with us and make out a sworn statement repeating what you told us here."

"I will. But I still don't think Oliver is guilty of anything but adultery."

Luciani took Paul's arm, and they headed out of the building. Newton stayed a moment.

"Are you sure about what you want to do, Professor Summer?"

Maggie nodded. "I'm sure."

"When will you be ready?"

"Five o'clock," Maggie said. "Unless I call you before that—five o'clock."

Did she really want to do this? She thought of Sarah, pale in that hospital bed, and Aura, missing her mother. Tyler, who was now living with his grandparents.

Now she understood more about Tiffany. But Sarah? It would take some time for the detectives to get

Paul's statement. Maggie finished cleaning the book-case he'd started on and straightened the papers still on top of her desk. She needed to keep her hands as busy as her mind.

Then she dialed Dorothy's number. Dorothy was somehow at the center of it all. "Dorothy? Are you free for lunch? It would have to be in the college cafeteria. I have a class at three, but I'd like to talk with you."

"I was just about to call you," Dorothy said. "I have news! See you in fifteen minutes."

Maggie pushed aside the feeling that perhaps she shouldn't see Dorothy now; she should let the police deal with what was to happen next.

How much did Dorothy know? And how much of what Maggie knew did she want to share with Dorothy?

By the time Maggie got to the cafeteria, Dorothy had already gotten a salad from the salad bar and a glass of iced tea. Maggie took a small salad and then, as she walked through the line of students and teachers, realized she'd skipped breakfast. She added two slices of vegetarian pizza and a large Diet Pepsi with ice and lemon to her tray. Even in the worst of times, a woman had to eat. By the time Maggie sat down, Dorothy had finished about a third of her salad.

Now what? Should she just broach the untouchable? Hey, Dorothy, I understand your husband was having steamy bondage sex with one of the single parents you sponsored! Do you think he could have murdered her? Maggie put a paper napkin in her lap and debated whether to use her fingers for the pizza or be civilized and use a knife and fork. The mounds of vegetables convinced her. Knife and fork.

Dorothy spoke first. "I just got through talking with Max. I think we have a deal."

"Yes?"

"He agreed he was a little overwrought when he talked with you yesterday. He said we were right. The residents of Whitcomb House can stay."

"That's a relief!"

"Yes and no. He did put one caveat in the agreement. But it won't have any effect on the students who're at Whitcomb House now. Just those in the future."

"The future?"

"Oliver and I agreed to resign from the committee that selects candidates for the program. We'll still sponsor Whitcomb House, of course, so we were disappointed, but I can understand, after the past week's events, why Max would feel that way."

Maggie was puzzled. "I didn't know a special committee determined who was offered Whitcomb House residencies and scholarships. I assumed that was done through the Admissions Office."

"Officially, yes. And then it's administered by the college president. But a small group of people consult on the decisions of the Admissions Office about those particular scholarship students. Bluntly, Maggie, since Oliver and I were putting up the money, we wanted to be sure we had some input about who received the scholarships."

Of course. That's how Sarah and Tiffany, who were roommates, had both been offered scholarships. It was beginning to make sense. "Sarah told Tiffany she was approached by someone at the diner where she worked, who told her about the program."

Dorothy shrugged slightly. "I had someone from the Admissions Office talk with her. The program was designed to help girls like Sarah."

"And now?" Maggie questioned. "That won't be happening in the future?"

"No. Max was quite clear about that." Dorothy put down her salad fork. "Actually, since Sarah was the only one I was specifically interested in, it doesn't really matter. I know the Admissions Office will select outstanding candidates."

"Do the current Whitcomb House students know of your role in their admission?"

"I don't think so. And Max has promised that no changes made now will affect the students who are already in the program. I think the house and its future are secure."

"Thank goodness! That is a relief, Dorothy," Maggie said, after another bite of pizza. "I was really concerned that Max might not change his mind. So—are you and Oliver still at the hotel?"

"No! The police left our house late yesterday, and we went right home. I'm not convinced our moving out was worth all the aggravation; I haven't heard that the police have made any progress in identifying whoever poisoned the girls, so they probably didn't find anything at our home."

"I just saw Detectives Newton and Luciani. They have some ideas they're going to pursue."

"Oh? Where did you see them?" Dorothy sipped her

iced tea. Her hand tightened around her glass.

"In my office. Did Oliver or Max or Paul tell you my office was pulled apart by someone looking for a briefcase that belonged to Tiffany?"

"No." Dorothy put down the glass. "I'm so sorry, Maggie. I didn't hear that. Whatever did they think was in the briefcase?"

Maggie was torn. She didn't want to tell Dorothy something that would hurt her, but Dorothy was going to find out soon anyway. Paul was down at the station now. "They have the contents now. There were photographs. Graphic photographs of Tiffany with her lover. The police think she may have been blackmailing him. He wanted to stop her. And destroy the pictures." Maggie watched closely, but Dorothy seemed strangely calm.

"And her lover actually went to your office to look for them? Why would he ever have thought to look there?" Dorothy's voice was cautious. Maggie wondered how much she really did know.

"Tiffany had been in my office Monday afternoon, just hours before she was murdered. Dorothy, I'm really sorry to have to tell you this, but the pictures were of Tiffany and Oliver," Maggie said quickly. "Oliver asked Paul to look for the photos in my office. He thought she might have left her briefcase there. And she had."

"Oliver asked Paul to do that? How clumsy of him," said Dorothy evenly. "That put Paul in a very awkward position."

Had Dorothy heard her? Maggie watched her face. "Dorothy—Oliver was having an affair with Tiffany."

"I know." Dorothy looked back at her calmly. "No, that's not strictly true, Maggie. I didn't know for sure that this time it was Tiffany. Oliver has so many affairs. But I suspected Tiffany was the one."

"How can you be so calm? Didn't you care? Your husband was sleeping with another woman!"

"I cared. Of course I cared. But I'm very conventional, Maggie. Oliver likes some activities that are not of interest to me. So he finds other women to play with. He isn't looking for love or commitment. He knows he has that with me."

Maggie had expected tears, screams, threats. Not this.

Dorothy looked at Maggie and smiled. "Don't be horrified. Oliver and I are very happy together. Our life is much simpler if we can concentrate on our relationship without cluttering it with behavior that just isn't to my taste. We don't talk about it a lot. But we both know what's happening. I told you we had separate friends, Maggie!"

"You've always known about his affairs."

"Yes; of course. Very few wives don't know when their husband is being unfaithful. But I know in Oliver's case it's only his body that's unfaithful, not his heart or mind."

Maggie thought too quickly of Michael, and of what she had not known about his behavior. Was she the only one who hadn't known? Was she the only wife who hadn't sensed what was happening? Was she so uninvolved with him that . . . But the issue today was Dorothy and Oliver.

"Dorothy, if you knew about Oliver's affairs, then

266

Tiffany wouldn't have been able to blackmail him by threatening to tell you about their relationship."

"Heavens, no. I would have laughed in her face. If she wanted to endure all of what he liked to do . . . that was her problem. It certainly wasn't a threat to me."

"And what about Sarah? Was he having an affair with Sarah?"

Dorothy paled. "No. He couldn't have. Wouldn't have. I can't even think about that, Maggie. Tiffany, yes. There were signs. She always made a point of talking to him at our gatherings, and the way she dressed . . . but— Sarah? I can't believe that of Sarah."

"But Sarah was poisoned. And so was Tiffany." But with different poisons, Maggie thought. Why would one person use two different poisons?

"Which is why the police need to get their act together and consider all the possibilities," said Dorothy.

"The police suspect Oliver poisoned at least Tiffany. Because of the photographs."

"That's ridiculous! Why would Oliver kill some girl just because she was stupid enough to think she could get some money out of him by having photographs taken? Oliver would never have done that." Dorothy shook her head. "He has some unconventional tastes, but murder isn't one of them. I'm sure of that. Do you really think they're considering Oliver a serious suspect?"

"They have Paul down at the station. They seem to think he may have poisoned the girls as a favor to Oliver. But that Oliver was in back of it all. If he isn't the murderer, then who is?" Maggie had to know what Dorothy would say.

"I have no idea," said Dorothy. "But I'm sure it isn't Oliver, and I thought Paul was brighter than that. But the police will figure that out. They wouldn't accuse an innocent man." She picked up her tray. "I'm going to the hospital to sit with Sarah; with all this focus on Tiffany's murder, no one is thinking about my daughter."

"Wait, Dorothy." Maggie put her hand on Dorothy's arm. "I think you're right. I don't think Oliver killed Tiffany. But I need your help in proving it."

Chapter 38

Arabian Illumination of Manuscripts. *German chromolithograph of Arabian maze designs, printed by E. Cochran in Stuttgart, Germany, c. 1880. From* Dekarative Varbilden, *a book illustrating decorative arts from different parts of the world. 10 x 13.5 inches. Price: $85.*

Maggie sat in the cafeteria for a few minutes after Dorothy left. Dorothy was clearly not threatened by either Oliver's infidelity or his sexual peccadilloes. Or by the possibility that he was a murderer. Or that he might have directed Paul to kill. Did she really know her husband so well she could be that sure of him?

Maggie had been sure of Michael. And she shouldn't have been. Even now . . . was Will faithful? He had never promised to be, nor had she. But there was an unspoken understanding. At least she felt there was. It was one of the reasons she'd held back with Paul

Monday night. Thank goodness. But did Will feel the same way about her? Did men and women place the same importance on fidelity? Or did they even have the same definition of fidelity?

Love hadn't stopped Oliver from having extramarital relationships. To "fill his needs," Dorothy had said. Was it impossible for all needs to be met inside marriage?

Maggie felt overwhelmed with information; she now knew more than she wanted to about Dorothy, about Oliver, about Paul, about Tiffany, and . . .

She needed to see Max. It was time. Max knew all the players; he was willing to compromise, clearly, because he'd agreed to let Whitcomb House remain open.

"He'll be finished in just a minute," said Jennifer when Maggie got to Max's office. "He's talking to the parents of a prospective student." Maggie nodded. The small reception area outside Max's office was clean and bright; the walls were filled with colored photographs of Max at campus events and Max with important visitors and Max receiving community awards. His aquarium was clean and the goldfish print was still on the wall. A goldfish. Could everything be that simple?

Maggie still hadn't gotten all the strands of possibilities straight when a middle-aged couple left Max's office, smiling and shaking his hand, and carrying the current "look-see" brochure and Somerset College catalog. Max beckoned her into his office.

"I assume you've talked with Dorothy or Oliver Whitcomb by now," Max said preemptively. "And, yes, I agreed to let the residents stay at Whitcomb House. But Dorothy and Oliver had to make some concessions, and

I'll change my mind again if anything else embarrassing should happen over there. Do you understand?"

"I understand." Maggie stood in front of his desk. "Has the media coverage started to die down?"

"Not at all. One of those television shows that covers unsolved mysteries called here this morning, wondering if we'd like the 'Somerset College Capers' to appear on their program."

"It's only been three days since Sarah collapsed and two days since Tiffany died. Isn't that a bit early to declare the cases unsolved?"

"They didn't seem to think so. Said they'd want to start on the program soon. To get in on the ground floor, they said."

"You mean you're going to let them do it?" Maggie couldn't imagine Max agreeing to that kind of publicity.

"I told them I'd think it over and then call them. They promised to give some background information about the college as well as about the crimes. It would give Somerset College nationwide visibility, don't you think? They'd be interviewing me, of course, and other key people, and we'd be able to talk about what Somerset College stood for: education, and a full intellectual life for all."

Did Max really think one of those television programs would showcase the romantic view of Somerset College that he liked to believe in? "I just came to thank you for changing your mind, and for letting the Whitcomb House students stay in their dorm."

"You don't have to thank me for anything, Maggie Summer. Thank Oliver and Dorothy for talking me out of doing something I still feel would've been best for the college. And I haven't decided yet whether I'm going to fire you."

"But I thought the situation with Whitcomb House was cleared up!"

"I agreed to let those students stay. I didn't say *you* were going to stay. You defied my orders. Instead of telling those students they would have to leave campus, you went around me. You went to Dorothy and Oliver and asked for their help. How do you think I feel about that, Maggie? I'm the president of this institution, in case you've forgotten, and I'm *your* boss. I have the experience and the knowledge to run this college. You don't; Dorothy and Oliver Whitcomb, for all of their money, don't. Do you understand me?" Max's voice was getting louder and louder; his face was red. "You got me to change my mind by enlisting Oliver and Dorothy Whitcomb. Just because they have money that this college needs. I'm not proud of myself for going along with that! If this college weren't so important to me, if I didn't know that in a few weeks this whole incident would have blown over, and we're going to need all of the financial help we can get to pull this campus back together, then I never would have gone along with Oliver and Dorothy. And you're the one who put me in this situation. You!"

Maggie tried to say something, but Max kept going.

"You think Oliver and Dorothy believe in goodness and light and educating the poor single parents of the county, don't you? Well, that isn't exactly the whole truth! Oliver Whitcomb has other interests in that house, and those interests are not exactly the kind anyone connected with this college would like written up in any newspapers or revealed on any television program. If you hadn't gotten yourself into the middle of all of this, then I could have closed down that place, and no one would have thought anything of it. Now who knows what will happen?" Max seemed to run out of steam for a moment. "And you're in this mess, too, Maggie. What happened in your office yesterday that required the police to come racing back to the college? I know: your office was vandalized. But why would anyone vandalize *your* office? A break-in at Admissions, I could understand. Or at the Bursar's Office, where the money is kept. Even my office, if someone wanted to make a political statement. But why did you call attention to yourself by having the police summoned to *your* office? I suppose *you'll* be on the six-o'clock news next!"

Maggie gritted her teeth. Max had always had a tendency to become overexcited, but this was beyond his usual temper tantrums. Way beyond.

"Tiffany Douglass left some photographs in my office, probably accidentally. She may have been using the photographs to try to blackmail Oliver. I don't know for sure who knew, or why, but Oliver found out and asked Paul Turk to find the photos."

"Turk? He's the one who dumped everything in your office?"

"He's down at the police department now, giving a statement. He thought he was doing Oliver a favor."

"Who has the photographs now?"

272

Claudia nodded. "I usually leave about now. Should stick around?"

"Could you stay a little later? Just in case."

"Just in case what?" Claudia asked eagerly. "What's going on, Professor Summer? I took those messages. I know something is happening. Can I help?"

"You can help by staying an extra half hour and answering my phone. Right now that could be a big help."

Claudia's face fell. "You're sure you don't want me to do anything else?"

Maggie headed for the hallway outside the American Studies offices. "I don't think so."

Claudia hesitated. "Like maybe I could loan you my gun. It would fit in your pocketbook."

Maggie stopped abruptly and turned around. "What did you say?"

"It's all right. Really it is. It's legal. I have a license." Claudia reached into the large gray leather pocketbook Maggie had assumed was full of chocolates and makeup and pulled out a small silver handgun. "It's loaded and all set to go. With these strange things happening on campus, a woman should be prepared to defend herself. I've had it with me all week. Normally I leave it at home."

"Claudia! You shouldn't have a gun on campus!"

"No. But there are bad people around, and I didn't want to be a victim like Sarah and Tiffany. No one knew I had it. Except you, now." Claudia gestured with the gun to indicate the whole area. "No one else is here. They've all left for the day. And I know you're in the

"I gave them to Detectives Luciani and Newton this morning."

Max inhaled deeply. "You gave them to the police?"

"They were critical to the investigation of Tiffany's death. And, possibly, of Sarah's poisoning." Max was clearly ready to blow again. Maggie could leave now or hold her ground. "I did what I had to do, Max. For the reputation of Somerset College, and for myself. I talked with the police. Maybe you should do the same."

Chapter 39

Helicopis acis; Zeonia chorinoeus. *A trio of primarily black butterflies, their color chromolithographed on a black-and-white steel-engraved background. Printed by Wyman & Sons, Limited, in 1896, London, for* Lloyd's Natural History. *4.75 x 7 inches. Price: $50.*

The students in Maggie's class, who should have been focusing on post–Civil War reconstruction, were restless, and Maggie could do little to bring them back to the issues in their textbooks. The outside world seemed to be closing in on all of them.

Monday night, less than forty-eight hours ago, Paul had asked her advice on keeping students' interest. It was a good thing he wasn't observing this class, she thought. Her mind was on Dorothy, who was making decisions about what she would do now; on Oliver, who had committed adultery, but whose wife didn't believe he could have committed murder; on Paul, who was making a formal statement at the police station; on Tiffany, and on Sarah and Aura. And on Max, and what he would do next.

No wonder the students' minds were wandering; their professor's mind was everywhere except on post–Civil War America. To everyone's relief Maggie declared the class over a little earlier than usual.

She went to the day-care center first.

"You came back!" Aura's smile was worth any hesitation Maggie had in taking the time to stop to see her. "I made this picture for you to take to Mommy." Aura handed her a picture of a big tree with two people labeled "Aura" and "Momy" sitting under it. They were both smiling, and the sun was shining. "And this is for you!" Aura gave Maggie a big heart with a smile on it. "You're my friend, and my mommy's friend."

Maggie couldn't stop the tears from coming. How could she ever have felt sorry for herself when this little girl was so strong and so sweet? She gave Aura a big hug.

"Don't be sad. The pictures are happy ones," said Aura.

"They're very happy. I know. Sometimes grown-ups do funny things, like crying when they're happy."

Aura didn't look convinced.

"These are very special pictures. I promise I'll go to the hospital and give your mommy hers, and then I'll go to my home and put my picture on the refrigerator," said Maggie.

"That's the best place for pictures to go," said Aura. "That's smart. The heart will make your house happy."

"I hope so, Aura. I truly hope so."

Maggie blew her nose and dabbed her eyes with a tissue, then drove from the parking lot of Wee Care back to her usual campus parking space. Was this going to work?

It had to.

At her office Claudia handed her the usual pile of pink slips and two chocolate Kisses. Maggie ate one of the Kisses as she looked through the notes. Everything was on target.

It was almost five. There weren't many classes scheduled for five; day classes were just about over, except for some labs, and evening classes didn't begin until six-thirty, to give working students time to drive from their jobs to the campus. It was a perfect time.

"Claudia, would you call Max Hagfield's office and tell him I'd like to see him? Now. Say it's important."

Claudia looked at her. "You already talked to President Hagfield today, didn't you? I saw Jennifer in the ladies' room, and she said you'd been up there."

"That's right. I was."

"You've been up there a lot recently."

"So it seems," said Maggie. "It's been an unusu[al] week." This was not the time to get into a deep discu[s]sion with Claudia about scheduling. "Let me know [if] there's a problem at Max's end."

A few minutes later Claudia stuck her head i[n] Maggie's office. "It's okay. Jennifer said he's alone. [But] he's not in a good mood."

Maggie nodded. Who was in a good mood t[hese] days? "If anyone else calls me and needs to know w[here] I am, tell them I've gone to his office."

middle of doing something dangerous. I can tell." Claudia looked at her closely. "You are, aren't you, Professor Summer?"

Maggie shook her head and couldn't help grinning. "I am, indeed, Claudia. But you shouldn't have that gun with you on campus under any circumstances, even if it is licensed."

"I know. Take it. It's loaded. Just in case." Claudia winked at her. "Just make sure you bring it back to me. And only shoot the bad guys, okay?" She handed the gun to Maggie.

Maggie hesitated. She hated guns. And she knew only a little about them. When she was thirteen, her father had taken her deer hunting. She had refused to shoot the rifle he'd trained her to shoot and had cried when he'd shot a doe. He'd been disgusted with her and never took her hunting with him again. She'd been relieved he hadn't asked.

The rifle he'd taught her to use was very different from the small handgun Claudia was handing her.

She hesitated and then took the cold weapon. "I'm not going to use this, Claudia."

"It's only for protection," Claudia said. "Or to scare someone. A woman's got to have protection sometimes. That's what my mother always told me."

Maggie wondered what other words of wisdom Claudia's mother had taught her. Against her better judgment, Maggie slipped the gun into her purse. Claudia was right. It slipped easily into the side pocket.

"I'll be right here when you get back," said Claudia happily. "Go get 'em, Maggie!"

Chapter 40

Say When! Lithograph from portfolio by James Montgomery Flagg (1877–1960), American illustrator known for his satirical portraits. His best-known illustration was the well-known "I want YOU!" World War I Uncle Sam recruiting poster. This lithograph shows a man and a woman facing each other across a low table. She is squirting seltzer into his glass; most of it is splashing onto the ground as their attention is on each other, not on the glass. Printed by Leslie-Judge Company, c. 1912. 10.5 x 13.5 inches. Price: $75.

Max was sitting at his desk when Maggie knocked on his open door. Jennifer must have left for the day.

"I thought our conversation was over, Maggie." His voice was strong, and frighteningly calm, after his tirade earlier in the afternoon. His eyes were hard and dark. Even across the room she smelled the faint odor of cognac and cigarettes. A Somerset College mug was on his desk. "You've ruined the reputation of the college, ruined my future. You gave those sick photographs to the police. It's just a matter of time before the broadcast networks get them. 'Philanthropist Uses Somerset College to Find Coeds for Kinky Sex.' Or maybe 'Scholarships for Sex'? The *National Enquirer* is going to love it! You're taking us all down, Maggie. There will be no jobs here, and no students, because you personally have ensured that this college is going to close."

"Is that why you did it, Max?" Maggie stood opposite him at his desk.

"Why I did what?"

"Why you killed Tiffany Douglass. To keep her from telling the media about her relationship with Oliver Whitcomb?"

He stared at her with eyes that seemed suddenly unfocused. His words were strong, but slurred. "Maggie Summer, you're not only destructive, you're crazy! I didn't even know about their relationship until you told me this afternoon." He picked up the mug and took a deep drink. Coffee, or cognac?

"Yes, you did. Tiffany told you, didn't she? She may have tried to blackmail Oliver Whitcomb with those pictures, but that didn't work. He probably laughed at her."

"That's exactly what I did." Oliver's voice came from the doorway. Maggie turned. Dorothy and Oliver were both there. So was Paul Turk. And in front of them were Detectives Luciani and Newton. Just as she had hoped and planned. They were all here. "I told her I wouldn't pay for pictures of me, and neither would my wife."

"I didn't need to see photographs," said Dorothy. "I knew what Oliver was doing."

"Don't try to get out of this, Dorothy!" The emotions behind Max's words were stronger than his voice. "You and Oliver think you're so high-and-mighty and sophisticated that such things don't mean anything to you, but pictures like that could mean something to the Board of Trustees. And to the media. How do you think it would look for Somerset College if its biggest donor turned out to be a pervert? Sleeping with a student in the college he supported? Tying her up and doing other things I don't think you would like to know, Dorothy! What you demented people thought was your own private sick business was going to take down the whole college. And every one of us with it!"

Oliver shrugged. "I assure you I wasn't going to pay Tiffany blackmail money."

"So then she came to you, didn't she, Max?" Maggie said.

"You have no proof of that! And none of you has any right to be in my private office. I want you all out of here. Now!"

"She must have come to you. Last week, or last weekend. Because you knew before the Whitcombs' party Sunday afternoon."

Max took another drink. "Maggie, you've absolutely no proof of what you're fantasizing about." His face was usually ruddy; now it was pale.

"Tiffany was poisoned with potassium permanganate, Max. That's how I knew."

"I'm here because the detectives brought me," Paul put in. "But I'm confused. What is potassium permanganate? Why would that mean Max killed Tiffany?"

"Exactly!" said Max. "Half the homes or garages in Somerset County probably have supplies of potassium permanganate! I'll bet your home does, Maggie. In fact, I'm sure it does."

"Not unless you were able to put some there when you tried to break in last night. A year ago it was in my garage, though. For the same reason you have it, Max.

You and Michael both used it in your garden ponds. It kills parasites on goldfish. I heard you discussing its use many times. You talked about having to be careful, because it was so poisonous; using too much would kill the fish as well as the parasites. I remembered when I saw the goldfish print outside your office. The print Michael and I gave you."

"So? There's no law against protecting goldfish!"

"But there are laws about mixing the poison with red wine and serving it to a human being. It's lethal to humans, as you well know, Max. That's why after Michael died I got rid of what was left in my house. The only reason someone would have it is if they had goldfish in outdoor ponds. Like you do, Max. Oliver and Dorothy don't keep fish."

Max was silent. Detective Luciani spoke up. "We had a search warrant issued for your home this afternoon, President Hagfield. We found the potassium permanganate, right where Professor Summer said it would be. Next to the goldfish food in your garage."

Max's voice contorted slightly. "None of you were thinking about Somerset College. It was up to me to make sure the college didn't go under. And I did. I risked everything! And then that dumb broad—that Sarah—drank the stuff I'd meant for Tiffany!" Max burst out. "She shouldn't have drunk the Bloody Mary mix. If Tiffany had drunk it, the way she usually did when she was with me—you weren't her one and only, Oliver!—then this whole situation wouldn't have gotten out of hand. It's all Sarah's fault. One overwrought young woman getting ill doesn't make headlines. But two? That's what raised questions."

Max had been at the Whitcombs' bar before Sarah had poured her drink. Max was the one who'd poisoned the pitcher of spiced tomato juice.

"How did you do it, Max?" asked Maggie. "Sarah was poisoned with nicotine."

"You're not as smart as you think you are, for a professor, Maggie," said Max as he walked around the front of the desk, holding on to the edge. "Nicotine is very potent. I just took the tobacco left in a dozen cigarettes I'd smoked halfway, soaked it in water for a couple of days, and strained it. All it took was a pill-bottleful to add to the pitcher of tomato juice. Oliver makes his Bloody Marys so strong I didn't think anyone would notice. I thought using two different poisons would confuse the police."

"It *was* you, then!" Dorothy's eyes glittered. "I was still hoping it had been some sort of accident. Some coincidence. But it was you! You self-centered idiot! You may have killed my daughter!"

For a moment the room was silent.

"Your daughter?" Oliver blurted. Everyone turned from Max to Dorothy. Anger and grief had just negated twenty-three years of secrecy.

"Damn it, yes! Sarah was—is—my daughter! I had to give her up for adoption years ago, but I was trying to make it up to her now. I was trying to ensure a safe future for her, and for Aura. And you"—Dorothy turned and walked toward Max, her polished nails pointing at him—"you selfish, idiotic little man, you ruined everything!"

She suddenly reached out and grabbed the pocketbook hanging on Maggie's shoulder.

"Stop!" Maggie yelled, and jerked her arm away. But Dorothy knew just what she was doing. She reached down into the side pocket where the gun was hidden. Luciani and Newton both rushed her, but before they could get there, the gun had gone off. The glass shattered in the print of Windsor Castle. Max's body slumped to the floor.

Dorothy dropped the gun, and Newton and Luciani each grabbed one of her arms. Maggie ran to Max and bent over him.

"No one can hurt me, Dorothy. It's already over," he murmured.

"He's still alive," said Maggie, "but I think he's poisoned himself. He was a smoker, but tonight he smells like Sarah did."

Behind them, they heard someone running down the hall. Luciani turned and pulled his gun as they all faced the doorway.

Claudia stood there, breathing deeply, taking in the whole scene. "Dr. Stevens just called, Professor Summer. Sarah Anderson's come out of her coma."

Chapter 41

Sarah. *Full-length, hand-colored lithograph of a beautiful dark-haired woman wearing an off-the-shoulder, red dress who is leaning on a white marble table. She wears one pink rose in her hair, which she has curled in ringlets, and one at her* *bust. A vase of pink roses is in the background. One of the N. Currier "lady prints," labeled #50; c. 1850. In Victorian frame. 11.10 x 8.1 inches. Price: $250.*

"So how did Dorothy know about the gun?" asked Gussie. It was nearly two thirty in the morning, but neither she nor Jim were ready for sleep. "The Broadway play we saw tonight wasn't a fraction as exciting as your week, Maggie. I want to hear all the details!" Gussie sliced another piece of the herbed cheddar Maggie had put on a plate for their late-night snack in the kitchen.

Maggie poured Jim a cup of cocoa. "I'm just so glad you're both here," said Maggie. "Coming back to an empty house would have been too, too hard tonight." Winslow stood on his hind legs and stretched toward the table. They had liverwurst and ham up there as well as cheese. His imploring look worked as well as he knew it would. Maggie tore off a small piece of ham and gave it to him. "Not totally alone, of course. Sorry, Winslow."

Jim laughed. "He isn't quite the same as a person, but he's trying."

"He does his best," agreed Maggie. "And to answer your question—Dorothy had called my office from her cell phone, just after I'd left for Max's office. She and Oliver were outside the administration building, waiting for five o'clock, which is when we'd all agreed to meet. She wanted to make sure I'd left at the time we'd agreed on, and she told Claudia she was worried about me. Claudia told her not to be; she'd given me her gun. She was even kind enough to tell Dorothy exactly where I'd put it. Luckily for Max, Dorothy knew nothing about guns. She hit Windsor Castle instead of him."

"And how is Max?"

"He must have been sipping the nicotine-laced cognac before we got there; he drank more than Sarah had. Of course, he would need to: he was a smoker, and it would have taken a lot more nicotine to kill him. The police found the solution of tobacco he'd made in his private bathroom. The last time the police called, they didn't know if he was going to make it. If he does, he'll stand trial."

"And Sarah?"

"She's going to need a lot of therapy and time, but Dr. Stevens says chances are she'll be all right in a few months. Oliver's already told Dr. Stevens he'll cover her medical bills. And he says Sarah and Aura can live with him and Dorothy after Sarah's released from the hospital. If they want to."

"So Oliver's accepted that Dorothy is Sarah's mother."

Maggie nodded. "It all happened so quickly that the future is hard to predict. But at least he feels guilty enough about the whole situation to try to make it up to Sarah—and Dorothy—for everything that's happened."

Gussie nodded. "As he should. He didn't kill anyone, but if it hadn't been for his behavior, none of that would have happened."

"Possibly," said Maggie. "Tiffany was blackmailing Max, too, so it's hard to tell. But certainly when Sarah is well enough to understand what's happening, she's going to have a major surprise: her mother has reclaimed her."

"So there's a happy ending after all," said Gussie.

"Except for Tiffany, of course. And her family. But at least no one else is going to be poisoned. Although I am afraid Max's nightmares about Somerset College's reputation may come true. The press is not going to be kind about this whole sordid situation."

"I guess you'd better keep your other job, then," said Gussie.

"My van is packed; I'm ready to set up at the antique show Friday afternoon," said Maggie. "Although the antique-print business is going to seem very calm after this week on campus."

Chapter 42

The End. *Lithograph from Maxfield Parrish (1870–1966), painting for the book* The Knave of Hearts *by Louise Saunders, 1925. Illustration of courtly gentleman in red robes bowing toward the audience against a background of Parrish blue sky, within a border designed to look like a classical sculpture. It was the closing lithograph in the book. 10.5 x 12.5 inches. Price: $250.*

It was almost dawn. Jim and Gussie had gone to bed, and Maggie had soaked in a hot tub scented with lavender oil long enough for her adrenaline to slow down and the skin on her feet to feel slightly puckered. The president of the Board of Trustees had called: Somerset College was going to be closed both today and tomorrow.

Two days off! The reasons were awful, but she planned to take full advantage of the extra time. She planned to sleep in and then perhaps be decadent and go shopping with Gussie and Jim, since they couldn't set up their booths until Friday afternoon.

The long bath had helped Maggie relax. She was exhausted, but now she was ready to sleep. She pulled on a clean flannel nightgown and walked to the kitchen to make sure Winslow had enough water for the night. With all the excitement she hadn't checked earlier.

Winslow followed her, weaving in and around her footsteps. His fur felt soft and warm against her ankles. November was the beginning of winter, not the end of fall.

The rap at the kitchen door was sudden and loud. Maggie's first impulse was to turn off the kitchen light and flee upstairs. She couldn't cope with anything more tonight. This morning, she corrected herself. The sky was a light gray now, tinged slightly with streaks of pink.

The police? By now they should have all the information they needed.

She sighed, picked up Winslow, and turned on the outside light over the back stairs. She looked through the window and relief flooded her chest. Quickly she unlocked the door. Will's secure arms folded around her.

Minutes later they sat at the kitchen table waiting for the kettle to boil. "Why did you come? You have a show to do."

"I have a radio in the van. What was happening at Somerset College made the national news. I knew it involved students at a single-parent dorm. I knew you were the adviser at Whitcomb House, and I know you don't ask for help. So when you didn't say anything about the situation in your e-mails, I knew you had to be in the middle of the whole mess. So I came."

Maggie put out her hand and he held it in both of his. "I'm glad you did."

"And I want to know everything, and hear everything. I was going to wait outside until it was a decent hour to knock. But when I drove up and saw your lights still on, I knew it must have been a long night for you. I saw Gussie's van, so I knew you weren't alone, and . . ."

"You knocked. And I'm all right, and you've driven all the way from Ohio."

"Started yesterday afternoon. I wanted to be with you."

Maggie stood up and turned off the kettle, and Will stood behind her, holding her gently, and then not so gently.

Center Point Publishing
600 Brooks Road • PO Box 1
Thorndike ME 04986-0001 USA

(207) 568-3717

US & Canada:
1 800 929-9108

288